Star Crowley Goes to High School

Star Crowley Goes to High School

BRIAN L. TUCKER

RESOURCE *Publications* • Eugene, Oregon

STAR CROWLEY GOES TO HIGH SCHOOL

Resource Publications
An Imprint of Wipf and Stock Publishers
199 W. 8th Ave., Suite 3
Eugene, OR 97401

www.wipfandstock.com

PAPERBACK ISBN: 979-8-3852-7655-4
HARDCOVER ISBN: 979-8-3852-7656-1
EBOOK ISBN: 979-8-3852-7657-8

VERSION NUMBER 03/26/26

To Patrick Pyles—for motivating this old man
to write another book

Acknowledgments

Writing any book isn't possible without a multitude of people praying and supporting it. I'm grateful for Leah, Zella, Mom, Dad, Al, Linda, family, extended family, the Bluegrass Writer's Studio, PCA family, Coastal Community ministries, my friends for beta reading, and everyone involved in the literary process at Wipf and Stock. Here's to more chapters. It's a blessing to work with all of you and see stories come to life.

Chapter 1

It's hard to believe a word I say, because I'm what the guidance office calls 'unfocused.' It started in the years before now, but suffice it to say, I am 'defiant' and other various terms used by my former elementary and middle school administration offices. Now, I am a collective problem for the high school officials. Ms. Begley, and I quote, said before my departure last year, "Now you're their problem." Today, it is 9th grade, and I am newly minted at the Idyll County High School. Our first day is sunny outside, and I can't wait to see who's joined me from Cascade Middle. I wonder if there'll be anyone else who proves 'difficult.'

My troubles started when I failed to dress appropriately. While I didn't exactly have a school uniform I had to wear like at a private school, I guess I always failed to see the point of wearing what school police considered 'appropriate attire.' For starters, the Cascade Middle school folks believed in a rationale that clothing should cover all of the male students and come down to at least the knee on us females (skirts included). Thank you, Ms. Begley & others, for always checking on this each day! However, this wasn't what drove them to write me up continually as ne'er-do-well. No. It was my outfit in general. I had what might be considered peculiarities in style, and this fell short of the prescribed Cascade values. My fashion was unique, I thought. I wore my favorite heavy metal t-shirts (sometimes missing large chunks in the fabric), and my jeans were sometimes more holes than material. I tried to explain that our washing machine at home was vicious in its bite, and it (rather than our dog) ate entire sections of my clothing in a single cycle, but they did not accept this as gospel. So, I saw more of Ms. Begley and Principal Weathers than any other single student.

Fashion was only one swath (forgive the pun) of the larger issue, they said. I spoke up too frequently and out of turn. I tried to relay that

I simply had a lot on my mind, but they only frowned and shook their heads when we met with Mom and Dad in the Main Office. I liked to express myself with frequent interruptions and had a tendency to 'disrupt' classrooms ad nauseam. I tried to explain that it was just my character makeup. *How does one put a sock in it, really?* So, I visited the couch in Ms. Begley's suite more than my homeroom and regular teachers all throughout 6th, 7th, and 8th grades. My classmates sometimes asked where I'd been all hours of the day, but I think many were simply happy to get through a lesson without me interrupting Geography or whatever was being taught. Principal Weathers said I had a "propensity for being difficult," to which I shook my shaggy head.

Middle school policy had enforced that kids needed to adhere to a code of conduct, and I always tried to the first week of school. But each year, as the school year progressed from Week One into Two, I found that others joined in following the book much more easily than I did. My parents fought back tears as I tried to tell them that it was just "Me being me." But I can still feel the pull of Mom's old brush struggling mightily to remove cobwebbed tangles from my hair. Dad pushing crumpled dollar bills at me, imploring me to, "Get nice clothes when we go into the store."

No matter how hard I tried, I just couldn't seem to get it like everyone else. There had been snickers from different girls and peaks sneaked by the boys all throughout those years. At first, it bothered me a little bit. I can still feel the eyes of Corine Bostic on my scalp and her pigtails shaking back and forth in a *tsk tsk* fashion. Not that I cared much what the boys had thought from 6th to 7th, by 8th, I remember grimacing a tad when Thomas Cranfill moved a seat away from me on the first day of school. (That had been the one school year I actually took a few of Dad's bills and bought a new sweater and jeans.) If it didn't help then, I didn't feel it would ever matter and so I gave it up after that one time.

Our 8th grade teachers let the students sit with a gap between me and them, and I only ever attempted to communicate with one other person regularly, Reagan Fieldstone. She didn't 'get' me, but I thought I 'got' her. So, without any pretense, I asked her if she'd sit with me at lunch, and she'd said, "Sure, why not."

Most of our conversations that last year in middle had been about collections we were working on. Reagan liked to collect Barbies and other trite things, but I figured I could make a mark on her. It proved largely fruitless, but I was happy to have an understudy. Plus, it got Ms. Begley & Co. off my back for a spell because it meant I couldn't be causing trouble if I was around Reagan. We sat in silence for large chunks of the day, but when we did talk, I always tried my best to show interest in her boy crushes and outfits she'd bought online. As she droned on, I kept reminding myself that this is what girls did. It mattered. So, I focused and sometimes answered her questions about style with almost inflection in my vocal cords. But usually, she caught me staring across the schoolyard to the fence barriers and beyond.

CHAPTER 2

Idyll High sits on a mountainside overlooking a placid lake called Chartreuse. The name fits, and the fish sometimes jump all the way out to show their bellies in the sunshine. I noticed this when the school bus dropped me off on the first day, and I noticed it again as my name was being called in our first Home Room of the year. My new teacher, Mr. Chethers (it might've been Cheethers), noticed it too, because I was called to his desk and told to pay attention or I'd be meeting the new principal if I wasn't careful. I asked him if he saw the fish jump, a bass more than likely, but he shook his head quickly and directed me to my seat. My new chair wasn't beside Reagan Fieldstone to my chagrin, but a skinny, new boy named Oscar Villanueve who smelled slightly of vanilla and had the beginnings of a mustache. He said hello as I sat back down.

Mr. C. (I'll ask Oscar if he caught the name later) droned on about classroom etiquette, school assignments for the year and what life would be like at Idyll High. Before I could get out a sheet of paper and start writing down some of the things Mr. C. was saying we'd learn, I felt a tap on my elbow and turned my shaggy head to see Oscar gesturing out the window, "I saw it, too," he said.

I smiled for the kind second it made me feel human, and I found myself nodding my head in agreement with the new kid. He took out a sheet of notebook paper and started writing with what I noticed was exceptional penmanship. To avoid being 'rude' as I'd remembered Ms. Begley said last year, I looked away and tried to focus on what Mr. C. was saying. I followed him for a second or two and was then lost again in words about tardiness and school violations. These all felt like curse words I'd heard before and tried so hard to not repeat. The classroom was stuffy, and it felt like August truly should in Chattanooga, Tennessee. Mr. C. had forgotten to open a window, I imagine, and the AC unit wasn't supplying any cool air, and my mind started to go a little fuzzy. Instead of passing out, I decided to focus on the classroom walls where I found spartan adornments you'd expect in a classroom with Shakespeare posters and witty tidbits of information like you'd find in any English/Language Arts classroom around the US. My eyes locked on an onomatopoeia design where the words *bang* and *crash* and *buzz* were twisted and designed to look like impressive sounding words. It struck me as silly that sounding words were still important enough to be studied, and I started to raise my hand to say such, but I thought of the countless trips to Principal Weather's office and restrained myself.

In the farthest corner of the classroom, behind Mr. C.'s desk, there was a map of some sort indicating a boat, a body of water, and a trajectory to what looked like an island. I was drawn toward the topographical features and found myself wanting to run my hand across the map; it looked as if it had raised lines along the mountain ranges and indentations to indicate the blue pools of water. Again, I tried to keep my hands at my side for fear that I might raise my finger in midair and trace the designs unknowingly.

Beside me, I could feel (and hear) Oscar still scribbling frantically at his station, and I wondered where he came from, what his previous year looked like. *Was he labeled trouble like me?* I hoped he was as exciting as he looked. The pince-nez glasses kept his longer, curly hair from falling into his eyes and gave him a scholarly look. I wondered if he read all summer before coming to Idyll. He wrote with long curly designs, and he bit his lip slightly as he focused on whatever his words were, and I tried to not stare at his efforts. The classroom held about twenty-five of us, and the seats were ordered like any stale classroom of the past one hundred years in a five-by-five design. Oscar and I were in the back row in the corner, and I thought about how it might've been by design for easier access to send me quickly to administration. *Where's that optimism from summer?* I thought. It didn't pay to be pessimistic this early on. No, I would focus on the good times ahead and pray there would be some.

Mr. C. pointed to the poster on his wall featuring great American classics in literature and said, "Do you see these books?"

After a few voices assented, he said, "*To Kill a Mockingbird*, *The Old Man and the Sea*, and *Of Mice and Men* are some of the finest works to come out of not just America but the whole world in the past years."

One or two students coughed in agreement or from nervousness. Then, Mr. C. asked, "Has anyone read one of them before?"

A girl in the front row I couldn't identify by the back of her head said, "I read *To Kill a Mockingbird* last summer."

"Good," Mr. C. answered, followed quickly with, "and please raise your hand, Corine, is it? When you answer a question."

My heart sank a little on hearing her name, but I'd kind of recognized the voice even before he confirmed it. *Great*, I thought. *Corine's back.*

"Yessir," her ponytail shook.

"Anyone else?" he asked, scanning the room.

Before I knew what was happening, my hand moved involuntarily to my body, and my mouth opened at the same time to say, "Mr . . . Chee—er, um. Weren't those books written like a hundred years ago? What about newer books?"

Mr. C. stared at my still raised hand and around the room like a hawk checking on other forms of prey. Then, he gestured for me to lower my hand, and he paused for what I imagined was maximum effect. When he still didn't say anything to me, I looked at him sideways and tried to not break eye contact. His beady, brown eyes squinted with crow's feet wrinkles. He cleared his throat and said, "They were written a while ago, I admit. But that doesn't make them any less monumental, Miss Crowley."

"Star," I replied. "My name is Freida Crowley, but I go by Star," I added, looking around the room to see if any heads would turn in recognition. Only Corine started to, but something held her head in place, like she was tethered to the front, staring at the board.

"Well, Star, I hope these outbursts won't be the norm," he smiled a Cheshire-grin. "While these books do come from the 20th century, it doesn't diminish their qualities in literature. They are some of the best forms of writing to ever grace us with their presence. Wouldn't you agree?"

I imagine he realized his blunder the moment he spoke these words, because no sooner had he said it, I noticed his grin fell to a frown of shocked horror, but I was already jabbering back.

"Well, American literature maybe, but what about Dickens and Tolstoy and Orwell? Don't you love Orwell? I think some of the best writing is found beyond the US, Mr. C. It is like only looking at the first few pages of human creativity and stopping there, don't you think? We should be studying totalitarianism and human regressions and cave walls as compared to text messages. That would be neat and applicable to where we are today, Mr. C," I exhaled, smiling at him, pleased with an opportunity to express these sentiments.

Mr. C. held a hand up with his index finger in the air, "Enough, Miss Crowley. Enough. It's Mr. *Chethers*, and I won't have you sabotaging what little time we have together each day. I have a strict three-strike policy, and if you run off at the mouth like that again, it will be a quick trip to the front office. Do you understand?"

"It's St—" I started to say but somehow managed to close my lips, there was a tapping on my elbow again. I turned to gaze at Oscar's fingernails touching the sleeves of my Quicksand t-shirt; he held one finger to his lips and pointed to a note in his hand. I bit my lip to say no more to the teacher.

"What was that?" Mr. Chethers asked, hands folded across his waist, coaxing more from me.

"Nothing, Mr. Cheethers," I said, placing an emphasis on the elongated name, pleased to know I was right the first time.

"Good," he replied, unfolding his arms, dropping his grin a little at not having an added fight. "You will respect this rule, or you'll spend the majority of the year doing administration's bidding. I won't have insubordination in this classroom. We will go over these texts, and it will be for the benefit of the entire room." I put my head down on the desk, but not before Oscar slipped the notebook paper into my open palm and whispered, "Read this, and we'll talk later."

My heart jumped a little, and I was ecstatic about a sudden shift in the day's path. The paper felt warm, and I knew it was from Oscar's frantic scribbling earlier. He wanted to be my friend, and I imagined what he might say to me later. I made a point to not catch Mr. C.'s eye for the remainder of the class, and the paper felt like an ounce of gold in my clenched fist. When I glanced down at it, I could see my name written in swooping curlicues, and he'd even erased and wrote it correctly as: Dear S-T-A-R.

Chapter 3

While there weren't dragons or sea monsters dwelling below Idyll High in Chartreuse Lake, there was plenty to distract me that first week. I kept trying to look down at the lakeshore and not think about what Oscar had written, but it was almost impossible. The note told me so much about him so quickly, and I marveled at how he could summarize his life like that. He'd told me where he was from: Idaho. I didn't know anyone else from out West. Idaho, I only knew the joke about potatoes. His family's reason for moving: a fresh start. And he was super competitive like his dad. He told me his favorite band, a super obscure metal band from the 90s: Extol, and his favorite food: pizza bites, when they'd cooled down. In that same note, he'd told me his favorite movie of all-time: Zoolander (who doesn't love a silly comedy about the modeling industry), and his biggest regret: not saying goodbye to any of his friends at his last school. What I took away from all that: he'd *had* friends. *I was so jealous!* But I really felt weird afterwards, because now I knew so much about him, and he didn't know a thing about me, except I suffered from interrupting cow syndrome in class. *Moo!*

So, that first week felt like forever, when he'd sit down beside me and try to strike up a conversation, and I'd look from him to Mr. C.'s beady eyes staring a hole into my retinas, and I'd mumble, "Let's talk later," and quickly survey the lake below our class windows. *It had to get better, right?* I panicked, my hands clammy and fingernails digging into my palms like talons. But it didn't. Each class bell would ring, and I would stumble throughout the day, not sure how to speak with any coherency. Even the lunch bell, signifying the sole thirty minutes we could talk at lunch, was interrupted by bullies like the ogre Elliott Bench and his cronies who tried to steal our food and demand our milk cartons at the start of each lunch. It was mayhem in the high school hallways.

One day, when I decided enough was enough, my cheeks flushed at the cafeteria table, I turned to Oscar and blurted, "Let's just skip lunch and walk down to the lockers."

He stared at me in what looked like mock amazement and stammered an eventual, "Okay."

"Great," I replied, unsure of my footing, and slowly stood to lead him out of the cafeteria.

Once we were past the cafeteria ladies and the foreboding lunchroom monitor, Mr. Kreig, we found ourselves in the eerily silent hallway, a row of lockers facing us.

"Which one's yours?" I asked, feigning interest in the metal wall, knowing he was three from the end.

"Down there," he pointed. "Yours?" he smiled, pushing his glasses up the bridge of his nose.

"Right here," I said, smacking the locker, testing its sturdiness, then putting my hands in my holey jeans, squirming a bit, wondering if I had any boogers in my nose.

He stared at it and rocked back and forth on his heels a bit, too, I noticed. He combed his hair back from his forehead, away from his eyes. They were an interesting green-blue, and he instinctively pushed his hair back down again.

"Your letter was nice," I said, tapping the locker again, kicking myself for not sharing anything else about myself.

"You looked like you needed a note," he said, clearing his throat a little. "Not that you *needed* a note, but you know what I'm saying. I thought it might help take your mind off all that stuff Cheether was saying," he stifled a laugh.

I turned to him, pausing my snare drum routine on the locker's door, "You said it the same way I did," I grinned. "Cheether. It makes me think of Cheetos. Do you like Cheetos?" *What is wrong with me?* I thought, instinctively smacking my forehead.

"I do," he laughed back, surprising me a little. "Flaming Hot. But Taqis are better."

"No way," I joined in. "No way. How can you say that?"

He laughed and said he swore by that.

"Thanks for telling me all that," I blurted back.

"What?"

"All that about yourself," I said, looking from him to the hallway floor, staring at my decrepit Chucks, once red, now a sad maroon color.

"You like a lot of stuff," I said, again wanting to hit my head against the locker. Don't say anything else like that.

"It's cool that you like old bands, too," he said, pointing to my shirt. I was wearing a Tool shirt today, and I was pleased he'd noticed.

"Anything is better than what they play on the radio," I said. "My folks listen to all that catchy pop and swear it's as good as anything in the past fifty years. As if," I huffed.

"As if," he agreed.

We stood in silence for a second, and I was about to ask him about his weekend plans, but the bell signifying the end of lunch rang and jolted me awake. The lunchroom door swung open and out poured the hordes of under and upperclassmen. We were soon jostled by warm bodies, and it brought us closer to my locker than I intended.

He fell forward a little when someone bumped into him, and I mock-attempted to catch him, but it was too late, and he was within inches of my personal bubble. I smelled the vanilla scent again, and his mustachioed upper lip was inches from mine, "Sorry," he grunted. "Personal space is a rare commodity at this school, I guess."

I laughed at him, and he stepped backward to regain his balance. "Cretins live here," I said. "Welcome to Tennessee, I'm Star," and I actually stuck out my hand.

And he played along and took my clammy paw in his, "Well, I'm glad there's one normal person in this place," he said, smiling with two distinct dimples showing.

We stood in place for a second, but I imagined I held that pose well past the bell ringing and the end of the school day. But the bell did chime, and he said he had to go to Biology or somewhere, and I was trying to remember my locker combination long enough to get an unexcused tardy for my next class.

Chapter 4

It's easy enough to guess why I preferred to be called Star. When your given name is Freida Crowley, you naturally gravitate toward something more insightful and catchier like that. My mom said I was born on a full moon, and Dad added that every star was out that night. I looked up what was happening on that night, and it did look like a bright one, so I stuck with the Star moniker. Even though no one else my age ever really got close enough to say, "Hey, Star, what's going on?" I still imagined them doing so. Now, I wonder and imagine how it'd sound coming out of Oscar's lips. He seemed like the best shot yet of getting to hear my nickname said aloud.

I am not fixated on astrology or anything of that sort, but I do enjoy knowing lots of things. And the solar system, like Latin, and music are just a few of the things I gravitate towards. Over the past summer, Mom could tell I was really getting into baking, and she got me a whole spice rack. I told her that she should use her hard-earned cash on things that meant a lot to her, but she refused to budge, and I ended up working with an entire alphabet of spices. My favorite dishes incorporated turmeric and mostly Asian-originating herbs. *Have you ever tried curry dishes?* And Mom and Dad taste-tested all of my good (and sometimes bad) efforts. I can still see their faces when I gave them a palak paneer dish with a poorly balanced ratio of spinach to spices. Fast forward to my last effort, and I am proud of the joy I brought to their taste buds when I successfully made samosas from scratch. It gave me a real thrill to give them something back. They work like sixty to ninety hours a week, and I am home a lot while they are still at the office.

When Oscar wrote to me that he liked pizza bites (not too hot), I wondered if I could make pizza bites from scratch and looked up a recipe online. Normally, I would say yuck, but I realize this is something that he enjoys and so I decided to withhold judgment. *Maybe this is something that friends do?* Sure enough, there was a fancified recipe online for pizza bites, and I discovered the dough basis would not be that different from samosas. It is worth a try, and I know (if they turn out okay) he might like them.

"Why are you making those?" I hear Dad ask, looking over my shoulder. "That's not what you'd normally do."

His tone rakes over me with condescension; he knows I'm doing something odd for me. I shrug nonchalantly.

"Well, I'm sure they'll be good, if you're making them," he rejoins, pinching my shoulder, walking from the kitchen to the living room.

"They're not for you," I say to his departing back.

"Aha," he bellows from the other room. "Busted."

"Dad," I groan, shaking flour from my apron. "Leave it alone."

He obviously does as that room goes quiet, and I turn to the recipe instructions before me. Like chemistry, baking can be achieved with focus and a little experimentation. I spring for the cake flour and gather the oil, cheese, baking powder, pizza sauce, and other ingredients and begin to make a small mess. Mom walks in and begins to say, "Clean that up after you're--" but I hold up my hand.

"I know, Mom, and I will."

"Good girl," she says, leaning in to kiss my sweaty forehead. "Remember to take a shower later, okay?"

I sniff and realize she's right. It's been a sweaty day, and I need to look fresh for whatever comes along at Idyll High tomorrow. I got the dough kneaded, rested, rolled, filled, and cut to where it almost looked like the picture on the online recipe. Then, I put them gently into the oven to bake to golden perfection. I think baking gets me closer to a satisfaction point than almost anything else. Maybe that's why I do it, I think. I set a timer and went upstairs to take a much-needed shower. As I gather my towel and washcloth, I can smell vanilla and envision the blue herons hunting for fish along the lake. The water hits me, and I think about the liters of water pounding against my shoulders and following rivulets down to the drain in seconds. *Where does it all go?* I feel guilty after a few minutes, imagining the entire aquifer below ground running dry at my expense. When I turn the nozzle off and pop my head out from the shower curtain, I can hear the beeping from my timer downstairs. Quickly, I towel off and put on some pajamas and leapfrog the stair steps two at a time.

"Careful," I can hear Dad hollering. "Don't want any ER visits."

I round the corner, grasp the oven mitts, plunge my hands into them, and open the oven door. They are still slightly opaque, and I give them two or three more minutes to arrive at the golden-brown cover. When they're ready, I open the door and take them out to cool. I will taste-test a few with Mom and Dad to make sure they're ready. Then, if they pass muster, I will package them up for Oscar to enjoy.

Chapter 5

The pizza bites feel like they burn a hole in my backpack as I carry them through the halls of Idyll High, first one flight of stairs, then a hallway, and another flight before reaching Mr. C.'s first block. I don't even waste time putting my backpack in the lockers for fear of spilling the contents, losing pizza bites all over the place. Mom put them in a tinfoil contraption that NASA would be proud of, and I imagine they could withstand anything I attempted, but I'm not taking a chance. So, at the door, I pause, and knock twice. It's still fifteen minutes before the bell rings, and I internally smack myself for being 'early' and somehow 'prepared' for the day. But the knocks do not elicit any activity from inside. Then, I reach for the knob to turn it when a smiling face greets me through the small, glass rectangle afforded by the Idyll administration. Mr. C.

But he's not his frowning (or, scowling) face from the previous week. Instead, he waves at me as if we've just met for the first time, and I can hear his not-quite-clear voice through the barrier, "Star, what a surprise. Did the bell ring?" he asked, glancing from me to the wall clock inside his room, to the left. "No, not yet. Just early?"

I think about bolting, because me and teachers and 'early' never yield anything substantial ever, but his inflection unnerves me too much to move from the spot. He waves again like the best friend I've never had, "C'mon in, Star. Tell me how this week is treating you," and the door is opened, and I'm ferried in before I can even realize my two feet are working.

"The early bird gets the worm, doesn't it?" he says over his shoulder, his gaze darting from the clock to his desk, peering at nothing and maybe everything all at once. Odd birds maybe, I think.

It does dawn on me that every crime show Dad has ever been keen on watching at night reveals psychopaths who lure victims into unwatched corners just like this, and I vaguely remember something in a school handbook (that I largely didn't read) about school policies prohibiting teachers from being alone with students one-on-one. *Was that just the opposite sex or what?* I can't remember. *Think. Think, Star.* But before I can tease any of this information out of my static brain, I hear the man cough. I turn back to Mr. C.'s desk and see him behind it now, leaning on the desk and trying to get my attention. One more cough for good measure.

"I can wait outside, Mr. Cheethers," I emphasize the elongated 'e' to see if I can get a rise. No dice. His whiskered cheeks don't even flinch. *How did I not notice the new whiskers since last week?* They looked to have sprouted overnight. Then, it hit me that he called me what I wanted, not my hideous birth name.

He waves his hand, "Nonsense, Star."

I do flinch a little.

"I've been thinking about the status of things, and we might've gotten off on the wrong foot last week. Know what I mean?"

When I don't like something, I twist my tangled hair around my index finger. This starts happening (I realize), as he offers a 'let's be friends' gaze.

"You are new to high school here at Idyll, and so am I. Did you know that?"

I did not. My purview was simply 1. survival at Cascade last year and 2. make friends at this place. I had no time for reconnaissance on teachers at Idyll High or their likelihood to murder students. So, I did what seemed best when trapped in a classroom with a schizo teacher and stood as still as marble. (I saw fainting goats at one of the Chattanooga fairs last summer, and I thought I could mimic them if absolutely necessary.) Then, when I realized Mr. C. was still gawking at me, I quickly shook my head.

"I am. Hand to God. The other ELA teacher, Mrs. Bottleheim, went on maternity leave at the start of school. Can you believe that?" he laughed with mirth. "I mean, who has a baby at the start of a school year? Talk about perfect timing! She is out indefinitely. Bottleheim has been teaching in this very ELA room for eons, according to the other teachers. And, *bam*! Now, I'm here to mold your young minds. Ain't that something?" he asked, clapping his hand on his khakis.

"Bottleheim," I heard my voice croak, sneaking a glance at the wall clock. The five minutes to 8 o'clock felt locked in a battle with itself. "Gone for a while?" I added.

"As long as maternity lasts. But you get the benefit of me, until then," he said, flashing a smile, eyebrows raised. "What do you have in the backpack? Don't you worry about having to put it in the locker. I am cool with you keeping it in class. Besides, lockers are a nuisance," he said, waving his hand through the air.

Did he say 'ain't' and 'cool' just now? I wondered, shaking my head as if in a daze. *Who was this guy, and didn't he know 'ain't' isn't proper English?* But before I could say anything, the bell rang and in stormed my peers with copies of *The Old Man and the Sea* begrudgingly held under their armpits and on top of binders.

I took my place and waited for Oscar to join us. My head craned from our classroom front door to Mr. C. like he might've eaten him and that was the reason for his 'too good' good mood. But neither Mr. C. admitted it, nor did Oscar come in after the tardy bell rang. My shoulders visibly slumped as I imagined not being able to tell him about the odd stuff that just happened or give him the pizza bites. Then I stared at the clock for a different reason and willed the time to stop. *Where the heck was he?* I wondered.

"Take your copies of *The Old Man and the Sea* out and lay them on your desks, please," Mr. C. said, looking from desk to desk, as the paperbacks *fumphed* down in succession. He patrolled from rows 1-5 and across the back row where I sat with an empty chair beside me. "Oscar not feeling well?" he stooped, whispering in my ear.

I shrugged my shoulders, still unsettled by this sudden kindness.

"Well, if you don't mind, Star, just tell him what he misses," he added, strolling back to the front.

Corine Bostic raised her hand and cleared her throat.

"Yes, Corine?" Mr. C. replied.

"Mr. Chethers, why do we have to read this book? It's sooo old. And didn't this guy like kill himself or something?" she whined.

I rolled my eyes and waited to see how this new and improved Mr. C. would respond. But before I could take a mental picture, he did the unexpected again and turned to me, "Star, what do you think our reason is for reading Hemingway?"

Too flummoxed to reply, I pursed my lips then thought about what would put Corine in her place quickest. Before I knew it, my mouth opened and came out with, "If it's considered classic literature, it must be good for a multitude of reasons. Regardless of who wrote it."

Mr. C., rather than scolding my smart aleck reply, turned to his desk again and looked to the wall where the map rested. Then, he turned and did the darndest thing and agreed with me.

"She's right. We can infer so much from such a tiny book, because it was written with such poignancy and depth. It's a classic, and I will fight anyone who wants to argue otherwise," he added, looking around the room.

With that gesture, Corine huffed under her breath and turned her torso to stare back at me in row five. I felt her smoldering gaze and somehow felt oddly satisfied in this brief moment, despite it being with the help of Mr. C.

The clock moved like an ant across a giant Sequoia somewhere in the vicinity of where Oscar came from, and I kicked myself for thinking about two bad things at once. Yes, time was moving slowly, but I didn't need to fret about Oscar. Not yet. *Maybe he was just taking a breather from all of this madness?* I reasoned. If he comes back, I'll make sure the pizza bites are in his chair for tomorrow. *Wait, do pizza bites need to be refrigerated?* I wondered. *Of course they do, you doofus. They have dairy and stuff. How could I be so silly about things like that?* Despite my brain synapses telling me otherwise, I lifted the tinfoil out of my backpack and placed it in Oscar's vacant seat.

When I took my eyes off the tinfoil, I saw Corine still gawking at me, and I stuck my tongue out. Juvenile, I know. But I was not ready to roll over just yet. Besides, Mr. C. was somehow different to how he was the last week, and I still couldn't believe he was being 'nice.' I shook my head and heard details about the novella in most of the students' hands: Santiago, Cuba, marlin, eighty-four days, Manuel, baseball. A few students yawned as Mr. C. recited from Hemingway's biography on the back of the book. He smiled and asked questions with alacrity, and I wondered what else weird would happen today. Before I could piece together anything else about our book, the bell rang. A harsh blackbird squawked outside, and class was dismissed.

Chapter 6

If I was allowed to get a cell phone, I probably wouldn't get one anyways. Mom liked to say that 'they' meaning her and Dad thought it was parentally wise to dodge any potential mishaps with cellular phone usage. Since I didn't know what parents thought about 24/7 or why everyone was so bent out of (or into) shape about socials, I simply shrugged when they told me to worry about it later. My 'nonexistent' friends all walked around school sneaking peaks at their pockets like burrowing creatures, but I found myself looking outside more anyways. Now that Oscar was in Idyll (and a 'friend'), I wondered if he had a phone. I would ask him next time I saw him. *Where was he?* I wondered, scanning my brain of images of our meetup at the lockers, his thin mustache. He didn't seem the type, but that might just be me casting 'aspersions' is what our pastor called it. No sooner had I thought this than I felt Dad's prodding elbow at my ribcage.

"Star, pay attention," he whispered, leaning down to my tangled cobweb of hair Mom had tried to fix.

I smirked but found my eyes raising to the pulpit and studying the lectern, Pastor Joe, behind it. We regularly attended the Idyll Community Gathering every Sunday, and I went largely because Mom and Dad were raised in the 'Bible Belt' of the South. Chattanooga had a lot of churches. Over seven hundred by my last count in scouring the zip codes, walking the neighborhoods, and asking people why there were so many religious buildings. Dad said people needed to believe in a higher power; we were wired that way. Mom agreed and asked if I had any questions about faith. It came out in her sweet, Altoid-scented voice in the van on the ride home, and I felt the real question beneath her tender vocals. *Did I believe in God yet?* I knew they wanted me to explore faith deeper, but I was content staring at the wooden platform where Pastor Joe, or PJ as the youth group kids called him, admiring the mahogany design, the etchings of 'This Do in Remembrance of Me' across the front panel with deep, intentional engravings. My mind jumped to things like this, but I could hyper focus if I needed to. Such as spending time counting all the churches I could find.

"Well, Star?" Mom asked, eyeing me quizzically.

I realized she wanted an answer. "God hasn't spoken to me yet," I replied, remembering some of the other youth kids saying this reply in church.

"He will," Mom beamed, then turned to Dad.

Dad kept both hands on the wheel of the van and guided us down Amnicola Highway and through some of Chattanooga's picturesque neighborhoods until we reached our split-level. I hopped out and slammed the sliding door on the aging Chevy Astro.

"Easy, Star. This van is quite a bit older than you," Dad said, not raising his voice louder than the clang. "We gotta treat her right in order for it to last us."

Until when? I wondered. The van was rusting on the side panels, above the wheels. It was older than Dad looked.

Mom unlocked the front door, and we entered the hallway, and I knew Dad or Mom was going to ask about lunch. I was ravenous and usually didn't wait, but today, I said unprompted, "PB & J, anyone?"

Both looked at one another, and I said, "My treat."

They stared at me as if they knew I was up to something, but I didn't relent. "Milk, too."

Mom smiled at Dad, then me, "Sure honey," she said. Then, "I'll get the plates."

I didn't mind that they 'thought' they could read my brain, but I knew they would never guess everything just exactly right. Without a phone, I had been racking my 'neuroplasticity' for non-phone ways to discover Oscar's whereabouts. With him missing class, the weekend had started and now almost ended without a clue. *Would a Google search be sufficient?* I wondered. Sometimes the Internet put people's addresses (and entire existences) online, and predators loved that, Mom said. In our house we were 'Luddites' Dad often proclaimed; he said we should wear the label like a banner of sorts. Again, I didn't put much stock in electronics in general, but I did see the output and benefits at school. We were given Chromebooks in 8th grade and showed how to write certain types of English papers. Then, when we were done, we turned them back in to the teacher with a 'cart' where all the black, plastic machines fell asleep and charged overnight. Like magic, they were recharged for the next time we needed them, and we could search for all kinds of interesting things during class.

Even though I spent most of my time at the Administration office in Cascade Middle, I recall the search engine screens flashing blank boxes across all of our student laptops. When I typed 'Australian koala,' (my favorite animal) for the first time a world of images had popped up of a creature I longed to see one day. Then, my next search, after I had 'backspaced' to the beginning and there were no words at all in my blank box, I had typed 'Taj Mahal,' and a million beautiful images of the white marble 'mausoleum' appeared. It was a miracle to see so much, so quickly. At home, I had to rely on the books on my shelves and what Dad begrudgingly searched on his cell phone, only after listening to me badger him for hours. So, the school laptops were a great delight to me when Cascade was so boring. *Dad's phone*, I thought. *That's it!*

After church, he always placed it in their room so that 'distractions' would be at a minimum. They worked so much already, it was important to have family time, he always said. Mom never argued. Their jobs always left them very sleepy when they got home at night. I made the PB & J sandwiches as quickly as a raccoon digging through a dumpster might, and I placed milk in three glasses at the dinner table. Then, when both Mom and Dad had changed out of their clothes (and I was certain the phone was safely put into their dresser drawer), I crept to the living room and waited for their familiar *thump thump* (Dad) and *swish swish* (Mom) noises to enter the kitchen.

"Star, well thank you," I heard Dad yell, shock in his voice.

"That was real nice, honey," Mom added. "Aren't you going to join us? We can say grace, but we'll wait for you."

I'd forgotten about 'grace,' but in my quick thinking, I yelled, "You guys go ahead, I need to get something, and then I'll be down."

It wasn't a lie, I told myself. I needed a way to search for something.

"Okay, girl," Mom said, and I could hear Dad giving thanks for the sandwiches.

As best I could, I tip-toed from the living room down the hall to their room, found the coveted dresser drawer (Dad's side), and opened it without a squeak. There, nestled under some of his well-worn white t-shirts, was the old, early-edition iPhone. I remembered how he'd unlocked it, swiping his fingers across in a box motion, starting with the top-left. It unlocked on the first try, and I stared at the Google search bar. *Why hadn't I thought about the words I'd use to find him?* I thought. That was more important than getting the phone or making a hasty search. It mattered more than any act of 'espionage.' But I thought about it, and eventually, I decided to just type his name and the city we lived in, because what else does one do with the blank box if you don't have much information? The computer figures it out; I recall hearing from some teacher at Cascade. Figure it out, Computer, I thought, as my chipped fingernails clicked into the search box 'Oscar Villanueve (his last name came up in Mr. C.'s class that first day) Chattanooga TN,' and I clicked the little magnifying glass image on Dad's phone. Nothing came up on the results at all, at least 'pertinent' to the Oscar I knew.

Scratching my frizzy mess of hair, I pursed my lips and backspaced to a fresh start. Then, I decided to type in his last place, 'Oscar Villanueve Idaho.' It wasn't a lot to go off of, and I felt like a complete loser not having more to get me started, but I also knew Dad and Mom would holler for me at any moment. *How long did it take to eat PB & J? Ten seconds? Fifteen?* I pictured them draining their milk at that very second. I really didn't want them to find me snooping, especially after having just come from church. The results loaded, and I saw not much about anyone I could determine was a kid, or close to Oscar's age. Then, before closing the phone, I realized there was a second page, and I clicked on it.

The third result on page two got my attention. The headline read 'Villanueve youth awarded Boise medal for rescuing drowning swimmer.' Below this heading, there was a mention of an 'Oscar Villanueve, age 13' and a thumbnail image of his shaggy (somewhat younger) head, pince-nez glasses and blue-green eyes. I held my breath in for too long and realized I might pass out. Then, the familiar, startling, "Star, honey?" came from the kitchen.

I shut the phone and slammed Dad's dresser drawer too hard. My steps down the hallway felt like walking on clouds that couldn't support my weight. I felt relief at knowing something else about my new friend, and suddenly, I felt something else akin to what might be pride.

Chapter 7

Monday morning and my alarm clock rang with a 'ferocity' like the bells of Notre Dame. My head ached from falling asleep face down on my pillow and feeling like I'd semi-suffocated in my sleep. I found my holey jeans in a pile on the floor, and I brushed my teeth with some Sensodyne. For some reason, my gums were agitated going from hot to cold food and drinks. I swished the fluoride around and spit it out into the sink. I wasn't vain, but this morning I looked in the mirror and saw bags under my eyes. *Not good*, I thought. I usually just put my bird's nest hair up in a ponytail and ran for the door, but today I considered a rare use of lip balm, and some perfume Mom once tried on me. Not sure what it was, but I spritzed it and walked into a horrid garden of Lavender and Rose. It would have to do.

"Almost ready, Sweet Pea?" Dad called from the bottom of the banister.

I slipped into my faded Chucks and lunged down the stairs two at a time.

Dad placed a cup of juice in my hand, and I found the Eggo waffles resting stiffly in the toaster. Not waiting for plates and conversation, I folded them into a paper towel and chugged the cranberry tartness. *I'll never have a UTI*, I figured. *Thanks, Dad.*

He gave me a hug and held the storm door open for me with one arm, "See you at bedtime, Pea. We both gotta work late again," he offered.

"I figured," I told him, giving him a peck on the cheek. "See you," I hollered over my shoulder, making my way to the squeaky-braked bus that had just arrived.

The bus swung open its doors, and I walked with a different gait past the driver, Mr. Holcomb, to my unassigned seat. It had peeling fake leather, and I liked the feel of the frayed edges when my fingers gripped at the openings. I dropped my bag and put my hand up for the inevitable lurch forward. Being one of the first two pupils on the morning commute, I had the benefit of Mr. Holcomb talking to me. The other (and first student) never made eye contact but stared straight ahead the entire trip. It was a tad odd, but I was fine with that.

"You okay this morning, Star?" Mr. Holcomb asked.

I held up my covered Eggos as a reply.

"Breakfast of champions," he grinned, steering the bus along the Chattanooga streets. "Good weekend?"

"It was better than I thought it'd be," I said, thinking of the search last night. My mind raced from where I sat to the future prospects of the day. *Would Oscar tell me about this stuff?* I wondered. I hoped he would sit down at lunch and tell me his whole life story. Plus, I couldn't wait to tell him how different Mr. C. had been last class. It was a good bit of anticipation for the new week.

"Your face looks a little different?" Mr. Holcomb added, but not in an 'insensitive' way. I liked that he was a non-creepy bus driver unlike the one that worked at Cascade Middle who had a tendency to always use the bus stairs as an opportunity to gawk at boarding students. I never called him on it, but if I was still with him this year, I would have. Somehow, I felt bolder than I had in previous years. It was empowering to know that school didn't have to be brutal and lonely.

"My face hasn't slept well," I offered, waiting to see if he would reply, staring at him in the rearview mirror.

"Oh, I wasn't talking about that," he laughed. "You just look a little more prepared today," he said.

"Nope," I said, moving my lips over the gloss, breathing in a little of the lavender. "You have a good weekend?" I redirected.

Mr. Holcomb, never one to waste an opportunity to chat, sped into a conversation with himself about gardening, motorcycles, and some trip planned for Seattle, and I only offered an occasional *Mm hmm* to keep him going. He liked the conversations to flow this way, because he never once paused on the whole trip to school except to admit new pupils onto his bus. It was only at the school's parking lot that he exhaled and said his 'Goodbyes' to me and the lot. I wished him well, and he said his usual exclamation, "Don't study too hard or you'll go blind."

I walked the stone steps up to Idyll High's front entrance and entered with one last glance toward Chartreuse Lake and the valley. It was beautiful with the sun coming up over Signal Mountain. If I tried really hard, I could almost envision people at Lookout Mountain preparing to descend to Ruby Falls for a photo opportunity and cooler temperatures. My day would be above ground, but for the tourists, it would be a trip into natural wonders and the inevitable stop at Rock City Gardens to squint toward seven states.

My hand pushed open the front door, and I walked past the Main Office with 'bravado' I'd never mustered in middle school. Since my first week, no teachers apart from Mr. C. had even threatened me with a trip to the principal. It felt like my redirect was from Oscar's good graces, and I knew Mom and Dad were happy that their phones hadn't rung since the start.

The locker combination worked on my first try, and I swung the door open and squeezed my grimy backpack into its narrow corridor. My copy of *The Old Man and the Sea* rested on top of my 3-ring binder, and I pushed my pencil behind my ear. Part of me wanted to walk toward Mr. C.'s class to see if he would be overly kind again, but a greater part of me was 'apprehensive' about testing it. Instead, I turned to walk toward the girl's bathroom to linger in a stall before the bell chimed. Before I could get more than a step away from the lockers, I felt a push in my back and high-pitched laughter. And before I could see my assailants, a foot or something came across my ankle and took me forward at breakneck speed. I barely had time to land with my palms turned downward to catch my fall, my book and binder sliding away from me. When I turned over, I saw Corine Bostic staring up at me with a mischievous grin on her face.

"Can't walk, Freida?" she cackled. "If I didn't know better, I'd say you were still learning to stand upright this year," she added, looking at her cronies, a brunette and a blonde, both standing icy still.

Rather than give them the satisfaction of watching me check for bruises or cuts, I collected my things and tried to control my rage. *Don't get suspended*, I heard in my brain. It would keep me away from seeing Oscar, learning anything, and I didn't want to see the looks at home. *These girls aren't worth it.* I brusquely pushed past them, my things clutched close to me, and I entered the bathroom, slamming the farthest stall door, collapsing into a heap on the toilet and finally letting myself breathe. "So, this was how it was going to be?" I asked no one but myself.

CHAPTER 8

Oscar came into class, and I noticed the pizza bites were still resting in his chair. I quickly snatched the tinfoil (knowing a weekend was too long to leave them there) and held it under my desk. He didn't let on when he saw the gift, and he took his chair without giving me a glance. I didn't register any coldness but noticed he had marks on his arms and legs that looked like he'd gotten into a fight with a cougar. Some of his marks were scabbed over, and I stared at his calves for a minute before my brain told me to stop. Mr. C. was rigid at his desk, marking attendance from his computer screen. *Is he back to his scary self?* I wondered. Before I could take additional inventory, he looked up and caught my eye. Then, quickly he scanned the room and marked two students absent according to empty chairs. We were twenty-three of twenty-five strong.

Rather than speak out of turn, I did the opposite and raised my hand.

Mr. C. gave a curt nod.

"Can I put this in the trash?" I asked the teacher.

"May I, and yes," Mr. C. replied, looking at the desk, where a copy of Hemingway's work rested.

I took the pizza bites and tossed them regrettably in the bin. *So much for that,* I thought. At my desk, I took out *The Old Man and the Sea* and pretended to mull over its contents. *How many times can I read this before class is over?* I wondered. It was such a short book. Hard to enjoy if you sped through it like I did other works. *It was no Dostoevsky,* I reasoned. But it was 'required reading' for the 9th grade year, and so, I agreed to what was in front of me.

Mr. C. crossed his arms and waited for the class to look his way. No one in the front row looked away as he stared at rows two through five. It typically took the successive rows a little longer to comply, but not when he stared at us. Something felt off, and I could tell it would be best to not speak up during the hour. Corine Bostic sat as straight as an arrow and never once looked backward at me. I tried to bore holes into the back of her head with my eyes; if it was humanly possible to make a dent in someone's body, I would be the first with my eyes.

Oscar took out a sheet of paper and scribbled in his fancy style again. I felt relief wash over me as he wrote something and hunched his body over his desk. *Maybe it would be another note? Something to 'summarize' the past few days.*

As his pen looped on the page beside me, I felt his intensity and waited for some guidance from the front. In American education, it is customary for teachers to teach in a largely 'archaic' style. The Socratic method (especially in English) creates a dynamic where teachers 'expound' and pupils listen at the feet of the master. The engagement level is largely minimal until the hour is up, some assignment sent home or posted on the board. Today, Mr. C. waited for something beyond our stillness to bring him to life.

My eyes kept to the pages of the book where I reread lines concerning Santiago's poor luck, no fish. *My life was a lot like the old man's,* I realized. *What do we do when it's been eighty-four days with no fish? We go out for day eighty-five,* I reasoned. But the going is easier said than done, because I never liked bullies in Cascade, and I certainly don't tolerate them now. I was already formulating how I would get Corine and company back. My rational brain struggled with bouts of 'instability' every time I came across someone who thought they were better just because of strength or dumb luck.

Mom's voice rankled my brain with her soft, "Turn the other cheek, Star."

I shook the reply away, and sure enough, there was Dad with, "Sweet Pea, don't sweat it. There's always a way through it."

My parents had that way of getting into my head space, almost like an MRI. It was all good things they wanted for me, I knew. For starters, in 9th grade they were all about teaching me time management, preparing for future academic goals (college included), and how to save for a rainy day. But I wanted to turn that 'logical' side off most times when I thought seriously about it. *I can do it better,* I thought. *Leave me alone.* And they usually went away when I simply shook my ponytail. I did it instinctively, and it looked like I was arguing with myself like a crazy person.

Here it comes, I thought. One. Two. Shake. And it worked. Just like that, I was parent-free again. Oscar, beside me, paused in his writing. He looked up for the first time, and he pushed his hair out of his eyes with his penciled hand. When I looked at my book with greater intensity, I prayed he wouldn't find me weird like everyone else. His lips turned into a smile, and he went back to the paper.

Mr. C. still glared at the remaining rows of students. When I didn't think I could remain silent any longer, he cleared his throat and finally said, "Mr. Villanueve, I want you to tell us what this book is about," without looking at the copy on his desk.

My stomach lurched because I didn't think Oscar even knew to finish the reading. He wasn't here to know what was expected of us. But without a pause, Oscar gently sat his pencil down on his desk, sat up straight, and met Mr. C.'s gauze.

"You read the book, didn't you?" Mr. C. smirked, shifting his stance from one leg to another.

Oscar fumbled to the paperback copy below his desk and brought it out slowly. The spine didn't even look cracked, and I knew he was a goner. With his eyes rejoining the teacher, Oscar opened his mouth and said, "Yes, sir," Oscar said, handling the 'pristine' copy. "It's a great novella," he added, with genuine warmth in his teenage voice.

"Don't try to con me," Mr. C. spat. "That book doesn't even look read. The cover is uncreased, and I bet you just bought it on Amazon two days ago."

Oscar looked down to his copy and back to his teacher. He politely said, "It's one of my favorites, sir. I don't know how many times I've read it, but it always makes me happy."

"Happy?" Mr. C. asked. "Happy how? There's not a bit of joy in it," Mr. C. said, finally unfolding his arms and walking toward Oscar and my chairs.

"Sure, there is," Oscar said, interrupting Mr. C.'s approach. "He learns perseverance even at his old age, and he teaches the boy to stay with it. The boy is there for him, and he's so happy to see Santiago upon his return. Don't you think?" Oscar asked.

Mr. C. exhaled loudly and looked from Oscar to the other rows. I kept my head down; it felt like a battleground, and I didn't want my new friend to be sacrificed. Mr. C. stared at his opponent, and Oscar looked from the book to the teacher with something I thought was genuine compassion.

Before the tension could reach a boiling point, I raised my hand and Mr. C. shook his head at me. It offered enough of a distraction that Oscar was able to look from our teacher to me and back again. Mr. C. turned to look at the clock, and I knew he was off again. It felt like a light switch going from illumination to darkness. He gave Oscar one more incredulous stare and walked back to his desk. *Something was definitely off*, I knew. It was only a matter of time before the answers would make some inevitable rise to the surface.

Chapter 9

The lunchroom felt oppressive with heat when we filed into it that day. Cafeteria ladies opened metal trays containing beefaroni and industrial grade vats of mashed potatoes. As they did this, steam rolled upward and out, over the Plexiglas barriers, into the room. I felt the heat so fully I imagined I could see it. When asked whether I wanted any of each, I just moved my head up and down, and the workers splatted the food onto each rectangle divider. If Elliott Bench or Corine or some other thug wanted to come over today and try to interrupt us while eating, they were going to have to go through me. I had to know what was up with Oscar. He pointed to a far corner of the cafeteria, not yet occupied, and I followed.

When we sat, he clasped his hands together and bowed. I sat awkwardly for a few seconds before noticing he now looked at this food.

"I didn't know you prayed," I whispered.

"Not always," he said, picking up his fork, pretending to enjoy the beefaroni as he brought it to his lips. "I forget a lot at school."

Now I wanted to ask him why he prayed, but I was interrupted by my silly brain. There wasn't much time. Looking at the slimy mashed potatoes on my plate and back to him, I said, "I did something immature, Oscar. I looked you up online, and I know it was wrong, but I couldn't figure out a way to talk to you, and you weren't at school so I went online and found this article about Idaho, and it showed you after rescuing a kid or something. Is it true?"

What is wrong with me? I thought, face reddening. *Would you just be quiet and let him talk?*

He put down his uneaten noodles and grinned, "I didn't think you had a cell phone."

"Oh, I don't. It was my dad's. I snuck into his room and looked you up that way. It felt like forever since we'd last talked, and I wanted to make sure you hadn't evaporated or something. Is it true?" I asked, finally exhaling.

He laughed but not at me, I noticed. "You're funny, Star, but in a cool way. I think you might be the only original thing about this entire place. Did you get in trouble for taking your dad's phone?" he asked.

"No," I said, looking at my milk, shaking the carton, then opening its tabs. I took a good long pull and imagined the calcium hitting my bones instantly. Then, I wiped my lips on my shirt sleeve and put it down. "I replaced it after making that search online. It was a two-minute job," I added, smiling back.

"My dad and I like to go mountain biking sometimes, and it takes us a few days away from the city. We go into the mountains around here, sometimes farther. He says we're going to bike all of the surrounding places that Chattanooga has to offer. Have you ever been before?"

I laughed out loud, glad I hadn't taken another sip of milk at that moment, because it would've shot out of my nostrils. Then, I shook my head.

"I bet you'd be good at it," he encouraged. "It's as much about your mind as the muscles sometimes. You have to want to get up the hills and some inclines are gradual."

"Nope," I said. "I've only ever taken bikes down suburbs and streets that are fairly flat. Not sure how I'd feel about going out into the woods with a bike," I said, blushing again that he thought I'd be good at something.

"It's how I got these cuts and scrapes," he said, pointing to his arms and legs.

I tried to not gawk at his body like I had in class. *Staring is rude,* I heard Mom say in my head.

"I was writing you a note in class to tell you about all of it, but I got interrupted by Mr. Cheethers. That threw me off, and I didn't get to finish it," he said, pointing to his pocket.

"You handled that interrogation extremely well," I encouraged. "He wanted to trip you up. That's what I wanted to tell you about but couldn't," I said, looking at his face, checking out my reflection in his glasses. "You caught him like we did the last week when he was all psycho. But when you were out, he was super nice. I don't know if you believe me, but it was the oddest case I've seen in someone before. Mom tells me not to psychoanalyze anyone, but it was like he had some condition. He went from being a menace to kind, almost caring, and then today back to terrorizing us. I wish you could've seen it. Do you believe me?" I asked, exhaling at the last word, louder than I meant to.

Oscar sat there for a minute, and I wanted him to hurry up. We didn't have a lot of time left, and the cafeteria was always unpredictable with 'testosterone' levels and other things. Finally, he bit his bottom lip and said, "Hmm."

I needed more than 'Hmm' to get me through to some form of understanding. This time at Idyll High could shift into Cascade Middle at a moment's notice, if I wasn't careful.

"So, he went from evil to polite and back to evil all in a few days, and he takes it out on us for no good reason at all?" Oscar asked.

"It seems," I encouraged. "I'm thinking he could have a bipolar tendency, but I figured you might know more about it," I said, looking at Oscar but trying not to be too desperate with my voice.

"How so?"

"Well, you're a guy, and he seems pretty good with the boys in the class, and last time he took it out on me. I thought maybe it made more sense to you. But then today, he took it out on you. Now, my hypothesis is falling apart," I said.

Oscar laughed. Then said, "Well, maybe you're onto something. Maybe it is a mental thing. I mean, what's the other solution? He's a werewolf?"

I looked at him and could tell by his voice that he wasn't being serious, but I had entertained that notion a little bit. Chattanooga could be a creepy place at night, resting in a valley, all kinds of mountains around it. Dad and Mom always told me to not go to magical solutions so quickly, but I knew there were things lurking beneath the surface, especially in places like Ruby Falls where fish didn't need eyes to see.

Seeing Oscar's stare, I wanted to add something like laughter to his offhand comment, but my vocal cords were static.

"Joking," Oscar offered. "All the werewolves stay in the Pacific Northwest I've been told."

It was my turn to say, "Hmm."

"Do you know anyone who's bipolar?" Oscar asked.

"I had an aunt who was diagnosed with it," I said. "Why?"

"We could investigate and see how it affects her and cross-compare the symptoms," Oscar said.

I was pleased that he went this far to show his interest (and seriousness) with my concerns for Mr. C. Instead of agreeing, I shook my head, said, "No. You're probably right. It's more than likely just something I took too far and imagined. I got in a lot of trouble at my last school, Cascade, and I'm supposed to do the opposite here. It helps Mom and Dad sleep better at night, too," I half-smiled.

"I believe you," Oscar said, touching my arm for a brief second, looking at me with his blue-green eyes. "Seriously. I can take better notice of him in our next class. That way we can confirm your suspicions or learn something else," he said, letting go of my arm.

I felt the warmth of that touch, and the cafeteria suddenly felt less stuffy but more inviting if that was possible.

"Star, you good?" he asked, looking at me again.

"Oh, yeah. I'm good," I said, picking up my lunch tray. The bell rang in symmetry with my action. I had the timing of my schedule already down to a science. Oscar rose, too. We dumped our trays but lingered at the cafeteria exit. I didn't want to leave just yet. Oscar hovered beside me.

"I think we should investigate," he said.

"Okay."

"Tomorrow?"

"Fine," I said. "Hey, have you really read Hemingway that many times?" I asked.

"No lie," he said. "One of my favorites. Still is. Hey, by the way, thanks for whatever was in the tinfoil. You didn't have to throw it out. What was it?"

"You don't want to know," I said, trying to not think about the silliness of baking for him.

"I do. I appreciate any gifts," he said, pushing his glasses up the bridge of his nose. "Especially ones from friends," he added.

My mouth formed a slight grin, and I uncharacteristically pushed a stray hair out of my face.

"Was it cookies? If it was cookies, they would've been great right about now."

"Nope," I countered.

"Brownies?"

"Wrong again."

Oscar licked his lips, and I was suddenly hungry again. Brownies did sound good right about now. I should have tried to force down a few bites of lunch. Now I would be 'ravenous' the remainder of the day, stomach rumblings and all. "Not dessert, but something you said you loved," I said, smirking.

"Oh no. You didn't throw away *those*," he half-shouted.

"Made from scratch," I smiled full-on now. "I didn't believe risking your health from something left in the chair over the weekend was safe. You know, salmonella, e coli, and all that family of bacteria. I didn't want you to die on me," I said.

The entire cafeteria was now empty, and the tardy bell was going to ring any second. I didn't want to move away from the spot, our privacy, but I knew a trip to administration was out of the question.

"Hey, we should probably go," Oscar answered for me. "You think?"

I nodded and walked beside him through the exit.

"You made me pizza bites from scratch and threw them away," he said. "Incredible."

"That's why you should attend school," I teased. "But mountain biking does sound way cooler," I said.

He elbowed me playfully, and I wasn't sure what to do with that gesture. I cleared my throat and wondered if I'd get written up. It would be a high school first for me. I imagined Oscar had never been in trouble. *He rescued a kid from drowning, didn't he?* If that was the case, he definitely didn't come across as someone serving any time in detention.

"You really rescued a kid?" I blurted out, immediately hating myself.

"Don't believe everything you read on the Internet," he smiled. "Things get blown out of proportion all the time."

"But you did it?" I said, raising my eyebrows a little.

"The boy lived," was all he said in reply.

I could sense he didn't want to go further with it, and I put a 'proverbial' zipper on my lips. *Who was this new friend, really? He prays before meals and saves kids?* It felt like I had a hero best friend, and Idyll High didn't even know someone so cool was gracing it with his presence. I felt bigger just walking beside him, carrying my binder and annotated Hemingway book. When we walked past Corine and her crew, I held my head high, intentionally pushing away thoughts of their 'shenanigans' last week. I felt forever away from the humility and the far stall in the girl's bathroom.

Oscar elbowed me just then, asked, "Are those girls always like that?"

"Indeed. And they never seem to change," I said, thinking of middle school and all that baggage from Cascade.

"Well, it's not important," he said. "What *is* important is our mission ahead of us," he smiled.

"Agreed," I said, pushing thoughts of mean girls away from my brain. Oscar turned to walk to his next class, and I suddenly didn't care about the tardy slip that awaited me.

Chapter 10

My preference was to walk along Chartreuse Lake and skip stones across the tranquil waters. Most of the boaters left the waters after Labor Day, and the water calmed down to a blue-green soup. The color reminded me of Oscar, and I realized that it was a fun comparison. When I left school, I thought of our conversation that day. He wanted the pizza bites, and I was glad I'd made them, even though the trash can was their home. I replayed what he'd said about mountain biking and climbing Chattanooga hillsides with his dad. It felt like an adventure within a town I thought I knew. He made everything sound so simple and 'accessible.' I crouched and selected a smooth, grey stone. It felt good to curve my fingers around its edge and send it skittering outwards from my body across the lake's surface, one, two, three, four hops. As friction slowed the rock, it eventually sank downward into the depths of the lake, and I looked out over the surface. There were blue herons perched above the dam where fishermen were casting their lines. It was the only activity besides myself, and I kept a wide berth and relished this solitude.

Mom and Dad never asked about these walks, because they trusted me, and they remained super busy with their jobs. Since I didn't have a cell phone, I asked them, "What about emergencies?" And they'd always said, "Don't have them." It was a running joke in our family and served as a reminder that technology didn't control us, we controlled it. Still, I wondered if they knew just how dangerous the world was. But these thoughts never lasted long, because I kept thinking about what I could discover in the city limits. There was so much to explore and investigate just inside town. Now, as I lifted another pebble from the embankment, I thought about the zones beyond. Places where Oscar went and what he thought of when he was getting whacked by branches on a less-traveled hillside. Then, I heard footsteps and quickly dropped the stone and stood up.

"Girl like you should be working on homework, shouldn't they?" a raspy, stern voice spoke from the steps above me.

I turned my head slowly, shocked that someone could sneak up on me so fast. The concrete steps built into the embankment led to the rocks along the shore, and it was not a simple landing spot for walkers. As I stared at the man, I took in his appearance in wide sweeps: thinning hair, tattered clothes, greyish pallor on his face, a walking stick instead of a fishing pole in his hand.

"You got a name?" he asked.

Considering all I knew about missing persons cases; I knew that it was all but impossible to find someone after the first forty-eight hours they went missing. If this gentleman tried something, I was prepared to scream as loudly as my fourteen-year-old vocal cords would allow. But I was too far away from the dam to be heard by the fishermen. *Here was that emergency I was talking about, Dad,* I thought. Then, just as quickly, I realized that this person looked more dead than alive, and I could push past him (maybe knock over) if anything. So, I relaxed my balled fists and turned fully to face him. "No homework," I offered, dodging the familiarity of exchanging names.

"Nice day for a stroll by the lake then," he said, his acne-scarred face trying to twist into a smile.

"It was," I said, emphasizing past tense.

"I won't disturb you then," the man replied.

Too late, I thought.

With no comment from me, we stood at an awkward 'impasse,' and I started to ball my fists again. If he was a study on human behavior at all, he would get the hint. But he put his weight on the hand holding the cane, and he winced a little as he did.

"How'd you get down here?" I heard myself ask, kicking myself for encouraging this dialogue.

"One step at a time," he said, then laughed. "How about you?"

At least he has humor.

I shrugged noncommittally and stared above him at my school in the background. *Would anyone still inside, a janitor maybe, be watching this unfold? Someone with a keen sense of impending doom?*

The glass windows from Idyll High sparkled with radiant sunlight, and I knew the only people still inside the building were desperately trying to get out, get home. It was a fruitless endeavor to hope for rescue.

Then, the man turned and looked behind him at the school on the hillside, and asked, "You like it there?"

"Not a lot," I replied, criticizing myself for offering more words.

"School can be dumb," he admitted, turning his gaze back to the water, my clenched fists. "You get into a lot of fights? I used to."

"Some," I said, trying to make my voice tougher than it felt. "I need to get started home," I added.

"Folks be looking for you, if you don't," he replied.

"Mom and Dad are expecting me," I said, wishing I was already past him on the stone steps.

"I'm Randall Tolley," he said, his raspiness turning to a cough at the introduction. "I used to work on things like the bridges here," he said, indicating the downtown area. "I was pretty good, too," he added, trying to smile again. The scars gave his face an almost clown-like appearance.

Again, I didn't proffer my name or anything beyond what he already knew. I didn't like him knowing I went to school right there.

"Slung a hammer for the city and for myself. Then got laid off. I turned to all kinds of dreadful things. Things you should stay clear of," he added, mimicking turning a bottle up with his bony hand. "I was here when that kid went missing over at Wolf Island," he said, pointing in the direction of the nearest bridge. "Sad story, you ever hear it?"

As much as I was ready to dart past this toothless guy, I scolded myself for suddenly wanting to know more. I shook my head 'no' and waited for him to continue. The sun was making its arc slowly downward beyond Northshore.

"Real sad stuff. A girl on one of those, what are they called? The thing where you stand on the board and use an oar to get around the water?"

"Stand up paddle board," I blurted.

"Yeah, paddle board. Real terrible way to get around if you ask me," he laughed, shaking his head. "Well, she was a visitor from somewhere. Ohio, maybe. Anyways, she didn't tell anyone she was visiting with that she was going to paddle over to Wolf and camp for the night. One of those 'I'm going to be Bear Grylls by myself' kinds of things. And so off she goes just before sunset one day. Right smack dab in the middle of downtown Chattanooga waters," he said, wheezing and spitting out something onto the rocks too close to where I stood.

I looked at him, shocked that some stranger felt compelled to tell me all of this, but still too fearful to get up on the steps with him. *I will wait till he passes*, I admitted. *If he passes by.*

"Anyways, the night got cold. It might've been in the teens. The girl stays out there that night and the next and the next and never comes back," he said, staring in that direction again.

"Hypothermia?" I asked, arms folded across my chest, trying to hasten the old man's tale.

"Nobody knows. Possibly. If she fell off that board and crawled on Wolf, she might not have been able to get a fire going. But I can't imagine how the search team didn't go over that place or someone on the bridge didn't see her. Can you?"

I shook my head slowly.

"The people looking for her didn't find her or anything else," he said, lowering his voice to a cautious whisper.

"Not even the board?" I asked.

"Nope. Or, the oar, or her clothes," he admitted, coughing again.

"Well, how'd they know she was there?" I asked, now confused.

"Her tent was there, and inside there was just a single book with her name in it," he grinned, pleased with his retelling, I imagined.

"Her book?"

"Yep, one she'd brought on her trip South, and the family identified it as her copy," he wheezed. Then, he looked at the sky and shifted his cane from one hand to the other. "Well, that's enough storytelling for one crusty sailor," he said, laughing. "I best get my steps in before the sun sets," he added, descending the steps and walking the opposite way from me.

"Did her family just stop looking for her?" I heard myself shout at his backside.

He turned slowly, looked at me with a puzzled expression and said, "I guess. They didn't have anything else. So, they stopped, and eventually got on with their lives. They didn't find her just like no one ever found that treasure on Wolfe either," he added, turning to go again.

My mouth opened to say more, but he was already limping farther away.

Chapter 11

September turned out to be the best month of my life, except for the creepy run-in with that Randall guy. My parents left cash for takeout, and I had a friend who was *sometimes* allowed to come over. Oscar said his parents were cool with it, as long as we didn't get into any trouble, and I thought that was very 'avant-garde' of them. Mom and Dad thought so, too, when they heard me tell it.

"No pregnancies, no drugs, no booze," Dad said, teasing me.

I didn't know or want any of what he said, but it was the way he said it that made me cringe. I kept all of that in a different dimension in my brain. There was 'life' and then there was 'damnation,' as our church said. I wanted the former and anything but something with the word 'damn' in it. So, I told them not to worry about me. I would be fine. Oscar was the last person on earth who I could imagine doing drugs.

"It's serious," Mom said, looking at me fully in my face.

"I was picturing Oscar with a drug," I said, stifling another laugh.

"She gets it, hon," Dad said, side-hugging Mom at my doorway.

"I just don't think she'd be laughing, if she knew what parenting was like," Mom said.

"Mom, Dad, really. I'm fine," I said, starting to shut my door.

"Okay, but it's still going to be just after school," Mom said, pointing her index finger at me. "And just until dinner (not when we get home)."

"Can we eat together?" I asked, looking at the card on the counter.

"If you have homework, you all can do that and eat on some nights," Mom relented.

My head instantly went to a word I'd never lived before, a 'date,' and I smiled at the thought of Oscar and me having some time to be ourselves outside of Idyll High School. It was a wonderful image in my head.

And the afternoons played out better than I could've ever imagined. Oscar would meet me outside the front entrance of Idyll High, and we would walk to my house toting our backpacks. He walked in silence mostly, but I could get him to talk when I shared some historical facts about Chattanooga. He really liked history, and I was in some ways his unofficial tour guide. "Just up here is where they buried that old president of the Ku Klux Klan," I'd say, and we'd file by in silence as I imagined Oscar was taking in the cemetery. Or, if we detoured a little on our trip to my house, I'd walk us past the monument marking where the Trail of Tears started and watch him closely as he stared at the flowing water across the channels.

"Can you imagine all of the chaos in uprooting so many people?" I asked him once.

"Can you imagine what the families felt?" Oscar replied, wiping his hair from his forehead, pushing his glasses up.

We took a long moment to think about such things, and I thought about what I always saw, a barefoot mom carrying a weeping child with another sibling in tow. Images of bleeding feet and skeletons trying to get to the middle of the US. All that pain and confusion and leaving the place once called home to a different destination that would never feel like the original. I shivered and wanted to change the topic, but Oscar was entrenched in it.

"Reservations are a terrible solution," he said, matter-of-factly, shaking his head.

"Indeed," I said. "But what's done is done."

"If our family left Idaho like Native Americans had to, I don't know if I'd stay put or just continue on to a different continent," he admitted. "What's the point in staying if it's not home and you knew it never would be?"

"That's what I was thinking," I agreed, adding, "without the Idaho part."

Oscar stooped and let his hand cup some of the pooling water. Once the water filled up, it overflowed down his pant leg. It was the first time he'd talked about Idaho since I'd brought up the rescue story. If he wanted to share more about whoever he was and whatever he'd done there, I was all for it. But it would have to be on his own terms. I bit my lip because I had so much trouble not knowing when to be quiet.

When Oscar stood up, he wiped the remaining water on his pants and said, "Lead on, wise sensei."

I laughed and led us through the streets toward my house. Once we were inside, I felt a slight jolt at having not just a boy in the house but a friend. It was amazing to have a chance to be someone, anyone else, outside of who I felt I was at school. We dropped our backpacks by the front door, and Oscar said, "Nice place, Star. We're still renting out at Hixson. Dad wants us closer to town, and he says maybe one day we will be. So then, we could just load our bikes and be at a mountain in a second."

"We've been here forever," I admitted. "My parents work *all* the time, so I have to create my own fun."

"What's fun for you?" Oscar said, like we'd just met. "You know everything about me, but I never got a note from you telling me all your likes and dislikes," he teased.

Admittedly, Oscar did share a lot in the note, but I felt there were ten thousand things he still hadn't opened up about. Now I was feeling nervous, because I didn't know how to tell him about my 'eccentricities' without scaring him away. Start slow, I told myself. Just don't overwhelm him.

"What would you like to know?" I asked, walking to the counter, picking up Mom's credit card from earlier. "Dinner's on me, by the way," I added, trying to sound cool.

Oscar laughed, flashing white teeth and an infectious smile. He said, "What should I know before this friendship goes any further?"

I loved how he could be completely himself and make me calmer all at once. Some people were great with numbers, and some could do like he did and put you at ease. It was a gift, I realized. For some reason, and I still don't know why, I decided to tell him about my run-in with Randall Tolley the other day. Not a great start, I thought. But maybe he would see more of my sense of adventure that way.

"So, this dude comes up to you, and you weren't scared? And you were alone? I would've split," he said.

"I thought about it, but I couldn't bring myself to leave. I dunno it was odd. It felt like he needed someone to talk to or something."

"And it was down at Chartreuse Lake after school?" Oscar asked.

"Yeah. I was walking along the shore, and he came out of nowhere, and I still don't know how he did it with that walking stick and being so weak," I said. The thought of Randall staring at me that day brought a shiver to my spine.

"And all he wanted was to tell you a story about some dead kid?" Oscar said, looking from me to the front door.

"Dunno. I guess, and before I realized it, I was too involved in what he was saying, and I didn't think I could break past him and go up the hill to school," I added.

"Spooky," Oscar agreed. "At least he didn't do anything or try to hurt you."

It felt good to know that my friend cared about that. I said, "I don't think he could've hurt me. He looked so weak and pale. Said he used to work on the bridges. Then he told me about the death," I trailed off.

"So many stories happen without us ever knowing about them, don't they?" he asked.

"Like what?" I said, curious.

"The one you just told, for example. It was delivered by an old dude to you about something that once happened here. You don't know if it did or didn't, but he was the one who told you. So, you'd have to do some real digging to find out if it's true or not. If it's not, you just got spooked by a really old stranger. But if it is, it's just one of millions that no one else really ever knows about or lives. Do you think a person can live stories?" Oscar asked.

"Of course," I said. "You're living one right now," I added, trying to not say anything too extreme.

"Like what?" he said, eyebrows raised.

"Take for example your trip to Chattanooga. You used to live in Idaho. Now, you live here and things you did there are a part of a story. It's only your story and no one else's. But it changes as you move from there to here. And since you moved here, you now know me. And before you were here, I was living a certain way and then you came to Idyll High. So, it changed the way each story was going. Ripples in a stream intersect and change shapes kind of stuff."

He gawked at me as I tapped the credit card on the counter. I was afraid I'd said something really bizarre. *Ripples in a stream,* I imagined. But he just laughed again.

"What?" I asked.

"That's really deep, Star. You have a unique mind, and I bet you are going to do crazy cool things when you get older."

"Tell me," I said.

"Go to the moon kinda stuff," he smiled. "You might help them develop some cure for cancer."

"Now you're just messing with me," I scolded. "I only told you that story, because I thought—"

"Seriously. I'm telling the truth. You have a way of thinking differently than everyone else."

"Tell me about it," I muttered.

Oscar held up his hand, calming my mind a little. "I meant it as a compliment. It's a gift."

Gift, I thought. It wasn't the way I'd labeled all the years of middle school. More like a curse and a penalty than anything. But his support changed my outlook a little bit. My stomach growled at that moment, and I looked at the card in my hand.

"I know what we should order," I said, surprising myself.

"What?"

"I owe you some pizza bites," I smiled.

Oscar didn't argue but licked his lips and agreed. After the order was placed, we had about forty-five minutes to burn, and I calculated the route the pizza delivery guy would most likely take.

"What do we do now?" Oscar asked, staring around the kitchen walls.

"I didn't tell you the most bizarre part of that Randall guy's story," I heard myself utter.

"Freakier than someone dying on an island?" Oscar said, frowning.

"The guy said they never found that treasure on the island either," I said, making sure to capture Oscar's blue-green eyes for a moment.

He looked dumbfounded and intrigued all at once, then said, "What treasure?"

Chapter 12

Mr. C. raced around the room. He talked about a lot of nonsensical things, and I tried to keep up. His voice went up and down in decibels, and it didn't ring true. I thought of a clown running out of air as he tried to shape balloons in the typical fashion. There was something else missing from the message of buried treasure. Mr. C. kept getting caught up in things about Shakespeare and Tim O'Brien and things that didn't matter. His eyes flashed from a green to a black shade, and I knew he was getting desperate. He banged the erasers against the chalkboard, and I wondered if he cared at all for the students he taught.

Oscar looked at me, and I stared out the window at Chartreuse Lake down below, and I couldn't help but distinguish between the pure and the error-prone, and I knew that things were better below the surface of the water. He droned on and on about hidden treasures and gold and riches. Oscar smiled, and I knew to stay quiet while the teacher huffed and puffed.

There was plenty to be seen and unearthed after class. There was a treasure waiting for us. I thought of gold trinkets and rubies and emeralds galore. Oscar put a finger to his lips, and I imagined us in a much different world. Mr. C. said, "See you all tomorrow."

The bell rang, and it was a slow-motion procedure of us moving outside the classroom, and then we were outside the walls and walking down the main halls and away from the eyes of the school. The remainder of the day went this same way, and Oscar must have suspected I was feeling grim, because he took my wrist for a second time and said, "Let's meet at my house after school."

I felt a whiplash effect, because I told Mom and Dad, I had a friend and was going to hang out with him for the afternoon. Dad launched into a tirade of questions about Oscar's family, their intentions in

Chattanooga. Mom smiled and was surprisingly quiet the whole time. Finally, Dad relented and said, "Be back by 9 PM. It's a school night, Star."

I ran at full speed to Oscar's house. Then, when I got there, he had two mountain bikes waiting for us. One was his, obviously he said. The other, he admitted, was his dad's. I asked him if it was okay to use his dad's bike, and he held up a hand. No worries, he'd already gotten permission. The way he said it made me believe that it was true. And just like that, he was slapping a riding helmet onto my head, the foam 'encapsulating' my skull and the chinstrap clicking into place. He did likewise, and we walked the bikes to the end of his driveway.

I started to ask where we were going, but he straddled his bike and said, "Let's go."

I climbed onto the bike and wobbly kicked off to follow in Oscar's path. The bike was surprisingly smooth, and I didn't know mountain bike tires could feel comfortable on a road. They were built for the hills, and I wondered if anyone else had ever tried this. When I caught up to him at a light, we leaned our bikes into a comfortable rest, and I said, "Where are we going?"

The helmet felt incredibly hot and muffled as I spoke, and I felt like a mummy under layers of warm garments.

Oscar turned to me, then pointed outward beyond the streets of Chattanooga, said, "Signal Mountain."

My jaw dropped as any sane human would because the distance looked 'astronomical' from where we stood at the intersection. As if reading my mind, he closed my jaw and said, "We'll go slow, and if it gets too intense, we turn back."

I believed him, but a large part of my stomach wanted to stay on the streets I knew so well. Before I could protest, the light changed, and the walking man appeared on the sign. We took off, and I felt confidence and apprehension tugging intermittently in a tug-of-war with my insides. The car traffic decreased as we turned onto a sidewalk which led to a hiking path. It allowed us to veer left and right in intervals along the bottom portion of signs pointing us up the mountain.

The switchbacks felt surprisingly nice, and I felt pride surging through my extremities as we went left and right. *This wasn't so bad,* I thought. I was climbing a mountain with my best friend, and it felt like we could go at this rate all day. Then, just as I was patting myself on the back, Oscar paused at our next turn and pointed uphill. My gut clenched like a hand wrapping around a wad of paper, crinkling it up. The path from this point on was almost straight up, and I felt what must be vertigo from the position we were in.

"I can lead, Star. If you feel it's too steep, we can walk the bikes. Okay?" he asked, leaning back on his handlebars, confident in something I didn't see.

I gave a weak nod, and gripped my handlebars looking up at the steepness.

"Dad's bike can do a lot of the work, but you just have to keep pedaling, and if it gets to a crawl, you can put your leg down and rest."

Again, I nodded, feeling less confident but not wanting to disappoint Oscar.

He started slowly up the hill and led at a pace I imagined must have been truly uncomfortable on his calves, but he didn't complain. He looked back frequently to check my progress, and I bit my lip and started heaving my legs in a grinding circular motion.

The bike did move forward with each crank that I gave it, and I noticed I was giving it forward momentum. The bike was moving me uphill, and I was better if I didn't look left or right to check my progress. When I did this, or glanced up ahead at the mountain looming, I lost my balance or freaked myself out, and the bike and I wobbled to a clumsy stop, me catching myself by sticking a leg out to break my fall.

True to his word, Oscar looked back and offered words of encouragement. His dad's bike was superior to his in so many ways, and I realized why he'd given it to me for this climb. We inched our way up the steep incline, and when I felt my legs burning beneath me, I finally gave the signal that I needed to walk to the next checkpoint. He came back and walked his bike alongside mine. The path was barely wide enough for two riders, but it felt good to have him beside me. Even though I felt horrible for slowing him down like this.

"You did so much better than I did my first time," he admitted.

I wanted to believe him, but it was hard to, considering how easy he made it look now.

"When Dad took us out here the first time, I tripped over a tree root going uphill," he laughed. "Can you imagine falling forward on this path?"

I knew I shouldn't, but I broke out into a laugh, and we walked and giggled with the image of him falling headfirst onto this steep path. If Oscar intended to distract me, it worked. We were on the next path, and the rest felt good for a moment. We sat our bikes on their kickstands, and we rested on a wooden bench placed conveniently at the top of this path. The afternoon breeze felt amazing on my sweaty shoulders and forehead. I pushed sweat away from my neck and helmet.

The next portion was just as steep, but Oscar swore it took us to the top of the mountain. While there were two more rest points, we only needed one of them. He said, "You're getting the hang of it already." The 'stamina' was coming to me much quicker than he remembered.

"What do you like best about this?" I huffed, trying to make conversation, anything to get my mind off of the burning calves.

He was quiet for what felt like forever, but then he said, "Doing it with someone else."

It was my turn to be silent, and I pictured him and his dad doing this on a weekend. It did feel better to have someone to talk to. I couldn't imagine climbing this slope with only my brain for company. Then, I tried to imagine Mom or Dad on this incline, and I laughed.

"What's so funny?" he asked, looking behind at my sweaty face again.

"Mom or Dad doing this," I admitted. "They would look silly."

"Everyone does the first time," he said. "Well, except you. You made it look pretty easy for a rookie," he added.

Part of me wanted to believe him. But I felt the tease and wondered if this was flirting. If it was, it felt good, and I didn't want it to stop. The larger part of me felt super weird about biking and trying to do something this crazy. I shook my head. "You're just messing with me."

He wiped sweat from his long hair, pushing it away from his glasses. They had fogged up on the last break, and he was trying to see through the condensation.

I laughed at him, and he gave a mock laugh in reply.

"Can you even see through those?" I asked, my sides hurting from the climb and laughing at him.

"Go ahead and make jokes," he said, offering a self-deprecating face. "I told you it was a workout."

"How much farther to the top?" I asked, wanting a break and not wanting the mood to change.

"It's just above that rise," he pointed, one hand steadying his handlebars.

There was a confidence in his motions that made me think he'd climbed this very hill countless times, even though he hadn't been in

Chattanooga long enough to do that. *Where had he ridden in Idaho to get so good?* I wondered.

"Are the paths out West anything like this?" I asked, breathing heavily now, wanting my mind to think of anything but the pain.

"They're gorgeous," he shouted back to me. "The trees, the terrain, and everything else. It's just different," he added, focusing more on his own way forward.

He's feeling it too, I thought. And the notion that he could get tired too suddenly gave me a little extra momentum. *I could do this. I was doing this!*

Instead of burning any extra energy on talking, we took to silence, and he incrementally crept up the remaining yards of the mountain, and I slowly followed. It was leg churning torture, and I thought of those Olympians who did this for gold. I remembered Dad watching the last Olympics on TV and announcers talking about how many years the riders had trained on mountains like the Alps. My thighs ached as I considered ranges steeper than what I was on.

"Almost there," Oscar huffed.

I pushed onward, and the gears groaned at me, and I leaned into the handlebars super hard, feeling the metal resistance. The bike remained solid, and I pushed a final time, and I amazingly came to a stop beside Oscar.

He was hunched over his handlebars and exhaling loudly. I did the same. When we finally regained our breath, he said, "You did it. Look!"

I steadied my gaze to where he pointed, and there was a platform and a few souls taking pictures of Signal Mountain scenery, Chattanooga below. We propped our bikes against a building, and Oscar said it was a coffee shop. I couldn't believe it. All the way up here!

"Let's take in the view and get a cup," he beamed, pride in his voice. "Celebrate your first time up the mountain."

I gave him a sudden hug and just as quickly let go. I felt embarrassed for such a quick reaction, but he hugged me back, and it felt great. I was proud of myself, but I was equally thankful for a friend who was there for me. The October air felt cool on my face as I removed my helmet and propped it on the bike's handlebar. The traffic and people at the bottom of the mountain looked tiny. We were so far away, and I tried to imagine how all of it was connected and together somehow.

Chapter 13

Before we left the mountaintop, Oscar closed his eyes and his breathing slowed. I asked him what he was doing, and he said he prayed at the tops of mountains with his dad. He asked if that was okay. I mumbled a half-hearted comment about it being fine, and he launched into a conversation with someone invisible. I stood there, eyes closed, because that's what you're supposed to do, right? And when he said, 'Amen,' I looked up, and he was smiling at me. I thought this strange but tried to smile back.

"What are you thankful for?" he asked, hands on his handlebar.

I fidgeted and searched for something to say.

"Really thankful for?" he added. "Like more than anything else in the world."

Before I knew it, the words were out of my lips, "Having a *friend* to do this with."

He looked from me to the elevations below; he scanned the terrain for something I was oblivious to. Then, he said, "It's nice, isn't it? Having friends."

"I guess so," I mumbled, still unsure of who this guy was.

"We get to bike up here after school and see the mountaintop. It's amazing how many of the people," he said, pointing below, "just go about their business without a thought of how this mountain got here."

I tried to see it from his vantage point, but he kept looking at everything like he was looking through it or something. *He's not crazy. Please not that,* I thought.

As if reading my thoughts, he said, "You're different, Star. You get this," he admitted, pointing to the coffee shop, the birds in the trees around the building. "It's so much bigger than anything we could do on our own."

"Please tell me where you're going with this," I said, stammering with words, praying he wasn't crazy.

"My dad . . . used to be a preacher," he said, voice soft, looking at me and then the skyline. "He said to look at things with a different lens. I'm trying to, Star. I want to listen to the voice of someone greater than me," he added, grinning with both dimples.

I took in his straddled stance above his bike. He looked uncomfortable and confident all at the same time. *How did he do that?* I fidgeted with the hole in my jeans and tried to imagine what his life was like back in Idaho. *Did he get into some kind of cult that Dad was always warning me about?* I hoped not.

Oscar must have sensed my discomfort because he said, "Hey, it's not like that. When Dad preached, it was always about grace and mercy and love. He never took a bible-thumping approach. He always let people reason it out themselves. I know being in the Bible Belt can't be easy. Everyone is looking at you, judging you all the time," he grinned. "Dad said that people look at you with rose-tinted glasses here. Not how it is, but how other people think it should be. I can't imagine how much stress that must be to live under."

I exhaled. He wasn't preaching a sermon but trying to level with me. I thought about all the times I wrestled with science, faith, and where the two intersect. He was a lot wiser than most of the preachers I knew around here. It was refreshing to have someone, a friend, so close to what I was going through. Then, I spotted a red-headed woodpecker and watched it whack away at a tree above us. It felt like we could both be up in the branches with it, hammering away at the wood for worms. It was wonderful and somehow silly all at once.

"Birds are your hobby?" he asked.

Finding my voice, I said, "No. I just love how simply they do what they do. They sing, mate, feed, and rest and do it all again."

He laughed and swiped sweat from his forehead. His glasses moved, and he attempted to take them off and wipe the water away.

"How do you bike with those things?" I asked, realizing it might've been too forward only afterwards.

"It takes as much skill as anything," he joked, putting them back on. "Dad says I should do contacts, but I can't get around to poking at my eyes."

"Have you ever tried?" I asked.

"One time I did. He took me to a vision place, and the people who worked there must've thought I was crazy. They tried and tried to get me in the office chair, hold me down, and put them on. It kept freaking me out. Someone touching my eyeball, you know? I bet I was there an hour or more," he added, laughing.

I tried to picture the scene, and it was funny. It brought a chuckle to my throat, and we fell into laughter. The sun continued its descent, and the birds chirped for a little while. The woodpecker grew bored or found what it was after, and the knocking subsided. The stillness brought me back to where we stood. The overlook was amazing. Cars circumnavigated the city streets below at a snail's pace. It looked like watching people in a far-removed grocery store. The streets were tracks for the carts to move around on, and the stop lights were moments where the people found the vegetables and items on their lists. I imagined that each stop was something I craved to eat, and it was funny for a while. I told Oscar about it, and he began pointing at each light and instructing what was there.

"Cheerios," he said, laughing, hands coming off the handlebars in a comfortable straddle of his bike.

"Coffee," I added, pointing to a light farther along the same road.

"Baking supplies," he gestured just down from my finger.

"Breakfast," I said, pointing to the next traffic light at an intersection.

"Do they move on to dairy?" he asked, looking distant, hoping they made a left turn.

"If there's time, and it's in the budget," I admitted, grinning as much as I felt possible.

"Cheese and yogurt, please," he laughed. "I could go for a bit for some mozzarella right now."

"A big cheese pizza with pepperoni," I grinned.

The thoughts of cheese and dough overwhelmed my stomach, and I imagined a pizza as big as a wheel. The thought made my stomach pang, and I wanted to go straight to Jett's Pizza or somewhere at the bottom of the mountain. The image of walking into the store and ordering a pie and asking for Coke made my throat constrict. I felt the carbonation on the back of my throat, and I wondered if Oscar felt similar. The combination of bread and soda made me intensely hungry, and I knew it was just a phantom. He leaned into my ear and said, "Let's get started back."

So, we did. The descent was a whirlwind, and I felt the wind whoosh past my ears. It was all a blur. The turns and the switchbacks went swiftly past us, and I leaned into the handlebars to let the bike do the work. The world went by in a whir, and it was a majestic autopilot moment as the wind carried us beyond the scope of the descent. Oscar looked back at me frequently as I navigated the turns, following his lead. The mountain was simply a navigation of one turn after another, and I knew he understood it better in a few months than I had all my life. I turned left and right and corrected as needed, and Oscar helped us get to the bottom of Signal Mountain before anything too treacherous met my eye.

At the bottom, he careened to a brake, and I followed suit. My bike braked with a screech, and it was rewarding to bring myself within half a foot of him. He looked over his shoulder and smiled as big as humanly possible. I felt my handlebars hot under the grip, and he said, "You did it, Star. The mountain welcomes us back to ground level!"

I didn't know how to congratulate this discovery, but I felt compelled to do something and so I said, "You're a good teacher."

He huffed a little under his breath and said, "Signal Mountain and back to ground zero."

I looked from the mountain's base to where we had been and it felt truly monumental. It was so far away and so quick.

"Thanks for doing that with me," Oscar said, glimpsing the fading sun and mountain above.

"I couldn't have done it without you," I admitted, checking out the steep incline.

"If you do that a few more times, you'll be ready for anything in town," he said, beaming.

"Don't kid. I'm sure you and your dad go everywhere," I said.

"He goes everywhere, but I am not that good," he said, encouraging me.

I felt a breeze sweep by my head and decided to step off of my bike. I stood side-straddle and walked my bike to the curb of a street. Oscar did likewise and walked his bike to the next stoplight.

"Where to now?" I asked.

"Lead on, pro," he said, pointing to the intersection and beyond.

I laughed and looked at him on the city street. The sun had fallen somewhere behind the mountains and the city life. The city felt familiar and distant all at once, and I admitted the top of the mountain was truly mesmerizing. While I didn't want to think about being back at the precipice, I realized I loved the two vantage points. Now, I was back to the street level view, and I wanted to show him what I knew. The street signs looked familiar, and I knew the way from Signal to my house intuitively. I hitched back over my bike, and I waited for him to do likewise. When he was back on his bike, I said, "Follow me."

He followed behind me, and I navigated the streets without a single missed turn on the way home. I followed streetlights and familiar signs. It was not too far from the base of the mountain to where home sat. Oscar hurried to catch up, and I hugged the corners imagining myself to be a speed racer. The bikes turned magnificently, and Oscar loudly exhaled a time or two. When we arrived at my home and driveway, we braked to a squeak.

"I could eat a horse," Oscar huffed.

"Me, too," I admitted, pedaling slowly up the driveway, parking the bikes at the shed beside my house.

Oscar stood to full height and wiped sweat onto his jeans. I felt my pulse slow as we checked to make sure the bikes were standing on their own. Then, I gestured toward the dark house, no lights visible from the driveway.

"Your parents okay with me being here?" Oscar asked.

"As much as I am," I said, wondering if that was completely true.

We entered the house, turned on the living room lights, and Oscar sat on the couch. I went to the kitchen and flipped on the lights. Inside the fridge, there were two La Croix cans Mom hadn't drank yet. I walked back to the living room and offered one Limoncello to Oscar. He took it, studied its look, and popped the lid. I did likewise, and we took two long pulls each. When we felt the carbonation hit us, we scanned the room and saw pictures of my family in various poses. I laughed at some of the funnier images spread around the room. One image of Dad, Mom, and me at the farmer's market made both of us chuckle. I was holding a crate of strawberries bigger than me. He took the picture down and studied it further.

"So embarrassing," I admitted.

"You look like a kindergartener," he said, holding the picture out for a better view.

"I was," I said, taking the picture away and putting it back on the shelf.

"You've lived here your whole life and never went to the top of Signal?" he asked.

I looked fully into his eyes and then back to the picture on the shelf, shaking my head.

"Not once?"

"Today was the first," I said. "Thanks for that by the way."

He scanned the room for other pictures. I wanted to know what he was thinking. His hands fell into his lap, and I noticed the scabs from his last excursion were healing.

"So much to see and do," he said. "I'm glad we could do that together," he added, looking at my face.

I wondered what he saw. *Was it a mess of hair and sweat?* I pushed my hair back from my face and tried to wipe the perspiration away.

Instinctively, Oscar leaned back onto the couch and took a long pull from the La Croix. I used this moment to survey the other pictures as well. There were images of Mom, Dad, and me from Christmas to Easter celebrating various moments in our Crowley household. I tried to land on one that would sum up my existence, something to give it all a message, but it felt odd. He was breathing a deep sigh of relief.

"We're just a predictable bunch," I admitted, some calm in my voice.

"You look happy," he said, glancing to the places I did across the room.

I felt at peace with the moment, and I reached for his hand slowly. He let me cup his palm, and I felt callouses there. Rather than pull away, he left my hand in his, and I wanted to sit like this forever.

Chapter 14

Corine Bostic stood a foot taller than me, and she wanted all of the attention from teachers. From Mr. Allstock in PE to Ms. Alleywash in History and everything in between, she raised her hand often and was most certainly wrong in most answers. When she answered a question, she reluctantly pulled her hand down and hid her error in a sweeping shake of her head. It was the effort that seemed to matter. She never let her wrongness show in her demeanor. Corine raised her hand anyways and always recited what she thought was her best answer.

I stifled a laugh anytime she was wrong, which was often, and felt out the answer for myself. It seemed she wanted to be liked as much in the subjects as she was by her friends. Her forte, if she had one, was winning people over to her side. She giggled and snickered with her crew anytime she had a chance. Her efforts with teachers was not much more subtle, because she would say, "Mr. Allstock, do we *have* to run all the sprints or can we simply say we did?" or more fittingly, "Ms. Alleywash, does history *really* repeat itself or is that just a nice way of saying we repeat our mistakes?" The teachers would pause to contemplate her assertion and usually rejoin with something the school board would want them to utter.

One day, Corine took matters into her own hands and said, "Mr. Deltweiler, I think I know enough to explain this lesson myself."

Mr. Deltweiler stood with mouth agape and finally said, "Okay, Corine. Tell us about the brain and behavior."

She launched into a tirade I figured any middle schooler at Cascade would understand, and Mr. Deltweiler waited for her to finish. Then, he said, "That's all very good, Corine. A particularly good understanding of the brain and its chemical functions. Anyone want to add to this?" he added, eyes pleading around the room.

When they landed upon mine, I raised my hand and launched into a summarized version of Freudian concepts and underpinnings of psychological behavior. He beamed with pride, and I knew I had ascended to whatever throne existed in the hierarchy of 9th grade classroom discussions. It was enough to make me toss my hair back and avoid Corine's gaze.

She tried to trip me on the way out of the room, but I was too quick and stepped on her foot deliberately with a full-weight twist. I heard her grimace, and it brought some sick delight to my heart.

When I found Oscar by the lockers, he asked me what was going on. I told him about the run-in with Corine. Without even a second thought, I told him that I had bested her in psychology, and he asked about the topic and questions. His mind raced through whatever maze he considered the foundations of psychology, and I waited for him to look at me again. When he did, I smiled, and I pointed to the notebook tucked under my armpit.

"You were prepared?" he asked.

"Like Dad always says, 'It's better to take note and be prepared than halfway do anything,'" I said, mimicking him.

"I guess I can agree with that," Oscar laughed. "Sounds like you've heard that one at least a million times."

"He says it a lot," I said, stuffing a notebook into my locker. "Your classes going all right?"

Oscar turned and glanced at my locker, my hold on the handle. Then, hesitantly, he said, "Yeah. I guess."

"What's up?" I asked, genuinely wanting him to share. He never shared anything more than his comments about his dad.

When he looked from me to the hallway, I knew it was something good. I didn't want to scare him away with my over-the-top delivery, and so I cautiously raised my eyebrows and looked at him with my earnest face.

"Stop doing that, Star," he teased. "Your face will stay stuck that way," he laughed.

"Seriously. What's going on with you?" I pried.

"It's nothing," he said, waving his hand.

"No, c'mon. I know you want to say it. What's going on?" I said, eyeing him skeptically.

"Did you notice how Mr. C. was eyeing his desk earlier?" he asked, some sort of uncertainty in his voice.

"No more than he usually does," I admitted. "Why?"

"He paced around it and stared at that map," Oscar said. "*That* map," he added for some emphasis I was unaware of.

"Yeah, he loves to scare us," I said, looking from my friend to the lockers and beyond.

"No, Star. He was bothered by something," he said, looking me fully in the face.

"What could he be bothered by?" I asked. "I mean, it's just some old map and us to deal with."

"Not us," he said, his voice sounding far away. "The map. It's tied to all of this. Don't you see?"

"Tied to what?" I asked, not seeing his point at all. The 9th grade class was 'lackluster' at best. We were a bunch of non-college tracked students. Other than me (and maybe Oscar), the group didn't look to be college bound.

"He wants to know what's on *that* map," he implored, voice rising, quavering a bit.

I thought of the map behind Mr. C.'s desk. It didn't bring up any familiar information at first notice. Then, I started to see it from Oscar's eyes. The topography, the mileage from one route to another. It looked to be familiar from something I had glimpsed on the bike ride yesterday. *Was it something from Chattanooga?* I wondered dumbly. The intersections and routes looked vaguely familiar in my mind's eye. *Could it all be tied back to something that simple?*

Oscar eyed me and then started scribbling inside his notebook. I wanted to peek, but my arm hair was standing on end, and I wanted to keep the one friend I had.

As he scribbled, I thought of the unspoken words between us, the hands held just the day before. I could still feel his callouses on me. It felt good and right and okay. I exhaled and waited for him to get whatever thought he had down onto the paper. The seconds ticked by. When he was finished he looked up, he asked what I was staring at. Him, of course.

"I write better than I think," he admitted, dimples showing.

"No duh," I countered. "Tell me what's on your mind."

He breathed in and exhaled loudly.

"Is the map really so special?" I asked.

"It's a map of Chattanooga, and I think it leads to something we haven't thought of before," he said, sounding wild, slightly delirious.

"Of Chattanooga?" I laughed. "That's preposterous. The map is just scribbles and dots and nothing reminiscent of here."

He looked at me like a crazy person and then to the lockers once more. He pounded it with his fist lightly.

"If it was a map of here, where are all the road signs and stores?" I asked.

He shook his head to deflect the sentiment.

I thought of the mountain we had just climbed and tried to restore some semblance of what the map offered. There were plenty of spots that could be mountains but none looked to be Signal.

"Star, it's a map, okay?" he offered, his glasses fogging up in the moment.

I tried to rack my brain for some sensible explanation of it all, but he only kept looking at me and then the locker.

"Okay, it's a map of here," I said, finding my voice. "So, what? Why would it mean that he's looking for something here?" I asked.

Oscar stared me fully in the face for the first time, and I suddenly wanted to believe everything he was saying. His blue-green eyes had a longing I hadn't seen before. The unexchanged words rang true in my head.

"Okay. What's the point of a map, of all of this?" I asked.

Oscar scrutinized the locker again before rejoining my gaze.

"Why would Mr. C. care about Chattanooga at all? He's just been here for a hot minute," I offered, hands folded outward.

"Don't you see, Star? He wants something. There's something in the hills," he said, pointing to some imaginary point on the metal, blue painted door.

I shook my head 'no.'

"Yes, there's something in the mountains that he's after. We just have to watch him closely. He's after something on the map. The map is the key to whatever he's after. If we can find out what, then the rest will come together," he said, sounding confident and looking to me for assurance.

I didn't have anything to give him, and so he kept looking at the locker for assurance. When nothing sprang up to his mind, he tried to meet my gaze. Again, I averted my eyes from his and wondered what he was after. He swooped the hair away from his glasses and pushed them as far up his nose as possible

"Maybe the map skips over the streets of the city and the famous landmarks," I offered, looking him fully in the eyes.

He bit his lip and imagined the map. I wondered if this was all we needed to do, but before I could insinuate more, he said, "Of course, the city!"

It was like looking through an image not fully developed, he shared. I tried to follow along, but he kept jumping to parts of the city I never visited or acknowledged. When he paused to see if I was with him, I offered a half-smile and it seemed to keep him dialed in. It went this way for about fifteen minutes, and I was pleased to offer him some form of miniscule support.

"The city is just a backdrop," he smiled. "It isn't what he's after at all," he added, clapping his hands together.

"So, if it's not the real focus," I said, "what's he after?" I asked, looking to the metal locker again like we'd been doing all along.

Oscar tapped the locker and looked to me for something extra. Not getting any hints from me, he stared at the hallway and no one in the space between us and the end of the building.

"What can an illegible map of Chattanooga supply him with?" I asked, leaning toward Oscar.

"Just the sort of thing you were talking about after you met that creeper at the lake," Oscar said. "He wants to find *that* treasure," he added, his voice fading to a whisper.

"What? The treasure that crazy guy mentioned?" I asked, leaning farther in, now just beside his ear.

Oscar nodded.

"But that sounded made up," I pleaded. "What if it all comes to nothing?" I asked.

"What if it's everything?" Oscar asked, not really talking to me.

I scanned the hallway for anyone else, but now the hallways were clear. I didn't want another detention and told Oscar this.

"Detention is the least of our concerns now, Star," he said, his voice far away.

I tried to imagine a treasure somewhere buried in the far reaches of town. The imaginary sequence ended in the dirt and debris of a trail somewhere in my mind. The outcome was as unsettling as my limited imagination. I shook the image away.

"Suppose it does exist," I said, wanting to say something to him. "What're we supposed to do with this, and a crazy teacher?"

Oscar waved the comment away like he'd done on any difficulties on the path toward Signal Mountain yesterday. He stared at the locker and envisaged what I imagined was a clear outline of what we should do.

"It's there," he finally said, pointing to the blue metal. "Mr. C. knows it. And so do we," he smiled, touching the locker's surface. "We just have to beat him to it now."

Not sure how to draw him from this reverie, I coughed slightly. He held his fingertip to the locker. Then, I coughed again, this time louder.

"Want to go on a treasure hunt with me, Star?" he asked, beaming with his bright eyes.

I offered my hand and uncertainly accepted whatever proposal he had. We were now on a treasure quest, and I had no clue where it was leading.

Chapter 15

Mr. C. brought in a packet of papers and all but tossed them on our desks. It concerned the life of F. Scott Fitzgerald and we found it dull. October and November came and went much this way and the seasons were lost to us, as we fought to look out the windows toward Chartreuse Lake. I wanted to stare out the window, but Mr. C. put up poster boards, and he read exclusively from authors I'd never read. Of particular note was Richard Connell's *The Most Dangerous Game*, and he read about hunting man for sport ad nauseum. It began to feel like a crowded cruise ship, and Mr. C. was both captain and cruise director. He told us where to look for significance and what we were apt to find.

I tried to pass a few notes to Oscar, but they were intercepted by Mr. C. and he had his second lieutenant, Corine Bostic, read the notes aloud. It remained embarrassing and okay, because I never put anything damning in the messages. They usually read like, *What's with him?* Or, *Can you believe Mr. C.?* And sometimes even, *He thinks he's so high and mighty!* But Corine read them all the same, and she smirked at the teacher and then to us. While I was somewhat embarrassed, I admit, I felt worse for her than anything. A teacher's pet was never the kindest place in the room.

Finally, Mr. C. decided to play ball and invited me to the front of the room one day. I reluctantly stood to my feet and traipsed to where he stood, beside the chalkboard. From there, he asked, "Ms. Crowley, what do you make of Mr. Connelly's stance on the human population?"

I remember his hands were on his hips, and I took the proffered chalk from his hand. On shaky feet, I wobbled to the board and wrote, "He wants to get people to fight against the dogs."

The answer only partly quelled Mr. C., because he took the chalk from me and began scribbling frantic notes on the board. Some of them pertained to us, but most were tied to something going on inside his head.

He wrote shorthand fragments about "longitude" and "temperature" and other items we didn't understand.

All the while, Oscar copied notes into his notepad and failed to look up even once at Mr. C. during the entire lecture.

I wanted to throw a chalk eraser at his head, but Mr. C. dismissed me to my seat without much fanfare. I was back to drawing squiggles and curlicues without anyone noticing. Some of the curlicues reminded me of Oscar's hair, and I fell into a daydream about the locks and potential for more.

Mr. C. droned on about habits of humans and their likelihood for predictable paths. He emphasized burying and search tactics. With each swoop of his hand, I noticed he grasped for something imaginative. It was as if he saw a treasure that the rest of the class failed to see. He clawed at the air and swiped like a hawk at some imaginary substance. I failed to see what he was looking for, but he drew comparisons to Robert Louis Stevenson and Poe. I considered the earth to be a buried treasure. There was something amiss and our 9th grade English class had to find it. It was a race against the clock, our teacher. *Where was the treasure buried?* I wondered.

Just as swiftly as the dirt was disturbed, I found Oscar tapping at his notepad, and he was laboring over some point I didn't understand. It took a full five minutes before I realized he was as much stuck as I was. It made me feel better about my inert problem-solving abilities.

Mr. C. said, "Connell's work makes us think of chasing man as the ultimate game. But he didn't want it to stop there. No, sir. There's still too much at stake," he added, coughing. "The person he's chasing, Rainsford, isn't just keen to sleep in his bed. No, he wants it all. Zaroff's treasure is much deeper than just a bedroom," he admitted, looking to the map on the wall, touching it for emphasis.

Suddenly, Oscar stopped writing and raised his hand. The abrupt movement, from someone usually looking downward, caught Mr. C's eye.

"Yes, Mr. Villanueve?" Mr. C. asked.

Oscar put his pen down and clasped his hands together, now deep in thought.

"I had a question, Mr. Chethers," Oscar said, his voice unlike any I've heard before.

"Shoot," Mr. C. said, admonishing a cold tone to his stoic voice.

"You know I've never thought too much about it, but the hunt between Rainsford and Zaroff always seemed one-sided. How do you feel about this story?"

Mr. C. blew out a fierce breath and smiled a hideous, toothless grin. He looked to be the devil incarnate, and I shielded my eyes for whatever tirade he was about to unleash.

Before I knew it, Oscar was raising his hand again. This time, Mr. C. waved him away to begin his soliloquy. I feared for the worst and prayed for the best.

"Mr. Villanueve, I think we can all take something away from what you just asked. General Zaroff is a bully. Simple and true. He held the hunting grounds and dictated the rules. He played by no rules but his own. The request to fight for survival rests solely on the shoulders of his participants. Rainsford is simply caught in the wrong place at the wrong time. Like a mouse in a maze, he must play by Zaroff's rules. The chase is afoot at the word 'Go' and there's nothing anyone can do. Do you believe that? Then, the people involved must run for their lives or be hunted on the closest proximity of the ground. It's not fair, and it's not even, no matter what anyone says. But, Zaroff believes this to be the best form of sport imaginable, because people will always surprise you. You know what I'm saying?" he asked, looking from Oscar to other students around the room.

Oscar cleared his throat to reply, but Mr. C. intercepted him, saying, "You can run and hide all day, but the alpha hunter will always catch you off guard, and he will put you in dire straits when you least expect it. The gun is always aimed at your head, and you in its crosshairs no matter what you do. Have you ever been there?" he added.

Oscar raised his hand obediently. Mr. C. finally acknowledged it, and the floor was my friends.

"Sir, I have never been on a hunt like this," he laughed. It felt forced, but I waited for him to go on.

"The story from Rainsford's point-of-view seems contrite and linear. He must simply run forward because General Zaroff has him pegged. Is that right?"

Mr. C. nodded in approval.

"If the only way forward is through, then the story rings true as a modern-day fable about the temptations we face and how we handle them."

Mr. C. obviously wanted more, because he dropped his smile and looked sternly into the face of my friend.

"Rainsford wanted to survive, and he cared nothing about the bed awaiting him in Zaroff's quarters," Oscar added, looking down to his calloused fingers.

"There's always more," Mr. C. encouraged, smacking his desk with his hand. "Always more. Anyone want to build upon what Mr. Villanueve shared?"

No hands went up, and the silence felt deafening in our small classroom. The Idyll High students looked to their desks, then the clock, willing it to cross into the bell ringing. While we waited, I felt compelled to defend Oscar. The story wasn't entirely fresh in my brain, but I knew enough to counter and get a little more from the teacher. I raised my hand slowly and by imperceptible degrees.

"Yes, Ms. Crowley?" he said, eyeing in on me directly.

His eyes felt like a ferret's gaze from a purse. I put my hand down and tucked it against my sweaty side.

"The Most Dangerous Game," I began, "is about realizing what it means to be human."

Mr. C. stared at me with a dumbstruck look.

"It's not about hunting at all," I countered, rubbing my ribcage.

"Oh really?" Mr. C. smiled, awaiting a chance to pounce.

"No. It's about human complexity, and the human mind," I said. "Rainsford doesn't want to participate at all. He doesn't want to run for his life. It's all thrust upon him, and he never once takes his eyes off the prize," I add.

"And what prize might that be?" Mr. C. asked, grinning like a Cheshire cat again.

"Survival," I said.

"He wants to simply survive?" Mr. C. asked.

"Yes, that's it," I rejoin, finding my voice. "He fights to live another day. The bed is only a consolation after the fight. He must fight Zaroff in the room. The battle only ends after the fight has occurred."

Mr. C. considers this for a moment, his hand wedged to his face. Then, he looks back to the map on his wall and again to the students before him.

"What battles have you been fighting?" I heard my voice ask, too late to retract the statement.

Mr. C. swiveled his head away from the desk to where I sat. He ruminated on my voice, the question, before answering. Then said, "Miss Crowley, I think you get the gold star for the day. I had never thought about it that way," he laughed. Then added, "People hunt people all the time in today's world. Whether it be through the news, the Internet, or wherever, no one escapes the critical eye of the masses. I am fond of believing in simpler times. But, no, today people have the ability to stalk anyone anywhere. Just pick up a phone and you are one search away from where anyone last left off. But to find someone, it's as easy as asking where they were last seen. Right?"

No one answered Mr. C. but kept their faces straight ahead. The chalkboard was our landing spot when he was asking a rhetorical question. I tried to train my eyes upon what the board read.

Corine in the front row pretended to write down some anonymous note. I felt her displeasure at trying to make the minutes pass away. Oscar was again scribbling notes beside me.

Mr. C. went to his computer and began doing an internet browser search. While we couldn't see his screen, I imagined that he was asking Google where the treasure was last seen, where whoever was once located, what the circumstances of their death might've been. It felt alien and akin to whatever Oscar wanted to know. The remaining minutes of class passed this way, and I was thankful for not having to answer any more of Mr. C.'s questions. There was a lot to consider, and for the first time in a long while, I found myself scribbling notes into my own notebook.

CHAPTER 16

Oscar wanted to dissect Mr. C.'s behaviors straightaway. We were back at my place, takeout money for Taco Bell, and I was midway into a burrito, when he said, "He's mad, because there's something wrong with his hunt for whatever treasure he thinks exists on Wolf Island. You saw how he flipped out when he looked at that map in class. He goes nuts and Mr. Hyde comes out. It's making him mad, and did you see the way his eyes bulge out when anyone asks a dumb question?" he said, wadding up his third taco wrapper, tossing it into my trashcan in my room.

"How do you eat those so fast?" I asked, wondering where he put all of the food, his lanky body, one tall skeleton.

He waved away my stare, and he opened a bag and began munching on cinnamon twists.

"Hey, keep the crumbs off my bed," I whined, wiping away at my comforter. Mom would kill me if I had crumbs on it, let alone a boy in my room.

"Mr. C. wants to get whatever he's after. I bet it's gold bricks. You never once heard anything about this 'treasure' that the old creeper mentioned that day at the lake? No idea what's supposed to be hidden out there? Don't you think that's odd that no one besides that one dude ever heard about it? And now, this replacement teacher comes in and somehow knows about it better than anyone? No way," he spat, some of his food flying from his lips.

Before I could protest, he was wiping that part of my blanket with the back of his hand and digging for another twist.

"You're like a savage," I laughed, trying to not think about germs. Mom and Dad forced germ topics into my brain. Anything since COVID was a cause for concern, and I never once thought of bacteria the same way. The air was swarming with particles and dust motes that wanted to kill me. All. The. Time.

He reached out his arm and offered his snack, and I pushed the bag toward him. *No thanks,* I thought. Even though I admitted it felt good having someone in here, someone to talk about things with.

I still had a packet of nachos and cheese, but the way Oscar was eating made me lose my appetite. Plus, I was now thinking about what he actually said. *Why was Wolf Island never brought up?* I wondered. There had to be a reason no one in Chattanooga wanted to talk about it. Apart from the rare discussions about the death, it was largely glossed over. Not good for tourism. Mom and Dad always told me to be home before dark, and I knew they were overly cautious, but maybe there was more to it. I had always chalked it up to too many Stephen King novels and news stories about murder. But, this was something else.

"Murder isn't anything new," I heard Oscar say behind his sleeve, wiping his mouth of some cinnamon sugar dust. "People get taken out all the time. Just look at the cartels and how many people disappear in drug trades," he said, point-blank.

My eyes met his, and I said, "How do you know so much about these things?"

"There was crime out West," he added, his voice cool, calm.

"There's crime everywhere," I argued. "What makes any difference where it happens?"

Oscar cleared his throat, pulled his cell phone out from his pocket.

I instantly felt a pang of remorse since I never had the option for getting a phone out. He pulled up his Google browser and typed in 'Wolf Island' in the search bar. I thought back to when I'd snuck into Dad's room to look Oscar up, and I suddenly felt guilty for some reason.

The search results yielded mostly articles about the supposed murder on Wolf, and a few articles supplied more details than the girl's disappearance spot, the tent. Farther down the browser page, a Reddit thread speculated on how so much could be overlooked, where facts were conveniently missing, and who could have done it and gotten away with it. It was an odd moment to lean over Oscar's shoulder and listen to him read about what happened. His voice rose an octave as he read about a potential weapon and the last whereabouts of the victim. He scanned his phone and zoomed in on the grainy terrain where the tent was found.

"This post from InternetSleuth99 sounds the most informed," he said, reading about the details not mentioned in the news articles, the 'conjecture' of supposed gaps filled in by him or her. I nodded my head like I understood all of this; my parents didn't even let me watch crime shows.

"How to get away with murder isn't a new thing," he added, looking me fully in the eyes, his blue-green irises boring a hole into me.

I was a little unnerved about his tone, but I was also thinking about what he hadn't told me yet about Idaho. He had rescued someone and was probably lucky to be alive. I wanted him to share that story with me, but I knew it wasn't the right time. He would do it, if and when he felt ready. *That's what made friendships special,* I thought.

"I'm not geeking out on you, am I?" he asked, glancing from me to his phone. "It's just, I like to think about things and solve things, and Dad says I sometimes take it too far."

"No," I said, "it's fine. It's more than I'm used to talking about death though," I tried to laugh.

"We can talk about other things," he said, putting his phone back into his pocket. "It's your call," he added, eyeing me quizzically.

"Do you want to be a detective when you grow up?" I said, trying to make my voice sound playful. "Is that why you're so excited about this? The mystery?"

He paused to consider me, and I thought he might reach into the bag and eat the nachos. I was fine with it, because my stomach was no longer feeling so great. I kept picturing terrible things happening to people like me when Randall Tolley stopped me at the lake. *Was that what it felt like to be truly scared? Would it feel like your stomach just dropped to your ankles?* I couldn't imagine having to run for my life, but that's what fight or flight 'psychology' was all about. *Would I be willing to fly when it mattered?* I knew I wasn't one to fight, except when teachers wanted to send me to the principal was the only time I got into trouble. Maybe I would fight. I didn't really know.

"Don't you like puzzles?" he asked, touching my arm with his hand gently. "Putting things together that don't make sense?"

I let his hand rest on my forearm for a second and then brushed it away. While it sent a slight shiver up my arm, I kept thinking about the mystery and someone disappearing. It wasn't a pleasing image, and I suddenly wanted to talk about anything else.

Oscar must have sensed this because he let it go and cleared his throat. Then, he stood away from the bed and began surveying my pictures around the bedroom. It was almost as vulnerable a feeling as the sickening thought of someone dying, but I waited in silence for him to scan pictures of Mom, Dad, and me on various trips.

"Looks like you had a good time at the beach," he said, picking up a five by seven frame, Dad dancing with me on the beach, Mom capturing it.

"Cocoa Beach," I uttered, thinking of the warm waters. "It was the time we went to Port Canaveral and saw the space station. Mom wanted to see a beach and so we drove a little farther after seeing the place where the launches occurred. Dad geeked out, but Mom and I just wanted to swim. So, we did," I smiled, taking the picture away from him, setting it back on my mantel.

"You went through a goth phase," he teased, eyeing a picture of me with Mom, pretending to headbang to some rock-n-roll song in her car. "I like it," he added.

"The black nail polish fetish was short-lived," I admitted. "The music is still good."

"Agreed," he said, looking from me to my dad's stereo, an old Magnavox. The left speaker barely worked, but the right one was still capable of delivering a blast. "So, did your dad just give you this?"

"It's one of our rules," I admitted. "No, phone, and so no streaming music or anything. But, I can play any of these CDs and cassette tapes he gave me. The others I found at yard sales or Goodwill on my own. It's my collection now, and it's slowly coming together," I said, pride swelling in my voice.

The music was strewn all over the floor and some under my bed. It was the one thing I didn't like to clean up, and Mom didn't make me. I felt like her and Dad took pride in seeing all of their older favorites clambering for attention on my bedroom floor. I stood from the bed and retrieved a partially hidden CD, David Bowie's "Aladdin Sane." I dusted off its cover and opened the disc, revealing the CD tray.

"Good choice," Oscar smiled, helping me plug in the stereo and loading the disc to play. As "Watch that Man" began to play, I returned his gaze, and he said my parents were cool. I admitted it was pretty nice to have all these albums and an old school stereo to play them on. Even though the stereo crackled and the one remaining speaker tried to work, it was much better than sitting in silence. We listened to the tracks, and Oscar read the liner notes to me. My favorite off this album was definitely "The Jean Genie," and Oscar agreed with me. As the sun fell outside my bedroom window, I imagined my parents working their jobs and trying to pay the bills. I felt guilty because they were gone so much, and I imagined getting a job next summer to try and help a little. Even if I made a few hundred dollars, maybe it would help out on something.

Oscar put the liner notes back into the CD and closed it. He said he needed to be getting back to his house; his parents would be wondering what he was up to. I told him to tell them I said 'hey' and 'thanks' for them letting him come over. Then, as he pedaled his bike away from my street, I turned off my bedroom light and peered out toward where Wolf Island would be in the night.

The silent driveway and single streetlight provided an eerie aftermath to Oscar's departure. I longed to know what had happened to the girl that night. *Was she truly murdered? Or, was she another runaway that didn't want her folks to know?* Oscar said they used to put people's faces on milk cartons. I thought that was an interesting 'tactic' for finding people who were lost. If she was still out there, I tried to imagine what would spook someone so fully that they'd just disappear. Then, the creepy posture of Randall Tolley came flooding back to my mind, and I shook my head vigorously. It wouldn't take much more than that to make me flee. And if that girl had met someone like him, it might've been enough to make her genuinely want to run away.

Chapter 17

Mom pulled back my blankets and found me covered in sweat. I must have overslept my alarm clock because she was picking up whatever clothes looked decent enough to put on my clammy body and tossing them at me. I heard some words but found them 'unintelligible' in my dream-like state. When I felt something cotton hit me in the face, I unfurled a tee shirt and put it on.

"Bring these to me tonight, Star. I need to do laundry, or you can if you beat me home," she said.

"I always beat you here," I mumbled, wiping sleepy eyes and putting the shirt on. "When do you plan on getting home?"

"It's Friday, so we'll be back sooner than yesterday. The weekend," she added, smiling.

"We ordering the usual?" I asked, stifling another yawn. Our 'usual' was Chinese from a small shop down the street, around the corner from the streetlight I stared at last night.

"Kung Pao and whatever else you want," she smiled. "Extra hot sauce for your dad."

I snatched the same pair of pants from yesterday on the floor and gave them the sniff test. Mom looked at me and gave another frown, coupled with an 'ew that's gross' look.

"Can Oscar come over and join us for movie night?" I asked, thinking of how I wanted to make up for the morbid stuff we'd talked about in my room. "Please?"

Mom shook her head, said, "No honey, it's the first time all week that we've been able to see you awake. It's protected family time," she said, not budging from where she stood.

"Besides, it'll be a chance for us to clean up all of this, and you could use a haircut as well. Look at that mop," she added, pointing to the top of my head. "Where's your brush?"

With a shrug of my shoulders and my best 'I don't care' face, she looked down at her watch and said, "Go. You're going to be late. It's already ten till, and I can't have any calls today. Remember our deal with high school?"

"Yes, yes. Do it differently than middle. Don't get into trouble. Come straight home," I recited, slinging my backpack over my shoulders. At my doorway, I considered turning to brush my teeth and remembered Dad kept mints in the kitchen drawer. I would grab those.

"I mean it, Star. We can't take off to come get you or spend any time in the office like we did at Cascade Middle. You promised you would do better, and we are counting on you to live up to that. Got it?"

"I know."

"Star—"

"I know," I repeated, descending the steps and grabbing the Altoids in a dash for the door. My feet barely felt like they touched asphalt as I descended the driveway and rounded the corner where the bus usually picked me up. With less than ten minutes for the school bell, I knew the bus was long past my stop (maybe already at the school). So, I sprinted down the sidewalk and heard the sloshing of my backpack, right and left, as I navigated toward Idyll High. The weightlessness of the sprint, coupled with the sounds of my pack made me laugh and consider gravity's pull on people. As people 'inevitably' grew older, their spines started to stoop more and more. They eventually looked more and more like shorter versions of their original frames. I vowed to stand up straight and try to remain my full height until I could no longer handle it. *Maybe by then, we'll be flying around everywhere and people won't have to walk on their legs anymore?* I thought, laughed at all those empty streets where people once walked.

Then, my mind flashed to the cane-wielding frame of Randall Tolley when we met that day at Chartreuse Lake. Suddenly, my feet found the asphalt and my back felt the weight of my pack as I slowed down at the base of Idyll's front steps. I felt a chill run across my neck, and I looked from the steps to the lake below. My eyes scanned the shoreline for figures, anyone matching the gait or description of this pursuer. Not seeing anyone, and only a single blue heron staring at something at the water, I attempted to laugh it off. *There's no one there, stupid,* I said to myself, then climbed the steps one at a time. The bag felt sticky-hot, and 'cumbersome' against my back now. Pushing the front entrance open, I heard the bell chime and the morning intercom kick to life for announcements.

"Good morning, Idyll High, this is Maria Thompson, your senior class president here to welcome you to another fantastic day at our great school! Please remember that Fall Break will be . . . " I heard her voice trail away, as I took my backpack off my shoulders and felt a tap on my sweaty shoulder.

"I'm going to class. Don't worry. I'm headed there now," I said, wanting to deflect whoever was beside me away. But when I turned, I realized the tap was from an unexpected person. The person before me was wearing a starched, denim uniform with the name Timothy embroidered onto the front. He held up one hand with a broom in it and stepped backward to signify he didn't mean any harm.

"I can walk you to class," he offered, pushing his ball cap back from his forehead a little, pretending to push the broom on the floor.

My nerves hadn't calmed down much since entering the building, and now I was wondering who this guy was. Looking him over, he had close cut blonde hair, deep brown eyes, and a thin-lipped smile. When I didn't move to join him, he leaned the broomstick against his arm and offered a big hand. He was tall, taller than Oscar or any of the Idyll teachers, but he looked no more than a few years older than some of the seniors I had passed at the school. Again, I kept both hands clasped to my backpack, resting on the ground in front of me.

His smile held, and I found myself wanting to stop running into such odd people at the school and 'adjacent' to it.

"Beats getting a tardy slip or being written up by the administration, doesn't it?" he smiled, pointing to their main entryway behind him. "They love writing people up in there," he added, and his familiarity with Idyll High's ways comforted me a little bit. It was enough to get me to pick my pack up and begin walking in the direction of first block.

He took the broom and began mock sweeping it in front of himself. As he did, I wanted the classroom to appear in front of us miraculously (and I couldn't believe I wanted to be in Mr. C.'s class more than here).

"Timothy," he said, from the side of his mouth.

"I can read," I said, pointing to his cursive name.

"Oh, yeah," he laughed. "I've only been doing this for a year and a half," he added. "I was actually a student at Idyll High the year before last. Some success story, huh?" he added, his laugh falling an octave.

"I thought you looked young for a custodian," I said aloud, happy for some of my deductive skills to prove fruitful.

"And thank you for saying that, instead of *janitor*," he mock-bowed. "So much better," he said, standing to full height again. The halls were empty now, and he stood almost as tall as the lockers. I wondered why I hadn't seen him before, but I figured I probably had, and he had been stooped over emptying trash cans or something.

"But, what I wanted to say before we get down there," he said, gesturing to Mr. C.'s classroom. "It's something I thought you should know."

Despite still feeling freaked out by this interruption, I realized 'Timothy' had a look of someone who just wanted to help. His face screamed 'do-gooder' and I needed to avoid detention, if at all possible. "All right, Timothy," I said, pausing for a second. "Tell me whatever you have to, and then, please help me get out of whatever trouble Mr. C. is going to create, because he's somewhat crazy, if you didn't know."

"That's what I need to tell you. He's not who he says he is," Timothy exhaled, covering his mouth behind his hand to where I could barely hear him.

"Huh?" I said, needing to lean closer than I wanted to. "He's not who . . . "

"He's not Mark Chethers," Timothy said in a rush, sweeping the hallway parallel to Mr. C.'s door. "We're out of time," he mouthed, then looked to the door where Corine was standing up to get the door.

She held a fat grin on her face obviously thinking I was about to be in trouble. As she reached to put her hand on the handle, Timothy said, "His ID fell out of his pocket one day, and he wasn't in the classroom. So, I went to put it in his drawer, and I saw some papers in the drawer and they said Mark Chethers, but they didn't match the ID name. Normally, I wouldn't notice something like that, but when I put the ID into the drawer I noticed the names didn't match up at all. Then, I wondered why afterwards, and I tried to remember the name. But I couldn't," he breathed loudly, the classroom opening.

Corine smiled and opened the door wide enough for Mr. C. to spot me through the opening, still standing beside my unannounced guest.

"This is gonna be good," Corine chirped.

Mr. C. opened the door wider, said, "You're late, Star."

I could tell all I needed to in just that one second, because he used my nickname. Suddenly, I breathed out and knew he wasn't going to try and suspend me.

"We've just started our lesson on characterization. You've not missed much," he grinned, beckoning me inside.

I tried to find my voice, but I couldn't and looked to Timothy for some summary of my whereabouts. Then, I glanced inside the room, and Oscar was waving me over with his arm. Behind me I heard, "She was held up by me, Sir. I am so sorry for the trouble. Won't happen again."

Without waiting for this awkward exchange to be over, I fell into my seat beside Oscar and only looked up when I had my notebook and pen in front of me. Timothy offered his hand, said, "Next time I have a question, I will ask someone in the front office instead of a student, Mr . . . "

"Chethers," Mr. C. said, meeting his hand and pumping it once. "I replaced someone," he added.

"Right," Timothy agreed.

"You look pretty young . . . " Mr. C. began, looking up to Timothy's full height.

"Timothy," Timothy said, pointing to his name. "Class of year before last," he smiled.

"Ah, so you are recent," Mr. C. said, taking in the custodian with fresh eyes. "Glad to make your acquaintance. Don't be a stranger in these parts," Mr. C. continued.

"I clean trash cans every day," Timothy answered. "See you around," he turned to exit and as he did, he looked over Mr. C. to where I sat. His brown eyes met mine, and I suddenly felt whatever panic he'd tried to relay just a moment ago. The door to our classroom clicked shut, and Corine raised her hand to ask if I was in trouble. Our teacher dismissed her with a simple, slow wave of his hand. Whoever our teacher was, he had two identities and one of them was locked away inside his teacher's desk.

Chapter 18

Oscar invited me over that night for his dad's famous chili mac, and I anticipated something from a can. Instead, Mr. Villanueve brought us all to the dinner table and said grace in his reserved voice. We held hands which felt odd, but I went with it. When he said, "Amen," I dropped Oscar's hand and his mom's. The clammy sweat wasn't something he noticed, or he didn't wipe his hand after holding mine. His mom smiled at me and said, "You're in for a treat, Star."

I looked at his mom and then at the girl dish in the middle of the table. Rather than looking like something made in a factory in a faraway land, the meat and cheese smelled divine, and the ladle in the dish beckoned us to dig in. My mouth watered, and I looked to Oscar for direction. At home, I would've just grabbed a spoon and stuck it in the glassware, but here I was a guest. So, I waited as best I could. My stomach grumbled as I glanced at the browned cheese clinging to the edges of the dish.

"Star, don't wait for us. You're the guest, and I only caution you that it's probably really hot," Mr. Villanueve said, pointing to the steam rising from the edges of the ladle.

"It looks a lot better than I imagined," I heard myself say, cupping my hands over my mouth in embarrassment.

"What did you think I was going to feed you? Dog food?" Mr. Villanueve asked, laughing and handing me the handle. "Not in our house," he smiled.

Reluctantly, I took the offered ladle and began to wrench the macaroni and chili cheese into a bowl Mrs. Villanueve gave me.

The family did likewise, and I bit my lip as they settled into their familiar spots. My chair, closest to Oscar, was empty most nights, I gathered. Mr. Villanueve glanced at the placemat and swiftly looked back to the dish. His wife did the same, and I knew there was something else happening.

"Do you have many people over?" I asked all three of them.

"You're the first in a while, Star," Mr. Villanueve said. "But, I bet you are good company," he smiled, wiping his hands on his napkin, placing it back on his lap.

Realizing it would be rude if I didn't take a first bite, I took a scoop of the mac with my fork and brought it to my lips. Before sinking my teeth into it, I saw the heat vapors and decided to blow on it. Oscar did the same, and we laughed at one another.

Then, I took a bite and let the cheese and sauce envelop my taste-buds. The family looked on, and I discovered something new that night. I shouldn't judge a meal by its name. *This was amazing!* Before I realized what I was doing, I clapped my hands together with the fork awkwardly in the middle.

Oscar took his first bite much slower, and he followed it with a long gulp of milk. I tried to pace myself with the dish in front of me, but it was so good.

"If all the food groups tasted this good, I would eat all the time," I said, wiping my mouth with a napkin. "How did you make this?" I asked, looking at Mr. Villanueve.

"Family recipe," he said, miming a zipper across his lips. "But my mom made it ten times better," he added, looking out the window and somewhere I couldn't see.

"Now I feel terrible for all the takeout I've been making Oscar eat," I said, smiling over my second bite.

"Don't be silly," Oscar said, playfully elbowing me. "I eat anything, don't I?" he asked, looking over to his mom.

Mrs. V. nodded and softly blew onto her fork.

When we finished the meal, Oscar asked if I wanted to see his music room, admitting it wasn't as 'robust' as mine. I fought past him to see what all he kept in the way of albums, and he was straight up lying to me. His albums were all over the walls, and he had instruments. *How many are there?* I wondered, scanning the room. I saw guitars, a drum set, and a keyboard.

"You play all of these?" I asked, hands on my hips.

"I'm trying to learn more on acoustic, but it's all basic stuff so far," he admitted, grinning with his dimples.

I turned on the keyboard and ran through a few automatic songs I knew. He stood to the side and watched me for a minute in silence. When I paused to consider playing something else, he said, "I saw you checking us out at dinner."

His eyes looked from me to the keyboard, and I could tell he wanted to say more but didn't.

"You're a dream family. Your dad even cooks," I smiled, looking at my fingers on the keys. "My family isn't even home at dinner."

"Not what I meant, Star," he said, slowly coming up to the board and clicking the power off.

"Hey, I was wowing you with my insane skills," I joked, but I could see his blue-green eyes narrow behind his glasses and knew he wanted to say more. "Sorry, what's up?"

"Something I didn't tell you before," he admitted, toying with the keys himself, avoiding eye contact.

"We're friends, Oscar," I said, looking at him. "What is it?"

"Mom and Dad haven't had company, a girl, I mean, in a long while. Since . . . " he fell away.

"Since what? C'mon," I urged, tugging at his sleeve, swatting at his hands on the keyboard.

"My sister," he said, voice barely above a whisper.

"Oh . . . ohhh," I exhaled, suddenly taking my hand away from his, realizing the severity of what he meant.

"She was little. Barely in middle school, and she went with me swimming one day at the lake," he said, looking at the keys and narrowing his eyes tighter into almost two small slits.

I sat silently waiting for him to continue, holding my breath in.

"Her name was Andrea," he said, more to himself than me, almost like he was trying to will her back into existence, I thought. "Her name was *Andrea*," he said, emphasizing her name this time. "She was swimming with me and a buddy, a classmate. She begged to come along. We swam at that cove all the time. But for whatever reason, me and the buddy swam out a little ways from her to talk about some dumb girl. Anyways, she starts yelling that she's got a cramp and thrashing in the water," Oscar said, sniffling and wiping his nose with the back of his hand.

"I'm so—" I started but cut myself off.

"My buddy turns to swim for her. He was the quicker swimmer, and I must've thought she was play-acting to get a rise out of us," he fake-laughed, still not believing it. "So, he takes off after her and gets to her in time. But when he gets to her, she doesn't calm down and keeps clawing and fighting with him and hanging onto his arms, pushing her weight onto his head, forcing him under. And he takes a big gulp of water and begins choking and goes under. Then, so does Andrea. I watched in horror and didn't move for what felt like an eternity. Then, I—" he said, voice croaking and his hands shaking in the air.

I was terrible at moments like this, but I knew I should console him in some way. Before I could think about it, I took his hands in mine and tried to get him to meet my gaze. He kept looking at his hands and trying to shake them.

"You don't have to say anything," I said, soothing him, my stomach filled with chili mac doing a backflip.

"I finally got there, and I couldn't see anything," he cried, sobbing into my shirt. "It was so muddy, Star," he said, biting his bottom lip as his chin quivered. "I dove down again and again and only felt him, my buddy," he said, putting his head fully on my shoulder now.

"You did the best you could," I said, trying to picture it, believing my own words but knowing they felt hollow.

"Her name was Andrea," he recited again, but this time his eyes came away from my shoulder red, swollen. "She was my sister, Star."

I gripped the edge of the keyboard and tried to hold in my own breath again. For some reason, it felt important that I not cry in front of him. *Was I trying to be strong?* I did not know, but he looked me fully in the face and waited for words I couldn't give. *Would it ever be alright again?* I wondered. Hearing him say all of this, it didn't feel true. I was amazed his family could still have faith after that. *Could I?* I thought.

When he wiped his eyes, his glasses moved up and down and almost fell off. I took them away and went downstairs to ask his mom for a glass of water. She gave me one, and I brought it back to Oscar's music room. When I tapped on his door, he wiped his sweaty hair from his face and repositioned his glasses firmly. I extended the water, and he took it down in two large gulps.

"Thanks," he said, then belched.

We both laughed awkwardly, because it felt so abrupt and sudden, given the topic just five minutes ago. He said, "Sorry for getting all mushy on you," and elbowed me in the ribcage.

"Don't ever apologize for telling me about that," I scolded. "Friends tell one another everything," I added.

"Everything?" he asked, eyeing me skeptically.

"Well, over time, but yes. Everything. Eventually, I mean."

He smiled a sheepish grin and said, "I'm going to remember that, Star."

Before I could chastise him about meaning it, he had already picked up a bass guitar and plugged it in. It only felt right to jam after something so serious and brutal, I imagined. Plus, he had cried in front of me. *Nobody had ever done that before,* I realized. Without waiting for instruction, I picked up the drumsticks and sat down in front of the snare.

"I'm not very savvy at drums," I said, half-yelling over the bass riffs to a Deep Purple song.

"Doesn't matter, does it?" Oscar shouted back. "Just play what you feel and go with it," he added, and before I knew it, I was playing along to something entirely new.

Chapter 19

My legs churned over uneven terrain, and I felt tree roots beneath my worn Converse as I stumbled through thick forest growth. The sun was somewhere above the tree canopy, and I felt the cool, thick air created by the dense copse of trunks surrounding me. My breath came in short bursts as my lungs pressed against my constricted ribcage. *Where was I running?* I couldn't tell, but the way ahead was simply a narrow margin of forest path leading to something that looked like the edge of the planet. I heaved and panted and fought for air and willed it into my nostrils and mouth as I held my arms awkwardly out in front of me, fearful of a branch smacking me across the face.

Time felt suspended and the sun just out of reach like a train distancing itself from me at a terminal. Nothing felt remotely familiar, and I kept lunging forward with my arms stretched outward. *Was this Chattanooga? Could it be a path that I took once with my family? Were they wondering where I was?* All of these thoughts sprang into my fevered brain, and I gasped for more of the elusive air around me.

As I looked toward the edge, some form of precipice ahead, I felt a tree root too late and my toe struck it full force and pulled me downward. In slow motion, gravity did its work, and I plummeted to the dirt and fell into a rolling somersault. The friction with earth banged against my left knee, and I winced at the pain and then felt the scrape across my uncovered face. My arms were too slow in coming upward, and I banged my elbow against a rock and grimaced as I felt the pointed edge slash a cut on me and the awkward buzz of the limestone sending a shiver up from my funny bone.

"Ouch!" I shouted to the darkness, gripping my injured arm and looking from the blood to my spot on the forest floor. "What is happening?" I asked no one but myself.

Then, I sat for a moment and considered the direction behind me, no one and nothing was chasing after me. To my right and left, not a creature stirred or chirped in reply. The darkness sent a different shiver across my neck, and I felt the cool air drafting across my sudden sweat. When I looked at the slight clearing ahead, I sat and considered what brought me out here. *Where was here?* I thought. *Did I take off in the middle of the night?* It wasn't like me to consider running away. Life was good. So was everything at home, except for never seeing my parents. *No, this was something else.* Slowly, I stood up, and my elbow throbbed when I brought my arm straight down. My knee ached from its impact with the ground. Even my toe hurt, and I cursed the exposed tree root at my feet thinking it looked somewhat snakelike and maligned as it S-shaped itself above the ground where it was supposed to be, hidden from all malice and deception. Out of anger, I kicked it with my injured toe, not thinking about it, and I bit my bottom lip hard. *Slow down,* I thought. *You fell over it.*

Stamping my foot on the ground for reassurance, I looked outward and saw what appeared to be the end of civilization again. This time, I wiped the sweat from my eyes and began to walk slowly in the direction of my original intent. The forest imperceptibly shifted from cold and remote to a lighter, more visible terrain. The path opened more distinctly as I carried myself, half limping at times, toward whatever my target was. As if on cue to my brain shifting, I heard a mourning dove cooing in the distance somewhere. My heart thawed somewhat to that familiar chorus I loved hearing outside my bedroom window, and I found the path expanding to where I no longer had to push branches and shrub growth away from my face and legs. The pain in my limbs subsided, too. I breathed deeply and felt renewed space in my lungs that was absent just moments ago.

As I walked, the light from the dismal canopy fell through the less densely grown branches, and I felt the sun on my arms, my face. I looked up and saw the piercing glow, felt the orange radiance, knowing that the earth was still alive. In this same discovery, I realized the edge was not some phantom ahead of me, but instead, it was the opening onto what was a lake and shoreline. *Had I been sleepwalking all the way to Chartreuse Lake?* I wondered, laughing at myself. But before I could dismiss the silliness of such a thought, I spotted what looked to be activity on the water.

I squinted my eyes outward toward the lake and saw ripples in the water. Fish were jumping or something. I kept my gaze where the sun reflected off the surface and scanned the shore for any other activity. No one was visible, and I imagined I was the only one awake at this hour. Dad and Mom were going to have a great laugh at this when I limped home, I imagined. But the ripples shifted almost snail-like from tranquil ebbs and flow to something much more choppy and erratic. I kept my eyes on the water and realized my breath came in shorter bursts again.

Before I could scan the shore for anyone else, I noticed a hand breaching the water's surface and grasping at thin air. Then, beside the disembodied hand, I saw more splashing and what looked like a head surfacing and gasping for morning air. As this happened, a shriek filled the expanse, and I swung my head toward another apparition to my right. There was movement and suddenly a body dove under the water and pursued the ripples and the thrashing closer to the shore.

I became lightheaded and realized I was holding my breath as the mysterious events played out in front of me. The body reappeared much closer to the shriek, but it was still a few yards away from where someone thrashed for their life. I need to help, I thought. But my feet remained planted to the edge where I was. No one else was coming to help, but I couldn't move a muscle.

As my limbs refused to budge, I saw the head go under the waterline, and the hand thrashed and miraculously brought its arm, head, and torso up to the sunlight in a burst of exhaustion. By this time, the approaching person wrestled with the other and fought to keep them upright. I noticed the dark hair, and something felt familiar. I forced the air out of my mouth and used equal energy to take in another unsatisfying breath.

"Oscar, she—" I heard, distorted by the water churning around the bodies.

"Where?!" Oscar shouted louder than the other.

Then, without waiting for the body to point, Oscar dove under and time ticked by slower than it had in the forest. When he did come up, he only took enough time to gulp in another burst of air and dove down again. He did this as time felt it froze completely, and I still couldn't move from my spot on the forest's edge. *What is wrong with me? Why can't I go help?* I pleaded with myself. *Just move out there!* But it was no use, I was completely rigid, and my body watched helplessly phantom-like as this scene played out.

When Oscar broke the surface for what must have been the twentieth time, he gasped and the other person gripped his arm.

"One more time!" he shouted.

"I can't hold up," the friend said, shaking his head, struggling to swim.

Oscar's face looked horrid, and it contorted into what hopelessness must've felt like inside him. I watched as he paddled and heaved and tried to swim in place, but he was struggling to remain above the water. As the friend turned to swim and sink toward the shoreline, Oscar reluctantly turned and began to follow, catching his sinking friend multiple times in the water. On this friend's last fall beneath the waterline, Oscar came up spitting and regurgitating water, pulling this man to the shore. There, Oscar spat and coughed and gagged and pushed his palms into his eyes fiercely. He was crying and shaking his head in disbelief. The friend collapsed near him, but Oscar only cried out once more across the tranquil water.

"She panicked—" the friend started to explain but was cut off.

Oscar stood on shaky legs and began limp-running over rocks on his bare feet toward something out of my sight. I tried to think of what was in that direction, and I came up blank. The friend stood and tried to navigate the rocky shoreline on his feet and stumbled many times.

"What're you doing?!" he called in the direction Oscar ran.

"My phone. If I can get to it, I'll call 9-1-1!" he shouted, beyond my vision.

"Man, she's gone!" the friend shout-cried back. "I'm sorry," he added, cupping his hands and crying again. This time he halted and fell to the rocky ground and sobbed facedown. "I'm so so sorry."

I felt my legs crumble simultaneously, and I was suddenly on the ground again. The rocks pierced into my jeans, and I felt the gashes against my skin. My entire body wanted to will itself to wherever Oscar ran, but it was immobile. All I could do was punch the rocks with my useless fists and bury my face in the surrounding dirt and scream. *Why? Why? Why?* I hollered. But no one came to answer or heard my cries, and I felt the sun on my back and suddenly realized it was all true. The water was placid once more and only the whimpering groans of this forgotten friend were heard below where I rested. I grabbed soil and rocks and driftwood pieces and tried to smash them in my hands. The resistance cut into my tender palms and held them there until I imagined eternal marks leaving scars for me—a reminder of this day.

Suddenly, I gasped for air and lunged forward in my bed almost heaving myself off the mattress. My back was soaked and watery indentions remained on the sheets beneath me. The dream was a nightmare, and I shook in my sweaty nightclothes, hugging myself and rocking back and forth. The images of Oscar's plight, losing his sister, almost losing his friend, these sights stuck in my head, and I wrestled with what to do next.

"Star? You awake, honey?" I heard from downstairs. "I made breakfast," Mom's voice called.

I groaned at the familiarity, thankful and disbelieving it all at once. *Why did it have to happen?* I asked myself. *To Oscar of all people!* But no sooner had I thought this, I heard, "Your favorite."

I could instantly see two pieces of French toast dusted with powdered sugar and topped with a little syrup waiting at my placement on the table. There was a glass of orange juice beside it, and I knew Dad would be pouring a steaming cup of his coffee from the carafe. Mom would be blotting bacon grease away from three strips, one for her, two for him and setting them on the table along with fried eggs. The morning routine before another day for them and me, and I felt sick to my stomach. Quickly, I grabbed the trash can beside my desk and threw up whatever liquid there was in my stomach.

"You okay?" I heard Dad ask, a coffee mug clinking on the countertop.

"Be right down," I groaned, trying to make my voice sound anything close to normal. "Just waking up," I added.

No more questions came from the kitchen, and I sat the can beside my bed, trying to regain whatever composure I could. Still, images of Oscar, his friend, the death of his sister all rattled around inside my head. It wasn't fair, and I felt more helpless than I had in the dream. Whatever sickness I was feeling, I suddenly knew Oscar had been through infinitely worse. Making my stomach churn even worse was the realization that what had been his worst day on earth was also what the town had called heroic. His Idaho supporters had labeled him a hero for saving his buddy, when all he'd wanted to do was save Andrea. While saving his friend was no doubt important to him, it was not what he'd been trying to do that disastrous day. My stomach tumbled again, and I lunged for the can with nothing to give but whatever was left.

Chapter 20

Our class filed into the dreaded ELA room, and I immediately longed for the comfort of Oscar's room, the instruments. The nightmare took some shaking, but I finally thought I was free of it this morning. Then, Mr. C. waltzed into the room with a gigantic grin plastered across his face. *Here we go,* I thought, elbowing Oscar as he took his seat beside me. Oscar waved me away in a 'placating' way like a grandparent might do an unruly child. I was immediately angry at him for doing this, but he mouthed something I couldn't understand.

Mr. C. took to the worn podium undoubtedly used by the teacher before him, and he scanned our assembled mass looking at us like a hawk does its grounded prey.

Corine raised her manicured hand, and he ignored her completely, his eyes resting on me uncomfortably.

"Star," he said, his voice filled with kindness, and instead of relaxing at his cheery disposition, I found myself further unnerved. I wanted to wiggle *into* the plastic material and composition of my chair.

"Ye-es," I squeaked, looking from him to Corine's straight, perfect blonde hair.

"Don't be alarmed, my dear," he said, putting up his hands in a conceding gesture. "I come in peace," he said and stifled a laugh. "Promise," he added, smirking and attempting what I thought was a face an alien might make.

"Okay?" I asked.

"You are familiar with trouble, aren't you?" he teased, lips still pulled into a deceptive grin. When I didn't answer, my mind jumping from Cascade Middle's administration office back to the present, he said, "I did some reading."

He's read our files at the front office, I thought. *Of course!*

"I'm not here to judge," he said, shaking his head. "No, quite the opposite, my dear," his voice sounding serpentine. "I want to congratulate you on sticking to your guns. Few your age actually care enough to go their own way, blaze their own trail. Know what I mean?" he asked, eyebrows raised.

"I guess," I muttered, my head swirling with hypotheticals.

"Think about it. Your age wants to be absorbed by distraction. Become one with technology and what have you. And I found it neat that you didn't back down from whatever happened last year. Now, here you are. In high school, and while you are starting over, you are still very much the same you."

I eyed him skeptically and forced myself not to break eye contact. *It's important to stand your ground here,* I heard my inner voice say. *Don't back down to bullies. Ever.*

He waited for something I wasn't going to give, then added, "See, I read *all* your files, and I can tell who's a natural born leader in this group and who isn't."

Mr. C. scanned the room and looked knowingly at everyone across all five rows. He paused only briefly at Oscar's desk and then resumed his monologue to me. As he droned on about intuition and human characteristics and famous literary figures who stood their ground, I saw Oscar pushing his glasses up further onto his nose out of the corner of my eye.

"Take Angeline Burnett here, for example," he rejoined, looking at a classmate at the end of the first row. Corine turned her head as her classmates did likewise. Angeline wiggled in place and crossed her legs nervously. While I had never spoken to her this year more than a 'Hey' in passing, I found her to be the least obnoxious girl in the class.

"Angeline is of solid stock. Dad owns a car dealership in town," he paused to sing the jingle to a commercial played on Chattanooga radio nonstop, then laughed at his own humor. "Mom is very active in the PTA, isn't she, Angie?" he asked. "Can I call you, Angie?"

Angeline nodded her head, eyes downcast, boring holes into her desk from embarrassment or humiliation or both.

"Angie's family does quite well for all intents and purposes here in the Scenic City. She makes good grades and never got into trouble once at her middle school. Her profile is as clean as a whistle," he said, tapping on Angeline's desk with his thick fingers. "And she's like 99.9% of others I've met. She stays on the straight and narrow like a good girl should," he grinned, looking her fully in the forehead. Angeline refused to make eye contact, and I couldn't blame her. Suddenly, I felt for her and wanted to tell her to put him in his place.

"But that's a game so many of you play, isn't it?" he asked, looking up and stepping away from her personal bubble. "And I find it boring," he said, placing an uncomfortable emphasis on the last word. "It's predictable, and how do you plan on ever learning anything, getting anything, from the world around you? Hmm?"

While I was waiting for him to break his own silence, I realized I was suddenly alarmed that Dr. Jekyll was trying to make some type of point. I raised my hand to go to the bathroom. *Maybe I could think better out in the hallway?* I thought.

But just as quickly, Mr. C. waved me away, and he said, "Not yet, Star. See, I have all but one in this room figured out. And I 'thank you' for standing up for yourself. It's inspirational, or should be, to your classmates. If they stopped being sheep for one second in their insulated lives, they would appreciate what you're trying to do," he admitted, looking from me to the map on his wall again.

Was that a compliment? Did he mean to give me a compliment? I wondered. It felt otherworldly and just as unnatural as anything else he said on his 'good' days. But my discovery was short-lived as he interrupted my thoughts with, "But it's not you I'm talking about, is it?"

Then, he pointed his stubby finger at my neighbor, and I realized too late that Oscar was his real target. "No, this one here. The out-of-towner, Mr. New Kid in School, Oscar Villanueve is who I mean."

Oscar sat upright from his slouched position, and I felt my hands go clammy on the desktop. When I turned my gaze to him, finally taking this as Mr. C.'s invitation to let me go, I saw Oscar place his pencil on his desk and look straight ahead at the teacher.

"Yes, Sir," Oscar said with a genuine inflection in his voice.

"And manners, too," Mr. C. clapped. "You really are cut from a different cloth, aren't you?"

"What do you mean, Mr. Chethers?" Oscar asked, looking the man fully in his face.

Mr. C. came around to our last row of desks and walked behind us slowly. He strolled to the wall and pretended to adjust a slightly askew poster of Herman Melville, one with the author posed with his arms crossed, a seafaring beard hanging down to his chest. *All he needed was a pipe,* I thought.

"You come to us with very little background, young man," Mr. C. said, dropping his hand from the poster, putting his hands in his pockets.

"My life is pretty normal now, Sir. Not much to say beyond I moved and my family lives in Chattanooga now," he said, turning his head to gaze at the teacher behind us.

"Quite the opposite, Oscar," Mr. C. said, inching closer to my friend's desk. "You have *some* stories to tell, and I know it's the stuff of novels."

"Nothing like Mr. Melville, Sir," Oscar said, pointing to the poster, trying unsuccessfully to laugh.

Mr. C. positioned himself between me and Oscar, and I forced myself to wait out this uncomfortable exchange.

"Few of us sail the seas," Mr. C. fake-laughed, his voice stifling whatever caused his Mr. Hyde to surface on unpleasant days. "No, not that. I mean, why the move? Why Chattanooga of all places? Surely there's a *reason* you landed here. It's not exactly a hotspot for world-class talent. And from what I've read in the news, your dad is something of an engineering wizard, isn't he?" Mr. C. asked, leaning down closer to Oscar's ear. "I just want to know more about that."

Oscar turned his head within an inch of Mr. C. and he looked the man fully in the face. After an awkward silence, I cleared my throat as much for Oscar's benefit as my own.

"What's there to tell, Sir? My dad is an engineer, and he's quite gifted, but he would be the first to say that it's all a gift from God," Oscar replied, swiping his hair from his face, peering genuinely at the teacher.

"God-given, huh? I read up on him a little and he's quite the Renaissance man. Engineer, inventor, Harvard educated, even explores and excavates sometimes. When does he find the time to do all that?" Mr. C. laughed, keeping his eyes pegged on Oscar.

"He rides bikes with me, too," Oscar interjected. "We try to do as much as we can together."

Suddenly, I felt immense pressure to defend Mr. Villanueve. I tasted the chili mac and cheese in my mouth, and I saw the facial expression of Mrs. V. looking at him across the table like they did the night I was over. Then, I removed their stoic gazes on me, the chair and placement I represented. I cleared my throat louder this time.

"Yes, Star. Is there something you'd like to add? It's rude to interrupt a conversation," Mr. C. said, elbowing me in the shoulder, his cologne a mixture of woods and citrus making my stomach lurch. *Don't throw up here,* I told myself. I couldn't give him the satisfaction.

"Oscar's dad," I said. "I've met him," then shifted my chair as much away from Mr. C. as I could.

"So, he's just as advertised?" Mr. C. continued, returning his stare to Oscar.

I nodded silently so that our teacher would have to glance back in my direction. Using this as motivation, I pointed at the map and found myself asking what we all surely wondered, "What's with the map, Mr. Chethers?" I made a point to stick emphasis on the name; however, I knew a different name tag existed in the drawer.

It appeared to be enough, because our teacher pulled himself away from Oscar and stood to full height. In a motion swifter than I imagined his stocky frame could accomplish, he pivoted and rounded the front row and fell behind his desk. His hands went to the drawer and instinctively pulled on the handle to ensure it was locked. Meeting the drawer's resistance, Mr. C. leaned on his desk edge and looked to the map behind him.

"This old thing?" he teased and pointed to a key printed on the bottom of the map.

"Yeah, I noticed you look at it *every* class, and it must be important for you to staple it to the wall. Am I right?" I asked and checked his posture for any changes, any rigidness.

He feigned interest and stroked the map key slowly before saying, "Like I said, Star. You're very astute. Nobody else has brought this up before," he said, waving his hand across all five rows of warm bodies. "Only you, and that's why I know you'll go places in your lifetime."

Again, if this was a compliment, I didn't want it. I realized he was a manipulative, unreliable person we were supposed to listen to. And it was all I could do to sit in my seat and listen to him rattle off lie after lie. *Who was he anyway? If not, Mr. C., then who in the world was this imposter? And how far was he willing to go to keep his identity a secret?*

"What if I don't want to go places, Mr. C.?" I asked, realizing I had never said the nickname aloud.

Rather than scold me, he chuckled to himself then said, "Mr. C. Hah! I like that." He smacked his leg in good humor, and I felt like the bell would never ring again.

"Sorry—" I began.

"No. No. It's fine. I realize all teachers must get some form of endearment or fun made about them. I think it's fun," he said, looking around the room at all of us.

"What I meant to say was, what if I'm fine just being me and living here in Chattanooga my whole life? Does that make whatever you said earlier any less true?" I frowned as I asked this.

"Not a bit, Star. It's more about who you are and what kind of DNA you have. Some have it and some do not. But, like I said, you have it," he beamed. As he spoke, I glanced above his head and stared at the map again.

"This heirloom is more gossip than anything else," he pointed again to the map key and moved his hand around the edges of the document. "Don't worry your pretty little heads about it. Just something I like to look at and ponder things from time to time. I'm not nearly as interesting as Oscar's dad. Now, he's someone I'd like to know better," he declared, looking at Oscar again and jutting his lower jaw forward. "Think you could introduce us, young man? I missed him and your mom at Open House last month. I'd love to pick his brain for a bit. If he's half the explorer and adventurer the local papers make him out to be, I am sure I could learn a thing or two from him. What do you say?" he asked.

Oscar pursed his lips together and gave a slight nod of his head, said, "Sure. But you're going to be let down, Mr. Chethers. He's not anything as exciting as you make him out to be. He's Dad at home and Javier to anyone at work or church. But, I can have him call you some time."

Mr. C. held up his hands in a 'stop' manner and shook his head slowly, "No. That won't do. I want to *meet* him. Ask him some questions about his work, his expertise, and I want to see him face to face. Would that be all right?"

Before I could stop him, Oscar said, "Sure. That's fine. Whatever you say, Mr. C."

Mr. C. grinned again at the nickname. He said 'okay' and clapped his hands together. The map was deflected in this way, and he tried to launch into some basics about *The Great Gatsby* and the 'elusive' Jay Gatsby, his neighbor Nick Carraway. However, our minds were rattling around, at least mine was, as I kept thinking about the ID tucked securely away in his drawer. If the custodian, Timothy, knew anything else about our substitute, I needed to ask him and fast. The last thing I wanted to do was let Oscar's dad be anywhere near this person claiming to be an English teacher here at Idyll High.

CHAPTER 21

Oscar said we should invite Angie over that night, and I immediately shook my head. *Why would he want to do that?* I wondered. A large part of me knew it was silly, but a larger part of me didn't want to share 'our time' with anyone else. Angie was a fine girl, maybe even could be a friend, but I didn't like the idea of a trio at my house. But Oscar stuck to his guns and said she could provide a balance to whatever he wanted to talk about, a neutral front like Switzerland.

"Switzerland?!" I asked, voice going up two octaves, laughing at his face.

"Think about it," he urged. "She's by the book. She can listen to whatever we say and make her mind up about whether we're being crazy or not?"

The part wrestling with the desire to keep our conversations private dwindled a bit in my mind. *She was a good listener,* I thought. She never spoke out of turn in class or the lunchroom, never got into trouble. I pushed my jealousies and rigidity aside. *Maybe he was scared to be alone with me suddenly? Was it something I said or did?* I imagined. *Surely not.*

To help push me the rest of the way into deciding, Oscar added, "Star, we need to look at this from a different angle. Just go ask her, please?" his eyebrows sticking in a quizzical glance.

"Why me?" I fumed.

"Because you're a girl," he laughed, like it was only natural.

It made me angry, but I was glad to be the one to make the offer instead of him. He was 'my' friend, and I wanted to make that clear to her up front.

"Fine," I agreed, clasping my arms across my chest. "Now where is she this next class?"

"I don't have her schedule memorized," he argued.

Part of me was glad for that admittance, so I said, "Well, you have Spanish next, and I'm in Biology and she's not in either of those, so, maybe History?"

He nodded in agreement and we took off for that class, knowing the tardy slips were worth it this time. Oscar walked shoulder to shoulder with me down the hall, and a senior cursed us for taking up half the aisle.

"Sorry," Oscar apologized, bumping into the football player's chest.

"Walk much?" he grunted and brusquely pushed past us.

"We should be efficient at it by this point, shouldn't we?" I joked but received no reply.

When we rounded the corner and arrived at History, Oscar said, "Show me how it's done."

Realizing I had never invited anyone over to my house before, except for the required birthday parties each year and getting all 'No's,' I breathed in deeply and exhaled like a high dive swimmer on the platform.

Sticking my head into the classroom, I scanned the room and landed on Angie's picture-perfect posture. She was sitting with her notebook already out, pencil lined up parallel, and her eyes were looking at the clock waiting for the bell to ring. *She's never had a front office meeting with the principal in her life,* I thought.

"Excuse me, Angie?" I called, my voice too soft to be heard over the din of students shifting into chairs and backpacks being flung to the ground.

"Angie?" I called louder, this time getting her to look away from the clock.

"Freida . . . I mean, Star. What are you doing? You're going to be late for class," she mouthed, losing some of her posture.

"Yeah, probably," I admitted. "Hey, I was wondering if you wanted to come over after school? I mean, we wanted to talk with you about something," I said, pointing to Oscar beside me.

She strained her neck to the door's entrance and saw Oscar standing awkwardly at its frame. Then, she smiled as he waved in reply. I didn't like the smile, but I needed to get an answer and so I stood my ground. "Well?"

Angie's shock registered on her face for a second. She probably never received invitations like this, and I never offered them. In a millisecond, she went from skeptical to more relaxed, I noticed. She said, "Yes, what time?"

"Right after if you can. It's important, okay?" I urged, sensing that the teacher was coming to shut the door. The bell rang as I waited for her response. The hubbub died down in the classroom and the teacher came to where we stood.

"Get to class you two," she said, reaching for the door to close it.

In my haste to finish whatever Angie might say next, I forgot about class and whatever was next. So, I boldly asked the teacher, "Can we have a tardy slip, Miss?"

The teacher paused only for a second, then replied, "Most certainly not. You're loitering in the hallway, and I won't have you disrupt my class," she spat, closing the door in one deft motion.

Taken aback, Oscar said, "We should go, Star," putting his hand on my wrist. I brushed it away and made eye contact with Angie once more through the glass rectangle of the classroom door. She nodded to me, and I turned and began walking the opposite way from my class.

Oscar hurried to catch up and panting said, "Biology is that way."

"I know," I huffed, a firm expression on my face. "I'm not going to Biology."

"Where are you going then?"

"You'll see," I chirped, not slowing down a bit.

"I have to get to class, Star. My dad will disown me if I get written up for skipping class," he gasped.

"I'm not stopping you," I said, rounding the corner to the gymnasium.

"What's in there?" he said, trying to put his hand on my shoulder to slow me down.

"If my intuition is right, the custodian will be in the gymnasium at this time emptying trash from yesterday's assembly. I need to talk to him. If you want to go to Spanish, you can. I'll tell you what I find out later," I said, putting my hand onto the door and pushing it open. Bingo! Timothy was on the edge of the court emptying a large black bin and tying the trash bag into a knot. Then, he shook open a new bag and secured it in place.

Oscar hesitated for a moment, and I knew his mind was made up before he said, "I'll see you then after school."

Not waiting for me to reply, he turned and hustled toward his Spanish class. I would deal with my trouble later, I reasoned.

Stepping into the gym, Timothy spotted me and threw up his hand.

"I knew you'd be in here," I admitted, proud of my recognition of human patterns. "Listen, I need to ask you if you'd been back in Mr. C.'s room? It's important because he's threatening Oscar now. Have you been able to get into that drawer?" I asked in a rush, finally exhaling.

"Hello to you, too," Timothy laughed. But he must've noticed my stone-cold face because he pushed the trash can on wheels away from us to a corner of the gym. "I have not. Have you?" he asked point-blank.

I was baffled. *Did he think I had lock picking abilities? A seasoned thief in my spare time?*

Again, he held his hand up but in concession this time. "Easy, all right?" he said. "I just thought you might've found a way in, or it was unlocked or something."

"Don't you have a key or something?" I asked incredulously. "*You* are the custodian. Don't you all have keys to everything in the building?"

He laughed again, and I felt my blood pressure rising. *What was so funny?*

"I'm not a superhero, okay? It's a common misconception."

"What is?"

"That janitors have keys to everything."

"Why wouldn't you?" I asked, balling my hands into fists, feeling a sinking feeling in my stomach. This was going to be harder than I thought.

"Privacy. You know?"

My bedroom door didn't even have a lock on it, so I didn't quite know what he was talking about.

"People's rights? I can't just go into people's personal effects whenever I want to. That's against the law. I'd get fired," he admitted. Then added, "Not that this job means that much to me anyways. I don't want to be a townie my whole life. I want to get out of here and see things, too," he said, looking somewhere beyond the doors I'd just barged through.

"But you said his ID didn't match what he's going by here at Idyll, right?" I asked, looking to him for some sort of guidance, but not finding any. "Isn't it against the law to pretend to be someone else?"

"It's sketchy I'll give you that," he said, eyeing me again. "But, if he changed his name or something, it's not against the law. I had a cousin who changed his from something he hated to a cooler name. He's so much happier now. Sorry if I got your hopes up about doing anything heroic about it before. It's just . . . I was curious, too. I mean, I can't imagine why he'd work at a high school and pretend to be someone other than he is. You know? If he was a criminal, then yeah. We'd need to report him," Timothy said, furrowing his brow.

"That's what I'm saying!" I all but shouted in reply. "What if he's a maniac and the school's just let him loose in here without a background check or anything!?"

"Well, they do background checks I know," Timothy said.

"People lie all the time," I urged, feeling the conversation was going nowhere. "People sneak around and do shady stuff, and it usually ends up on the news too late."

My mind lurched to images of Oscar's family being harassed by Mr. C., and I shook the sight away. *Was I overreacting? Did Mr. C. just say that to creep Oscar out? He said nice things to me and then said that to him,* I thought.

Either way, I didn't want to leave anything to chance. So, I put my hands together and suddenly felt like a beggar. "Please, Tim. All I'm saying is if this wackjob leaves his ID outside of his desk or drops it on the floor, would you be so kind as to take a picture of it and tell me what it says? That's all I'm asking. Pretty please?" I asked, trying to not get sick at the thought of what I was doing.

The custodian eyed me for another full minute and finally said, "Sure, kid. I can do that. That's not going to get me into any trouble I don't think. I can't be getting into any mishaps. I gotta get out of this town, you know?"

I said, "Of course. Please and thank you. And, I will owe you big time for doing it. But I don't think this is just a case of changed names. Know what I'm saying? I have a bad feeling about this," I cautioned, looking him directly in the eyes before turning toward the door.

"If he's a criminal, it'll come out in the end," he said to my back.

"I'm not waiting till the end, okay?" I said, turning around to him once more. Then, I marched out of the gymnasium and went straight to the front office not waiting for whatever the Biology teacher would say.

Chapter 22

The front office did as expected and launched into a 'tirade' about performance and standards and how my presence was necessary in all high school classes. The teacher had already sent my absence notification down to the office by way of electronic communication, and I found myself marveling at technology and how buttons controlled so much of everyone's lives. *At least it's done,* I thought. *Let's get this over with.* And I crossed my fingers that the sentence would be simple—detention, a dreaded phone call straight to Dad or Mom's voicemail. But the principal stared at me for a second longer than necessary, and I knew something was being cooked up in his brain.

"I've been checking your middle school folder," he began, lips puckered in some sort of sick delight, and I knew it was not going to be that mild.

"You're a repeat offender, Ms. Crowley," he frowned, trying to hide some administrative smile that read 'I got you.'

"It's Star," I replied, scolding myself for knowing I better play nice to avoid further consequences. Then added forcefully, "Sir."

"I'd like to think a person changes over the course of their lives, wouldn't you?" he questioned, scanning me then the sheets of paper again. "But a summer usually isn't enough time to get them to shape up. The stream takes longer and has to wind more than this," he added, pointing to the paper again. "Forty-five unexcused absences, thirty detentions, and two suspensions, if I'm reading this right," he exhaled in a resigned manner. "You took a lot of time building something like this. I mean, were you trying to avoid school?" he fake-laughed, closing the manila folder.

I shrugged noncommittally like he'd just asked if I liked frozen yogurt. Then reminded myself of what was at stake and said, "Sir, I was under a lot of pressure at Cascade. It was a trying time for me. You know middle school girls?" I offered, looking at him with what I hoped were apologetic eyes. It sickened me to play such a game, but I knew I needed to stay on the right path, as Oscar needed it.

"Why do you think I'm at the high school?" he laughed, not delving further into adolescent traumas. Something in the way he said it made me think he might've been bullied, too.

I nodded in agreement and felt a little tension fall from the room. I clasped my hands together and decided to go deeper in the abyss saying, "My parents aren't home all that much, and I was trying to make the best of a tough scenario in middle, Sir. I ran with a tough crowd," I said, feeling instantly bad for my lie. The truth was my friendless-ness was what kept me so guarded all those years.

"Been there," he agreed, looking out his large, expansive window. I followed his gaze.

The lake was below the glass, and I imagined him staring at the tranquil scene anytime he needed a 'reprieve' from high school problems. Part of me wanted to know why someone would take a position to serve students when so many bad memories might be associated with it. *Maybe it was his way of getting back at the bullies?* I reasoned. Then, I heard him clear his throat, and he pulled his eyes from the scenery outside.

"What I wouldn't give to be fishing," he replied, tossing my folder onto his desk.

"I've never been," I heard myself say, trying to make some positive moment with him, anything to get me out of the office quicker.

"Never?" he asked incredulously. "That's what I do on all my weekends . . . if the weather's good," he added, gazing out the window again for a second.

"Dad wanted me to go, but I always made up some excuse. When he was home, I wanted all three of us to be together and do something to make memories as a family, you know?" I said, not sure why I was being so honest on that topic.

"Fishing can be a family affair," he countered, looking me fully in the face. "I take my wife and kids."

"It's not that," I agreed. "I just didn't want even the fishing part to distract us. Does that make sense?" I asked, hoping he would get it.

He thought for a moment and put a finger to his lips stoically. Then, he picked the folder up and walked toward his filing cabinet slowly.

"Mom always liked to go on country drives, and I knew that being in the car would get us to talking, and I liked those better," I said, watching his hands, willing the filing cabinet to open.

"I think I get it," he suddenly said, pressing the metal button and pulling the handle to release a million files for review. "You wanted to protect the time together, right?"

"Yeah, that's it," I said, a little too eagerly.

He turned to hold my folder, my shortcomings, in midair above the files arranged alphabetically in their sad little homes. There was a gap in there for 'Crowley,' and I prayed he would search for it and return it to its resting place.

"Cascade is not so different from Idyll," he said, pointing to the room around us. "What happened over there *can* happen here. I hope it doesn't, Star. You have a chance to do things right and make a name for yourself. Know what I'm saying?" he asked, eyeing me fully for what felt like a full minute.

I nodded in slow agreement, and I realized he would be the perfect person to ask about Mr. C.'s background, if he was only trustworthy. But, I quickly tossed the notion away. A simple rule of thumb for all students was to not trust the administration. They were the ones who called home at the slightest disturbance. And if something did come of a bit of gossip, the administration always sided with the parental unit. So, I felt my hope rise and fall in a quick instant. *How easy that would be though!* I imagined. *If only this principal was different and willing to shoot me straight,* I thought.

"Do you all keep files on everyone?" I heard my voice croak, realizing it was stupid the moment it came out.

"What do you mean? All students, of course. We have one on everyone for the year," he beamed, proud of the record-keeping skills of the front office.

"No, I meant more on the faculty side," I said, squirming in my chair a bit, feeling stupid for carrying this out.

"Oh," he said, frowning a bit as he looked for my file's placement in the cabinet. "That would be something HR manages. Why?" he asked, finding my spot and forcing the file into its tight-fitting.

"No reason. Just curious how all of this works," I said, waving my hand around the room to imply the entire school system. "It's so many moving parts," I added, trying to laugh.

He eyed me again and said, "It's a jigsaw. You're right. It takes a village to make it run, you know?" he laughed, trying to contain what looked like pride at running the school.

Rather than run the risk of too much flattery, I kept quiet and waited for him to bask in the school's functioning all by himself. He closed the file drawer and turned once the filing cabinet lock clicked into place. He went to his desk and sat down across from me. This time he stared for what felt like an eternity, then said, "Star, I think you get it. Now, you just have to make a point to do it, my dear. It's easy to sit here and talk about it. The hard part is actually taking that first step and doing the right thing. If everyone in school did what we're talking about, I wouldn't ever have a dismissal or feel the need to background check someone."

For a moment, I didn't know if he was talking about students or personnel, and I tried to keep my mind from racing in thoughts about Mr. C.'s employment profile.

"Can you imagine a world free of dishonesty?" he asked me, looking me fully in the face, his eyes staring through me to the walls possibly beyond the administration office. "I can't, but I'd like to see that someday," he added wistfully. Then, he walked toward me and I held my breath as he leaned into me, whispering in his stale coffee flavor, "You can try though . . . to be good, can't you?"

I nodded my head and longed for the freedom beyond the room's cramped space. If that was what coffee did to you, I didn't want any part of it. Dad could keep his nasty coffee habits and Mom, too. *Not for me,* I thought.

He leaned past me and twisted the door handle to an opening just wide enough, and I stood to full height. He smiled a reluctant grin, and I felt some form of heaviness in his posture. His body stooped forward from some weight he seemed to carry, beyond the write ups and disciplinary actions on his desk for the day. The principal bid me good day and encouraged me to make an example to the others I saw. I commented that I would try my best, and I scooted from the office.

Rather than venture to the Biology classroom and face my betrayer, I looked to a clock in the hallway and saw the day was all but done. Just fifteen minutes before the final bell rang. I walk-jogged to my locker and took my backpack from its metal peg. Then, I decidedly exited the school's entryway and began a swift sprint to my house knowing that Oscar and Angie would soon follow.

Chapter 23

Angie arrived first and nervously rang my front doorbell. She shifted from foot to foot and stood on the stoop like a lost puppy. I permitted her entry and asked if she saw Oscar outside. She shook her head 'no,' and I offered her some Chex Mix from a communal bowl Mom kept on the counter. Surprisingly, Angie stuck her hand into the bowl and took out a big handful, cupping it in both hands.

"Bowl?" I offered.

She sheepishly accepted and poured the contents from her hands into the bowl, "Thanks."

"Sure," I said, sizing her up, wondering if she hung out with many people, or if she was a loner like myself.

"Oscar gave you directions?" I asked.

"He did," she said as she scanned my kitchen.

"We're glad you could come," I said, feigning delight, unsure of why I was being this way.

"Why did you all ask me over?" she asked, eyebrows raising honestly.

"Let's wait until Oscar shows up. He can probably fill you in quicker," I said, looking at our family clock on the wall.

The seconds ticked by, and I knew I was being exceptionally harsh to Angie. She had never done anything to me. Like I was thinking before, she could be a friend, if I gave her a fair shake. But something caused me to keep my guard up, and I couldn't let it down. I heard a stamping of feet at the entryway and a knock on the door. For some reason, Oscar had a habit of trying to knock dirt off his shoes, even when it was clear his shoes were clean. I opened the front door and permitted him entry.

"Good," he said, taking in me and then Angie. "I was hoping you'd beat me here."

I offered him a drink from the fridge and started to launch into my "We have the credit card speech," but he waved me away.

"No time, Star. Let's just get upstairs and start talking about what we need to do," he said, pointing up the flight to my room.

I liked the urgency, but I hadn't seen him take charge like this before, and I felt like I was back on the Signal Mountain trail with him leading us uphill. It felt odd but also comforting. I put Dad's card back on the kitchen table and led them up the stairs, taking them two at a time. Oscar hustled behind me, and Angie walked at a slower, firmer pace taking in the scene for the first time.

In my room, I kicked my shoes off and said forgive the mess, pointing to the mounds of clothes still resting beside my bed from a month ago. It should have embarrassed me in front of a 'new' guest, but I didn't mind. It was me who lived there, not Angie.

"Sweet room," Angie muttered, and I couldn't tell if she was being serious or not.

"Thanks," I said, jumping onto my bed and staring the two of them down.

Oscar fell onto the bed similarly and Angie lingered at the doorway, scanning my music, posters, and whatever else her beady eyes could settle upon.

"Okay, so what's so important that she had to be here, too?" I heard myself say, not liking my own tone.

"Star, it's important that we have a bigger crew, if we're going to get at this thing all the way to its bottom," Oscar said, holding his hands up in concession.

"What thing?" Angie asked, her blank expression saying more than words.

I took in Oscar's spectacled face, and he pushed long hair from his eyes. He stared at me to get it going, but I didn't, and so he turned to Angie and breathed in and out deeply.

"You all are odd," she tried to joke.

"Angie, we have noticed some things at Idyll," Oscar started and trailed off.

If that was my cue to match his delivery, I rested my head on my hands and resisted.

"What things?" she asked, looking from him to me and back again.

"We wouldn't bring you into this, if we didn't think it necessary," he added.

"Okay?" she said.

"What have you noticed since the start of ninth?" Oscar asked.

"She probably hasn't noticed it," I finally countered. "It's something you have to do some digging to really understand."

Angie eyed me quizzically and came into my bedroom a little farther. She toyed with my Ramones poster and stood in front of my vanity mirror. I wondered if she was checking herself out. If so, she would be hard-pressed to find a single hair out of place on her head. She never appeared to be disheveled.

"How weird Mr. C. is?" she offered, looking at us in the mirror to check our reactions.

I held her gaze in the mirror and slowly shifted to check Oscar's face. He didn't have nearly as good of a poker face, and he bit first, "Right. That's part of it."

"And?" Angie pried.

"And we think there's a whole lot more going on than anyone knows about," he said, grinning and giving a conspiratorial look to me.

"Like what?" Angie asked, looking directly at me this time.

I didn't want to give her the satisfaction of seeing into our plans, but I knew Oscar wanted this and so I took a moment to think about how to say what I wanted to say.

"You guys are freaking me out a little," Angie admitted.

"Mr. C. is not who he says he is," I finally blurted, checking her reaction as I said it.

She opened her eyes wider and tried to laugh it off, but I held up my hand.

"Seriously. He has a different name than the one he uses at school. The custodian, Timothy, found his ID laying on the ground one day, and it didn't match his teacher name," I said, looking her fully in the face.

Angie gradually took her eyes away from me and looked to Oscar for guidance, but he just froze and waited for her to say something else. Finally, she said, "And you both saw the ID as well?"

We glanced at each other on the bed, and Oscar shook his head.

"So, you're taking the janitor's word for it?" she said, her voice rising in a skeptical tone. "Isn't this what Corine makes fun of you for?" Angie asked, meaning me.

I stifled my initial reaction to lash out at her and bit my tongue.

"Let's leave Corine out of this," Oscar pleaded. "If Timothy saw this ID, what reason does he have to lie about it?" he added, looking from Angie to me.

"And Mr. C. acts completely different from day to day," I chimed in. "He's friendly one class and half schizo the next. What do you make of that?" I asked.

Angie held her hands up, said, "I'm not picking sides, okay? I'm just saying, isn't it possible that this Timothy could be mistaken?"

"We need you to pick a side," I heard myself say too quickly. "He's not who he says he is, and he's threatening Oscar's family now. So, you need to listen to what we're saying, because it's about to get really real and fast."

She looked at me like I was a crazy person, and I met her gaze and held it. Oscar did likewise, and he said, "Angie, it would mean a lot if you could hear us out, and if you don't like what we say, you can head home. No big deal. But, if it adds up, would you consider sticking by us on this?" he said, flashing a hopeful smile and pushing his glasses up the bridge of his nose.

Angie hesitated, then said, "Fine. But I don't like speculation."

"That's fine. Neither do we," he added, pointing to me and then himself. "But what we've seen is just too convenient to be random."

"Mr. C. is someone else," I argued. "He's got a different ID locked inside his teacher drawer at school. He studies that map all hours of the day in our class—"

"What's with that map?" Angie interrupted, but I held up my hand.

"He's interested in Oscar's dad now, and he knows about the—"

"Supposed treasure," Oscar chimed in.

"What treasure?" Angie asked, loud enough to interrupt both our thoughts.

"Should we tell her about that?" I asked Oscar, not glancing in Angie's direction.

"It's a part of this, Star," he pleaded. "We need to be upfront, *if* she's going to help us."

I lifted my chin and stared at the glow-in-the-dark stars stuck to my ceiling. They came to life when all the lights were off. Then, I refocused on Angie and thought about the story Randall Tolley had told me that day. I realized it sounded like crazy 'conjecture' when we pieced this together to a third-party. But Angie was our only baseline across the weeks since the start of school. No one else had heard any of this, and I wondered if it sounded as bizarre to her as it felt saying it out loud.

"Guys, what treasure?" she asked again, shaking me back to the bedroom. She took a handful of Chex Mix and popped one piece at a time into her mouth, waiting for me to deliver the story.

"I met a guy at Chartreuse who told me about a person going missing on Wolf Island. He sounded crazy at first, but it wasn't the missing person that stuck with me. It was what he said at the end of his story that felt really odd. He said something about a treasure never being found on Wolf, and I told Oscar about it," I said, pointing to my co-conspirator. Oscar leaned forward on the bed and nodded his head in agreement.

Angie's eyebrows raised, and she pursed her lips; she turned from the vanity to face us directly.

"The map, in Mr. C.'s classroom, is the exact outline of Wolf Island and downtown Chattanooga—"

"You can't be serious," Angie protested.

"Albeit a really old map with a key and everything," I added, gripping my comforter in my hands. "He's after whatever treasure is supposedly out there, and he means to use Oscar's dad to find it," I said, breathing out in a loud rush, looking from our new guest to Oscar for support.

Then, Oscar said what I'd hoped he wouldn't, adding, "We *think*."

Angie's gaze became crestfallen, and she pivoted from my mirror and desk to the bedside, asking, "You think? So, that's all it really is. You think this is where Mr. C. is going?"

"We don't *think*," I countered. "We *know* he's up to no good, and he means business, Angie. It's just a matter of time before someone gets hurt. Timothy isn't lying about the ID, and I know Mr. C. really isn't Mr. C. You have to believe us," I said, sounding more desperate than I intended.

"Why should I believe this? Any of it?" she asked, waving her hand around the room.

"Because you are the most likely to support us, if this all goes too far," I said, trying to motivate like Oscar would. "And we think that's where it's headed."

Angie rummaged through my albums and picked up a CCR copy of "Willy and the Poor Boys." Then, she placed it back on the pile and scanned Oscar for some chink in our proverbial armor. Not finding any, she folded her arms and studied me for a moment. "I always thought we could be friends," she said to me.

"I'd like that, Angie," I answered, eyeing her for some decision she seemed to be on the verge of.

"I don't have many friends at Idyll yet. And you two seem to stick pretty close together. How do I know that you're not just trying to make fun of me?" she asked.

"Angie, that's not who Star and I are," Oscar soothed. "We are being real with you."

Coming from Oscar, the sentiment seemed to mean more to her, because she unfolded her arms again and said, "Okay. I believe you. But, what do you plan to do about it? What can any of us do about it? Shouldn't we bring in the cops or something?" she asked, matter-of-factly.

"No cops," I answered. "We need proof, before anything gets that real."

"And cops are always going to spin their own story," Oscar attested, his voice taking on a defensive tone.

I thought of the story about his sister, his supposed heroism in Idaho. At that moment, I felt for him, and I wanted to grab his hand but thought better of it.

"So, what's the next step?" Angie asked, looking at us both on the bed.

"We're going to break into his drawer and make a copy of whatever we find inside," I heard myself say.

Oscar's breath caught in his throat, and so did Angie's, because I had never said this out loud to anyone. And now that I had, it left a truly tangible weight in the room.

Chapter 24

The plan was simple in our collective mind—Mr. C. would take the ID home and so breaking into school after hours was pointless. So, we decided to use the 'lunch period' to our advantage. It gave us a solid fifteen minutes, even if Mr. C. only went to the teacher's lounge for half of the thirty minutes. The teachers always complained about waiting in line for the microwave, and we prayed that he needed to heat something up. The time in line could add five to ten minutes to our time spent trying to pick his locked drawer. But even if he only went to the lounge to get something out of the fridge, say a tuna sandwich and carrots, he would still eat it there like the other teachers. It was a well-known fact that teachers didn't hang in their rooms for fear of being intercepted by a student on their 'hallowed' lunch break.

So, Angie served as a diversion outside of his classroom to halt Mr. C. in case he should return too early. She asked a million questions, but I told her to just think up something to keep him confused for a bit. Angie asked 'What?' and I'd said 'Anything!' Because I didn't really care as long as he wasn't suspicious that I was *inside* his room, without his permission. Oscar gave even more resistance, because he didn't like the idea of something he called "the sin of the problem." I'd asked him what exactly he was talking about, and he'd said that his folks didn't believe in stealing anything, even if it didn't matter that our teacher was an imposter.

With all of these roadblocks, I finally had our team in place, and Oscar was to wait at the water fountain and offer a bird whistle, if Mr. C. was spotted at the corner, where the teacher's lounge was visible. Then, he would tip Angie off who was to pound on the glass rectangle and tell me to "Hurry!"

While it wasn't a foolproof plan, it felt good, and I was confident in my lockpicking abilities. Both had asked me where I learned such a skill, and I shrugged, relishing in my secrets, even if they were some simple YouTube videos I had practiced on Dad's storage shed behind our house. The classroom door was no problem; I didn't even need to pick it. I simply stuck a piece of gum in the latch and it kept the lock from engaging. So, I was able to enter the classroom with all but no resistance. Once inside, I sprinted to the drawer and got on my hands and knees. The clock above me moved much quicker than it ever had during class. I felt sweat beading on my forehead. *What was my plan if he came back early?* I thought. *I was eager to ask him a question.* That felt too dumb to be remotely believable.

Oscar said he would pretend to be drinking from the fountain, and I thought about how much water he would down just trying to look believable as people passed. Angie said she would lean against the wall and look 'bored,' and her facial expression, while pretending to file her nails did look realistic. I was impressed with her acting abilities.

But I knew they both were nervous for me. I took a second and inhaled deeply, holding my breath for a five-second count. When I exhaled, I took the paperclip from my pocket and unfolded it like the video had shown. My prayer was that it was a wafer or cam lock and not a pin tumbler. Using the paperclip, I funneled it into the hole and twisted the two ends to line up with the mechanisms inside. Feeling them catch hold, I turned and felt one of the prongs fall off. The other edge held and felt snug inside the hole. Twisting my hand just slightly, I used my other hand to steady the loose end and navigated it slowly to the other spot again. This time, it fell into place, and I forced both prongs firmly into place. My mind was abuzz with what the video mentioned, and I tried to turn them both simultaneously, but the lock would not budge.

Perspiration fell from my face in drops to the floor beside Mr. C.'s desk chair. Instinctively, I wiped the sweat from the floor like an expert thief, but I suddenly felt tired and nervous like my confidence was disappearing. My hands shook as I took the paperclip from the desk lock and tried to straighten them a little more. *Why didn't I bring more than one clip? What if this one broke off?* I glanced out to Angie in the hallway. She was perfecting her fake manicure, and I willed myself to not glance at the clock again.

The seconds ticked by, and I imagined Oscar getting water-logged from consuming so much unnecessary water. *Focus, Star. Focus.* I told myself. When I straightened the edges of the clip again, I placed them into the hole where I thought the edges of the locking mechanism were.

The two ends found purchase, and I pressed firmly into their notches. This time, I said, "Please God. Just this one small miracle" and turned the prongs in the invisible space. The lock moved simultaneously with my wrist and clicked open.

Without waiting for anything else, oblivious to the noises in the hallway, I flung the drawer open and scanned inside for anything matching Mr. C.'s face. I looked on top of the files where I thought his ID would magically rest but nothing was there. My fingers flipped through the folders and all that was there was paperwork. My eyes roved over the bottom of the metal box for anything resembling a lanyard or plastic ID sleeve but to no avail. Begrudgingly, I pulled away from the drawer and stole a glance at Angie again. This time, she was standing to full attention and beckoning me to hurry up. I didn't hear any whistles through the classroom wall.

As I flipped the folders forward and backwards, I blamed myself for being so stupid. Then, as I was about to clang the drawer back into place, I saw a small plastic shape at the bottom of the drawer resembling a key chain. Instinctively, I picked it up and noticed it was a USB drive. Without a thought on how I would return it, I picked it up and pocketed it along with my paper clip.

Angie said loud enough for me to hear inside, "We really need to ask you a question, Sir."

Oscar was beside her at the door, nodding his head fervently in agreement.

"Can't it wait until I get this Tupperware put away?" Mr. C.'s voice, angrily chimed in.

"It'll just take a second," Angie implored, beckoning Mr. C. away from the classroom, toward the lockers and out of sight.

"It better," he scolded, walking with them out of sight.

I couldn't remember if the lights were on or off and decided to leave them on. I checked the desk one more time for any other signs of forced entry and walked out, easing the door closed behind me. It was only after I had passed the water fountain that I remembered the gum and thought better of leaving it alone. The thumb drive felt heavy in my pocket, and I was exhausted from this one simple heist.

Chapter 25

We waited for what felt an eternity as the school day drew to a close. Every time the classroom doors opened, I ducked my head like a guilty party to something that only I knew about. If other classmates noticed my odd behavior, they said nothing and chalked it up to me being me. I laughed at this consideration completely, and for once, was pleased at my limited number of friends. Simultaneously, I wondered if Angie and Oscar were behaving similarly in their remaining classes. When I got up to get a drink of water, I scanned the hallways for a raving Mr. C. Not seeing him, I took a deep sigh of relief and took my time returning to class. In the last block, I asked to go to the restroom and fell into the 'solace' of knowing he wouldn't darken the female bathroom. It felt oddly quiet and safe in the puke yellow space, and I leaned on the porcelain sink and stared at myself in the mirror. Thoughts of stealing his flash drive invaded my brain, and I shook the notion away. *It was worth it,* I thought. *To catch him at whatever he was doing.* Suddenly, the bathroom door swung open, and the unmistakable exchange of giggles interrupted my reverie.

"What are you going to do?" Corine's flighty voice asked.

I spun from the mirror and leaned against the sink with my full weight.

Corine and her two friends halted to attention, and I waited for whatever insults would come.

"Playing sick?" she asked, her voice fixed at a high pitch. Her girlfriends laughed, and I cheerfully couldn't name either. It was a point of pride not knowing such characters at Idyll.

I rested casually against the edge and folded my arms across my tee, covering my Rolling Stones lips.

"She's dreading going home," Corine chirped. "If she *has* a home to go to," she added, falling into laughter at her own joke.

Her posse did likewise, and they breezed past me to the other mirrors and began applying lip gloss and checking their hair for misplaced locks.

"You just going to stand there and stare at us or make like a bee . . . ?" Corine asked, pausing in her second application of gloss to her upper lip.

"It's a free country," I spat. "So, I'll leave whenever I feel like it, okay?" balling my fists against my ribcage.

Corine paused, then chuckled at my retort. She looked at herself and me in the mirror and then looked to see what her friends' reactions were. Not wanting to lose any ground with them, she took a different approach and said, "I saw you ducking out of lunch and Melanie said she saw you in the hallway with that Angie doing something. She says Oscar was with you," she added.

The one who was Melanie nodded in agreement and smacked her lips for a second or two, the lip gloss glowing on her face.

Corine paused in her admiration of her picture and leaned closer to my personal space, and said, "I'm going to find out what you were doing, *Freida*. I know you are up to something with those two, and I'll get it out sooner or later."

I kept my face as motionless as I knew how, and I smelled her intoxicating lavender scent. *Did she use the whole bottle on herself?*

"It seems you'd have something better to do," I teased, keeping my posture static. "I'm quite boring," I added.

"That's just it, Freida. You might think I'm dumber than anyone you messed with in middle school, but I know that's one thing you are not . . . boring," she said, smacking her lips to make sure the gloss was fully visible.

"A popular girl like you has to have a million things to do besides check up on me," I smiled, unfolding my arms. "You have a school to run, don't you?"

She put her makeup away and shook her single stray hair into place. Then, she looked at the girls and gave them a nonverbal cue that their work was done. Both recognized their leader's gesture and put their tubes back into their pockets.

"Besides, I'm trouble, Corine. You wouldn't want to get too close to me, or it might rub off," I admitted, laughing and straightening my shirt as I stood to full height.

Corine's smile fell from her lips, and she seemed to be thinking about something else, because her hand fell to her pocket. She pulled her cell phone from her pocket and said, "Shoot. We're almost done. Bell's going to ring any second. Meet me at the lockers?" she said to the two girls.

The girl named Melanie and the other one filed past us and exited the bathroom in single file. Corine waited for the door to swing closed all the way and said, "You aren't half as smart as you think you are, okay?"

"Meaning what?" I said, teeth gritted.

"You are so easy to read. If I didn't know better, you were trying to harass some teacher or worse, trying to get some teacher to show you *special* attention," she chided. "You're the type to do something like that," she added, laughing at her own sick joke.

"Gross," I uttered below my breath.

"Just saying," she said, raising her hands up in an apologetic way.

"What gives you the right to say that to my face?" I said, fuming beneath the surface. A large part of me wanted to smear her lip gloss off on the porcelain rim of the sink, but in divine intervention, the bell rang.

"Your lucky day," Corine grinned.

My back felt sticky against my tee, and I pushed off from the sink and walked away, leaving her standing in the bathroom alone. In the hallway, students were pushing against me, and I couldn't help but feel sickened by her insinuation. *Why would she stoop so low? Who did she think she was?* I never flirted with a teacher in my life. It was so gross that I lost my train of thought and bumped into a student trying to get into the bathroom. She didn't say 'Excuse me,' but I heard her grumble, "Walk much?" as she passed.

Corine came out of the bathroom and saw me gawking at the door. She grinned a devilish grin and said, "I bet it was Mr. Chethers."

Hearing her say his name unnerved me more, and my face must have given me away, because I heard, "Oh my, it *was*, wasn't it?"

Rather than stay for more abuse, I turned toward the front doors and sprinted around people milling outside their classrooms and lockers. It was my one goal to get outside, and I felt the hallway spinning and my vision dimming. When I got past the melee, I found myself at the bottom of the school's front steps and didn't know where I was headed.

With my stomach churning, I walked downhill and found the base of the hill and the edge of Chartreuse Lake. Images of my run-in with Randell Tolley flashed across my mind, and I felt bile rise in my throat. Without thinking, I ducked onto the path and dry heaved on the trail leading to the closest edge of the water. I leaned down and felt the emptiness of my stomach seize against my insides. I spat what little saliva there was in my mouth onto the dirt and wiped my mouth slowly. *Why couldn't I eat something like a normal person?* I thought, scolding myself. Then, remembering that we'd been too focused on getting into Mr. C.'s room to eat anything, I laughed at how long the day had seemed. *It's hard to eat when you're busy breaking into a classroom.*

My head felt dizzy, and my legs were wobbly from this all-day fast. Spotting a bench along the path, I swayed to it and sat down to steady myself. My brain surged with what could possibly be on the flash drive. I felt around inside my canvas bag and found it resting on the bottom like a piece of discarded plastic. Instinctively, I pulled it from the bag and held it to the light. To anyone watching, it would look like I'd gone insane. But I knew that something had to be stored inside it. If it helped get to the bottom of who Mr. C. was, that would be great. I wanted to walk back into class and see him for *what* he was.

"Who are you?" I heard myself say aloud.

The plastic thumb drive, black and shaped like a key didn't even have a name on it. Oscar, being more tech savvy than me, would probably know how to get something good off of it straightaway. I didn't know if Angie had used a drive before, but she could add something. If Mr. C. was someone with a criminal past, I prayed the damning information would be on this. *But who would be dumb enough to store all of this on a file?* I thought. *And where did his ID go?* Suddenly, my heart started to sink as I imagined the drive offering up little to nothing about what we needed.

A blue heron rose from its hunkered pose to full height and half flew half skimmed across the lake, landing safely (and far) away from me. When it settled on the opposite shore, it shook its feathers and seemed to taunt me for a second. Then, it crouched and began stalking into the water to look for its next fish. When I put the flash drive safely into my pocket, I noticed the stone steps where Tolley once stood. I thought of his tale about the disappearance on Wolf Island. *How does someone just disappear?* I wondered.

Chartreuse Lake provided a beautiful scene with sunlight bouncing off the ripples that fish made when surfacing. The heron stalked and peered downward into the shallows and maneuvered its awkward head backwards and forwards. No boats sped across the channel, and I was thankful for the silence and space to think. The weather cooled and gusts of wind flitted around my bench as I shielded my eyes from the bright sunlight. Suddenly, I found myself thinking an odd thought, wondering what else Tolley might know about the island and its lore. It felt magical, and I shook away images of fairies and pots of gold.

Then, I remembered the nightmare about Oscar's dead sister, and I felt a chill rake across my body. Several states and months away, I imagined where his sister had drowned in a similar body of water. I tried to not think about the thrashing of water that I'd seen in my sleep, but it was there and wouldn't release me. I saw the hand protruding from the water and imagined I saw it here, on Chartreuse. The streaking flashes of Oscar's friend trying to go beneath the surface to save Andrea met me full force. The panicked swim of Oscar and his countless attempts to bring her back in time. Then, him saving his friend, and the loud, reverberating cries he groaned from the shoreline. It felt as if it was happening right beside my bench, and I put my head in my hands. My vision blurred, and the sun made me even dizzier.

"Why, God? Why?" I said aloud, raising my head, looking outward to the lake, the bird stalking its prey.

Met with an unquenchable silence, I wiped my forehead and felt my pocket to ensure the drive was still there. Even if the files provided nothing of use, I resolved to check every one of them. I owed it to Oscar, his sister especially. If Mr. C. intended to do anything wrong, I was going to be there to point a spotlight at him.

Chapter 26

Oscar agreed that the best spot for testing out the drive would be his house, because his dad had a super computer and my only option was sneaking onto technology when my parents were asleep or away. Angie was adequate with technology, but she was quick to point out that she didn't want anything 'malicious' on her home computer. So, we decided to meet over winter break and see if there was anything worthwhile on the device. We waited a few weeks until the semester ended, because it was something we needed to build up to. Oscar said some drives were encrypted and alert the owner if someone tries to hack into them. I didn't know anything about this, and so I trusted him on it.

My prayers were that the drive wasn't tricky and it would open right up. The one obstacle we didn't need was something tipping Mr. C. off that we were the ones who took the thing. He had acted odd over the remaining weeks of school, odder than usual, and he continually blamed students for stealing things from his desk, his room. We three feigned ignorance and never made eye contact with him. A few times, Corine had turned around to stare at me point-blank in class, but I had shrugged my shoulders and asked her what her problem was.

True to his word, Oscar secured access to Mr. Villanueve's laptop and even asked his dad if he could use it for a while. I was floored by how much trust he had with his parents. It made me miss the absences of mine at home all the more. I wondered if Angie was ever left at home alone for long spells. It would be something I could ask her about, if we were ever alone without Oscar.

Oscar whizzed through his dad's login name and password prompts. When the computer came to life, he clicked 'delay' on updates and other items needing his dad's attention for work. I wanted to ask Oscar what his dad did exactly, but I felt the time wasn't right. Besides, we had more pressing business, and I watched him as he took the flash drive and plugged it into the computer port.

"Moment of truth, guys," he said, cracking his knuckles and waiting for the device to be recognized.

The seconds felt like an eternity, and I held my breath and gazed across what Oscar called the 'OLED screen' to meet Angie's eye. She grinned a hopeful half-smile and just as quickly her smile fell as the flash drive image popped up in the bottom screen bar.

"Is that a good sign?" I asked, knowing my knowledge was not good here.

Oscar held up his hand and double-clicked on the drive picture. When he did, the flash drive morphed into an open folder and there were two columns of what appeared to be files.

"Bingo," he said, clapping his hands. "The drive is unencrypted and standard security. Dad would say it's not Fort Knox," he added, laughing at some family joke.

"So we can get to whatever might be on it?" I asked, attempting to read some of the file names, but they were all seemingly gibberish with long-tailed names featuring unintelligible letters and numbers strewn together.

"Yes," Oscar said, looking first to me, then Angie.

"Good," Angie chimed in. "I don't like messing around with other people's stuff."

I wanted to tell her to 'Think about *who* it was,' but didn't. The files stared back at us, and I wondered what Oscar might click on first. With no set course of action, I knew it might take a while to get any sort of 'coherence' from the files. His fingers hovered over the first file in the first column, and he looked at us both with a 'here goes' as he clicked it.

The image appeared grainy and looked to be some unmarked trail. The quality was so poor that I pointed at a sign and said, "What's that say?"

Angie shook her head, and Oscar hovered over the next file below it. He clicked it, and another image of slightly better quality popped up. This one featured an open area on what could possibly be the same trail, but it was hard to discern. There was no sign visible, and the ground was muddy and leaves were strewn across the path. The season I recognized as Fall, because the leaves were various hues of gold, crimson, and apricot. But not much else was identifiable.

Oscar clicked on the third image, and it brought up a blurry photo like it was taken in haste. There was an unidentified hand pointing at something on the ground, and the leaves were covering most of the forest ground. From this shot, it was all but impossible to interpret what the photographer was pointing at. I frowned and thought about taking the mousepad away from Oscar. *Maybe if I just clicked through all of them and opened them up in quick order something would be recognizable?*

Oscar opened a fourth and fifth file and more clues escaped us. The images all appeared to be shot by whomever while walking and quickly scanning the trail. The open ground was the only spot that had more than one recurring image devoted to it. There were numerous pictures detailing the open space, and I wondered if Mr. C. took all of these, or if this was just some dumb flash drive he'd taken from a student. My heart sank.

Not waiting for Oscar to protest, I pushed him away from the keyboard and ran my finger over the mousepad to the second column. The first file opened after I triple-clicked it too quickly, and the file simply read 35.0561849°N, -85.3005134°W. The files below it read the same but with slight identifiers such as 'Hopesfall Trail' and 'Tent Site.' I looked from the images Oscar had clicked open to the simple messages displayed on the parallel columns.

"It's his research into that island," I said, without waiting for either of them to comment. "See how the first column matches the notes?"

Angie tilted her head sideways and didn't protest as she surveyed the files. Oscar clapped me on the back like a sibling might, and I didn't know if I liked that or not. But he was grinning, and he said I was right. He took his phone from his pocket and began punching buttons in a rush.

"Hey, what's this?" I asked, clicking on the file at the bottom, separate from the two columns.

Before either could respond, I was staring at a PDF document that looked to be multiple pages in length. The image that popped up on page one was a younger version of Mr. Villanueve. My jaw dropped. As I stared at Oscar's dad, Angie said, "What's that?"

Oscar stopped staring at his phone and his eyes went as big as saucers. "What the—" he began.

I scrolled past the familiar picture of a man who served me chili mac not too long ago and what appeared to be his work profile, his engineering firm, to the next page. It brought me even lower, because I saw an old, faded copy of a social security card with the name Edward Clarence Munson on it.

"That's not my dad's name," Oscar started to protest.

Angie said, "What's . . . what's going on?" her voice ringing hollow across the bed. "Who is that then?"

"Don't you all see?" I asked them both. "It's the mother lode," I added a little too eagerly. "It's Mr. C.'s real name. This must be the file that he kept all his important stuff on. One place. It is *his* flash drive!"

Oscar was too shocked to match my giddiness. His blank expression showed fear and concern instead of excitement. Angie backed off the bed slowly and held her hands up. I scrolled past this, imagining what else might be stored here. And the final page did not disappoint. It featured a Cayman Islands account with the same name of 'Munson' attached to it. I clapped my hands in surprise at finding so much. *We didn't need the ID after all!* But when I looked at my two other sleuths, their faces showed anything but glee.

"What's wrong?" I asked, looking from one to the other. "Don't you see how lucky we are to find this? It gives us what we need."

Angie's face turned a deep shade of red, and Oscar turned his phone to both of us, not making eye contact. The Google search showed 'Wolf Island' as its result, and I saw that he'd typed in the numbers from the file.

"It's coordinates. It's what Mr. C. is after," he admitted, dropping his phone on my bed and looking away.

I was baffled. Now was not the time to pout or get defeated. I climbed off the bed and grabbed Angie's clammy hand. She looked at me with reservation and shame. I didn't know what to make of her reactions, but said, "We're in this together, right?"

She looked away, and Oscar stood silently for a moment, scanning my room and looking anywhere but at me. It was the first time I'd seen him lost. Well, except when he spoke about his sister. But this felt different. The room was drained of its energy, and I didn't know why.

"We have everything we need to nail him," I offered, holding up my hands in petition, pointing back to the laptop half-closed on the bed. "His goose is cooked," I said, laughing at my own stupid delight.

"Why does he have so much on my dad?" Oscar finally pleaded. He turned and looked me fully in the face and there were tears there.

"We don't know that . . . *yet*," I said, grabbing his hand and holding it like I had Angie's. "But, we're going to find out," I added, trying to sound as confident as I felt.

"I can't get my dad into trouble," he said with his teeth clenched. "We were just starting over since . . . "

"Star, Oscar's right. This is so much bigger than us," Angie said suddenly. "I think we should take it to the police. It might be the smartest thing we do."

I shook my head 'no.' It was too simple. Cops had a way of explaining away things like this. *Didn't these two watch crime shows?* The cops were usually the least helpful and would somehow pawn the problems on us, kids bored with their town, their lives, making mischief and more work for them in the end.

"Do you think they'll believe us after having stolen his flash drive?" I asked. "Of course not. They'll put us in some juvenile track for being delinquents. I know how these things work," I said, suddenly ashamed of my middle school track record.

"And the Cayman account?" Angie asked.

"Tax privileges and discretion," I admitted, thinking of the heists and times criminals tried sending their wealth elsewhere.

"So, Mr. C., er Munson, is doing all of this to try and get at whatever is on this island?" Angie said, her face no longer as red as before.

"It all fits," I agreed.

"Why the name change then?" she said, glancing from me to Oscar who remained motionless, still holding my hand.

"Criminal, no doubt. He's done something somewhere, and he doesn't want to risk using anything but an alias."

Oscar dropped my hand suddenly, and I felt the sting. He folded his arms across his chest and glared at me. I didn't want to create a divide, but his dad was someone coming into the picture now. *Why was he Mr. C.'s interest?* As if reading my thoughts, Oscar picked his phone up from the bed and put it forcefully into his pocket.

"We'll figure this out," I pleaded. "Don't give up on this now. Oscar, you know we can't do it without you," I offered, trying to look as desperate as I felt.

He paused in his walk to the door, his back to me and Angie.

"We don't know the full scope of it, okay?" I tried, once more. "It might be nothing."

"This was a terrible idea, Star," he muttered, not turning around. "And I'd appreciate it if you leave. Both of you," he leveled at the door.

Too stunned to respond, I felt my face flush like Angie's had, and I looked to her for support. She was already walking past Oscar and toward the main foyer. It was the first time he'd spoken to me like this, the first argument ever. Not wanting to lose ground or give up on this, I fumbled for the flash drive in his dad's laptop and stuck it in my pocket. He waited for me to exit his room, and he shut the door on us before we could say 'goodbye.'

Angie marched quickly in the direction of wherever home was for her, and I lingered at the front entryway for a moment. I turned to peer up at his bedroom window, and I could hear a bass guitar come to life and begin playing forceful notes. The sounds cemented me in place, and I knew there was too much at stake to simply walk away.

Chapter 27

Oscar avoided reaching out during the remainder of Christmas break. Angie ran into my family once in the Hamilton Place mall, but her eyes only locked onto mine long enough to say 'I'm sorry,' before her parents led her along to Bath & Body Works. I was demoralized because I thought these two would rally around the cause. It *did* involve Oscar's dad. I tried to rationalize why neither of them wanted to plan our next move, especially Oscar. I thought of his hand holding mine that last time in his room, and I felt the warmth of his body next to me still. It was silly to linger on such notions, but he was my best friend. And I didn't want to go back to flying solo like at Cascade Middle. So, I gave him and Angie as wide of a berth as possible, and if it took all of the holidays to recover, I was fine with it.

Today, it was New Year's Eve, and I vowed to find something that would entertain me while my parents made plans to party like it was 1999 and joked about going downtown this evening. They had just celebrated their twentieth anniversary the month prior, and I was glad to see them so eager to not talk about work or upcoming projects. Mom asked me if I was going to prom, and I told her freshmen don't usually go to prom. We laughed at her silly oversight, and Dad sided with me.

"No need for prom dress shopping," I chided her.

"Touche," she replied.

Dad asked me what I would do while they were out for the night, and I said I would keep the mayhem to a dull roar. He elbowed me and slipped me the faithful credit card.

"Two hundred dollar limit?" I teased.

"Funny," he replied.

"You all going to dance?" I asked, thinking of how Dad had swirled Mom around the living room earlier like teenagers practicing some routine.

"We might cut a rug somewhere," Dad answered.

"No one says that anymore," I groaned.

"We'll be back in the new year," he added, pointing to his watch. He still wore one, and I often remembered taking it from his wrist and playing with the metal clasp.

Part of me admitted that I would miss them and felt like they needed to stay, but I tossed this notion away as I considered how much needed to be attended to regarding the drive. It felt heavy in my pocket, having kept it all of break, and it still rested in my jeans pocket. I felt it against my palm, and realized I was about to go into uncharted territory.

As the hours drew toward the end of the year, Mom dressed in an evening gown, a pretty sleek number and asked me what I thought. I nodded noncommittal and Dad asked the same. I pushed him away, because he always wore the same business clothes to everything. The navy blazer now looked threadbare against his shoulders, and his consistent brown and blue-striped tie hung down his chest like a worn dishrag. I asked if he was going to wear the lighter blue dress shirt or if he wanted to mix it up. He patted the blue shirt against his belly and said he never messed with tradition. I didn't argue but let the two of them become giddy in my sight. Oddly, I felt like a grandparent or something as they dressed and sprayed perfumes and colognes in my presence. The room smelled abysmal with competing scents, and I felt a headache forming.

"Are you two almost done?" I asked, sounding angrier than I intended.

Dad stopped and stared at Mom. His expression dropped a little, and his face slackened to a droop like his tie.

"If I didn't know better, I would say she's trying to get rid of us," he said to Mom.

Mom *hmphed* and unfastened a pearl necklace, handing it to Dad to put around her fragile neck. Once the necklace was on, she looked in a standing mirror and surveyed herself.

"Not a day over twenty-five," Dad beamed.

Mom play-punched his arm, and the two gathered purse, wallet, and keys. Mom draped a shawl across her shoulders and patted it firmly. Then, she turned to me and said, "No boys, Star. None. Not even that Oscar, okay? I mean it."

"Go, have fun. I'll be fine. Happy New Year and all that. See you in the next one," I smiled.

"Star?"

"Yes, no boys. I don't have anyone else I could call," I admitted, scolding myself for saying it out loud.

"We'll be back, and in the morning, we'll have breakfast together. Whatever you want," Dad smiled, planting a kiss on my cheek. "I can make French toast, hmm?"

My mouth watered at the mention, and I nodded in approval. I could taste the cinnamon-y sugar already. "Fine," I agreed.

No sooner had the minivan exited the garage, I was stumbling around inside their room looking for our old family laptop. Knowing it never came out except for rare occasions when Dad wanted to look something up like planning a family trip or doing taxes, I hunted under the bed first. Part of me wished it was right there, but it was not. My brain rumbled over moments in time and tried to think of when it'd been used last. It had been a long time since last tax season and so Dad would've used it since then. We went to Mammoth Cave on our last family trip last June, and I remember Dad mulling over websites about cave exploration. When he'd put it away, he went into the bedroom, but I couldn't imagine where he'd put something he didn't intend to use again. Under the bed was the logical choice. *Out of sight, out of mind.* But, when I didn't find it there, I looked next in the closet. Mom's and Dad's work attire were hanging on old metal hangers awaiting their next trip into the offices. The boxes in the corner all held random contents like scrapbooks and photo albums. I pulled one of the underwear bins out and looked behind there, but there was nothing to see except some solo socks that had hidden from view.

I closed the closet doors intent to leave it just like I found it. Their dresser beside Mom's jewelry chest was next, and I pulled the drawers open one at a time. Inside, it only contained more clothes and various receipts and spare change. I looked around the room and realized I might not find the computer. *It had to be in here!* I tried to channel how Dad put things away, and it led to a sinking feeling, because he was as chaotic as I was in such matters. He liked to move things around and temporarily leave them as he saw fit. As I was about to give up and go search the living room, I turned and noticed their bookshelf with books in anything but an organized order. On the bottom shelf, partially hidden by a stack of three-ring binders, I saw the old Dell laptop poking out slightly. With held breath, I bent and retrieved the computer from its semi-hidden view. Thankfully, beside the binders, the charging cord rested like a snake long resting in hibernation. I took it, and the laptop, into the kitchen and plugged them into an outlet to charge.

Not being patient enough, I opened the computer and saw it was at one percent. Then, the messages popped up that an update was needed. I clicked 'delay' more than once, and the computer slowly came to life. With shaky hands, I took the flash drive from my pocket and stuck it into the port. The computer gave a spinning wheel and eventually recognized the USB drive as in use. I opened the file (as Oscar had done), and the two columns and the solo file at the bottom appeared. It felt like success, even if only for a moment. I knew our home printer was long since gone from having ink, but I didn't plan on printing anything out, anyway. Once I had all of the files open, I scanned them in painstaking order. I took a notepad out and wrote all of it down on a piece of paper. Then, I went to the Chrome browser and typed in *Edmund Clarence Munson* and hit 'search.'

The results were less than desired as his name populated only a couple of times recognizing all three names. My brain rattled around knowledge about 'expunged' records and how courts did that in different states. The names 'Edmund' and 'Munson' generated some generic Facebook and Instagram accounts and zero met all three words. The states associated with both his first and last name most often were California and Kansas. I tried to make myself think of how he spoke and any noticeable accents he gave in class. Sadly, Mr. C. was largely an amoeba and knew how to mask anything reminiscent of a dialect or tone. I shuddered at the thought of how many states he might have lived in before Tennessee. More to humor myself than anything, I clicked on 'images,' and it provided a small list of 'Edmund Munsons' sprinkled throughout the Internet. One was a high school athlete dressed in football gear, and he looked young, the picture dated just from a year ago. Another image showed a farmer sitting atop a tractor in Arkansas with a link for 'Top Yield Crops of the Year.' The man wore overalls and grinned a large grin with pride in his accomplishment. He didn't resemble Mr. C. at all, even with my biggest attempts and imagination. A final image revealed a man with a thin, blonde mustache and a receding hairline with a leather cowboy hat sitting snugly on his head. He looked more adventurer than rodeo spectator, and he squinted, as if he was looking directly into the sun. While his face wasn't quite smiling, his lips were slightly apart, and he looked pleased with himself or someone. I drew in a deep breath as I knew that maniacal gaze from morning classes. The caption read, "Local man finds Ming Dynasty Bowl in backyard," and I clicked on the article. It led to a brief news piece about an Idaho man named 'Edmund Munson' who dug up the exposed portion of a vase in his Pocatello backyard to find that it was an original 15th century lotus bowl from the Ming Dynasty in China. The story revealed that the bowl was estimated to be worth a small fortune, and the owner had no plans for selling it or returning it just yet.

I hovered over the image and felt my pulse racing. My eyes scanned the bottom of the search results but it stopped at just the one page. There was no mention of what came next, and I couldn't stop there. So, I typed in 'Edmund Munson' and 'Idaho' and nothing popped up except for the image (and story) again. Then, I tried 'Edmund Munson' and 'Pocatello' only to arrive at the same crossroad. I bit my lip and let out a loud groan. My stomach grumbled, and I pushed away notions of ordering Greek food. I could always eat later.

Hovering over the keyboard, I racked my brain for anything else that might yield a result. I wanted to know what happened next, and so I typed 'Ming Dynasty vase' and 'Idaho.' Again, the only article and picture were the ones tied to Munson's story. *What happened next?*

If he'd sold the vase, he would be rich now. He wouldn't be working at our crummy high school. And a better question might be, why would he? I paused to consider things he'd said in class, why he was so obsessed with that darn mask. It was all he looked at when he wasn't scolding us or making us feel like objects he could push around. His Jekyll and Hyde routine only made me all the angrier, because it couldn't be that he was simply insane. *Could it?* I could hear Oscar telling me to let it go. His dad was in Mr. C.'s crosshairs now, and it wasn't safe to play with someone so unhinged. Part of me felt bad for Mr. Villanueve's face being displayed on the flash drive, but a greater part wanted to know why this was happening.

The last PDF file had Mr. Villanueve's face, his work, Edmund's social, and the Cayman Islands account. It had to be the key to all of this, but I just couldn't reason it out. *Did Edmund have some vendetta against Oscar's dad? The Idaho connection couldn't be random, could it?* I looked up how many people lived in Idaho - about two million. Tennessee was listed at over seven. *What were the odds of them living in the same city now?* On a map search, Pocatello was less than three and a half hours from Boise, Idaho. I pushed away thoughts of Oscar's sister drowning in a lake. In many ways, my mind assimilated the words 'Idaho' with her death. I knew the real story there about Oscar's heroism, how he felt about it.

The article about the found vase was written by a Herbert Anglewood, and it was dated from five years ago. The author's name was highlighted blue, and I clicked on it. The link took me to the Pocatello Gazette website. On its reporter page, the man's name was listed with an email address and phone number. Not having consistent access to a phone, I decided to click on the email and send a message using my school email (one I rarely thought about). In the subject line, I simply wrote 'Question about Vase Article,' and in the body message I said, "I'm inquiring about the Ming Dynasty vase and whatever happened to it. Loved the article. Would like to know more about its story." Then, I signed it "A freshman writing an English/Language Arts essay" and clicked 'send' on the submission box.

I felt no closer to returning to school in a few days and celebrating our heist, bringing closure to Oscar's worries. But, *this* discovery was something. I prayed that Mr. Anglewood would write back quickly, and I imagined his email would provide something of use for us. Whether Angie or Oscar wanted to help me solve this or not was not my concern. I had to see this through, because I couldn't let Mr. C. or Edmund Clarence Munson get away with whatever he was planning. Even if it meant challenging him in front of the class, I was ready to take him on.

Chapter 28

The January air chilled my bones getting off the bus and walking into Idyll High. I was nervous Oscar would still be mad, and I knew to tread lightly on anything concerning the flash drive. Angie met me outside of Mr. C.'s class and gave me a hug, said, "Sorry for leaving things like we did."

"Me too," I heard my voice croak through her coat's fabric. She released me from the thick puffy coat, and I gathered my breath.

"Christmas gift," she smiled, showing off the rich purple hue. "I got it the day you saw me at the mall."

"Cool," I said. I looked down at my jean jacket and patted one of my band buttons. "Same coat as before," I joked.

"You have such great style," Angie said in her kind voice. "Seriously. I love your look."

"It's definitely a look," I answered, not sure how my style stacked up to mall shopping.

"I've got your back, if Corine tries anything," Angie added, walking past my desk to her front row spot.

It felt good to hear her say it, even if I felt like I could hold my own. She was the first girl friend I had ever had in school. It was a good feeling, and I sat down, not waiting for Oscar like I normally would.

Mr. C., or Edmund, took roll and made little eye contact. Something was different about him, and I studied his hideous expressions for longer than I wanted to. The light blonde mustache was back on his face, and I immediately thought of the photo online. It made me certain that two plus two equals four. If I had a leather hat, I would have put it on top of his head to cover the balding hairline. *It was a definite match!*

"Get out your copies of Bradbury's *Fahrenheit 451* and review it for five minutes. I'm giving a beginning of term test, and I'll hand it out after the five minutes are up. If you have questions—"

Several hands in the front row shot up, all except Angie's, I noticed.

"I'll answer them after the exam. Last semester the lowest quiz grades were dropped. This round I'm not dropping quiz or test grades. What you earn is what you earn," he said matter-of-factly.

Corine's hand went up again, and Mr. C. ignored her entirely as he went to the filing cabinet and collected a fresh stack of printed packets.

Rather than wait for Mr. C. to acknowledge her, Corine said out loud, "Sir, we didn't know the test would happen today and—"

"Silence!" he boomed, then collected himself and straightened the papers neatly on his desk. "Five minutes, and I'll pass these out."

Corine's face went a rare red, and I could tell her posture slumped. She leaned forward and covered her face with her arms. I wondered if she was going to cry. If it was last semester, I would have delighted in her agony. But now, the circumstances were way larger than her, and I tried to not listen if whimpers came from her desk.

Angie scanned her copy of the novel even quicker and looked for portions of the book she had underlined. I watched her for a moment and began scanning my copy as well. My mind couldn't focus on the lines that I read and reread, because I kept glancing up to Mr. C. and seeing his face online.

The classroom door opened, and Oscar came in. He went to his desk without bothering to close the door. I thought Mr. C. would protest, but he only glanced at Oscar's appearance and back to his attendance file on his computer.

When Oscar dropped his backpack, I leaned over and told him, "Test in five. Bradbury. Hope you brought your book."

My rationale was to 'synthesize' my words with him, maybe bring him back closer this way. Our last talk felt like forever ago, because December *was* last year. He nodded in some form of acceptance and rummaged in his pack for a worn, tattered copy of *451*. I tried to not stare, but I could tell that his book was annotated unlike any I had ever seen. There was no way Oscar would fail this test, even if he waited five years to take the exam. *Anyone who marked a book up that devotedly would remember its details like riding a bike,* I thought.

Before I could refocus on Guy Montag and whatever was happening on the page, I heard a timer go off, and Mr. C. said, "Books away. Now!"

Groans emitted from all five rows, and I noticed Corine's head was still down on her desk. I never thought I'd feel something akin to sadness for her, but I guess I did now. She hadn't even been able to get a question off. Now, we were putting pencils adjacent to our bodies and tearing sheets of notebook paper for scrap paper.

"Here are the packets, as promised," Mr. C. said, blankly. "You have twenty minutes. Anything longer, and it would show me that you didn't read the book. Plain and simple."

He passed the packets out from the front row to the back and only gave us the 'go ahead' when everyone had the packets before them. The clock on the wall read 8:05 AM, and I made a mental note of 8:25 AM as our buzzer. Writing *Star Crowley* and today's date in the top two lines, I scanned the four pages of paper and noticed it featured multiple choice, short answer, matching, and two essay questions (asking for one page each). *There was no way to finish in twenty minutes!* This time, I waited for Corine to protest, but she sat stoically in the front row and only started writing on the page when nudged by her friend, Melanie.

My tactic was simple when under duress; to go with what I knew on the matching and multiple choice, then the short answer, and after doing this as quickly as possible, jump into the essay questions and write as frantically as I could. The book held some space in my head, but it hadn't been a favorite. Because I didn't have Oscar to visit, and Angie I only saw once, I read *451* twice. It was a big accomplishment for me, but I did it largely out of boredom. I related to Guy Montag somewhat, as he remained disconnected to his totalitarian society and was largely friendless. I guess, I channeled his loner-nature and discovered I could connect with a character on a deeper level. Plus, I wondered if burning books was a fun hobby.

I shook my head to clear it of anything associated with Mr. C., or Oscar, and I began scribbling and circling what looked like correct answers. The short answer section came swiftly, and I filled up the spaces provided on the packet. When I arrived at the first essay prompt, I glanced at the clock and saw I still had twelve minutes. *Six minutes for each,* I thought. *They won't be great essays, but at least they'll be on the page.* I read a prompt about why Guy Montag would hide resources he knew he was required to burn and how the ethics applied to such a decision. I wrote quickly about personal choices and morality and governmental involvement. After crafting my thesis, I wrote a weak body paragraph, and began closing my final thoughts when I heard, "Pencils down."

"But we still have seven minutes left," Melanie cried out this time. "Sir—"

"Silence! Or, it's off to detention," he spat, not giving her time to speak.

She, like Corine before her, placed her pencil on the desk and then she cradled her head. I could hear slight sobs beginning from her chair.

"I change my mind," Mr. C. said nonchalantly. "Instead of twenty, I mean. Thirteen minutes is enough," he smiled, pleased with himself, his fabricated authority.

Oscar sat motionless beside me, and I saw that he hadn't even opened his packet. There was no name at the top, and his pencil was where he had first placed it. This unnerved me more than anything, because Oscar always did his work. He knew this book probably better than anyone apart from Bradbury when he wrote it. *Why would he not start it?* But as quickly as I thought it, I answered my own question. He was taking a stand against this imposter before us. Even if he wouldn't talk to me, this was something I could rally behind.

Mr. C. began collecting the unfinished exams, and I thought Corine might be bold enough to ask for a curve or bonus points, but she relinquished even this control. He went around to all twenty-five chairs and gave small *mmms* in approval. I could see him grading these later tonight and relishing in the satisfaction of giving everyone a grade (or two or three) below their normal marks. He collected mine and seemed less satisfied, as I was almost two-thirds finished. *Maybe that was the most?* Then, he came to Oscar's chair and whistled. "I need a name and date, young man," he laughed to himself, no one else joining in.

"Wonder how you think you did?" he continued, breathing stale coffee breath onto both of us. "What's Mr. Villanueve going to think of this?" Mr. C. chided, holding up the blank packet for the entire room to see.

Oscar didn't move to sign and date it, and Mr. C. shrugged his shoulders, said, "I'll know which one is yours certainly."

After gathering them all, he sauntered to the front desk and unlocked his cabinet drawer that I had picked just weeks before. I noticed he scanned the room as he did this to see how many were watching, and he made brief eye contact with me. *He was still bothered by that,* I reasoned. It gave me a little pleasure to know that I had gotten one over on him. Without saying anything else about it, he dropped the batch of unfinished work into the drawer and closed it. He pocketed his key and went to the board and began scribbling feverishly.

Once the board was filled up, he stepped back to marvel at his handiwork and said, "See this here?"

No one spoke, but most heads nodded in the affirmative.

"It's a history lesson of your fair city," he said, putting his hands on his hips. "Well, not mine and Oscar's, but everyone else's. I hit the high points because there's a lot to say about living *here*. I want you to write down all of this and then write an essay about your experiences living here. Ten pages. Due Friday," he said, placing the dry erase marker back in its slot.

Everyone seemed shell-shocked, because no one spoke or issued an outburst. Oscar sat with his gaze fixated on the person pretending to be someone else. If he lost his cool, I felt it was my job to hold him back. The classroom scribbled onto notebook paper whatever existed on the board, except for Oscar and myself. As he stared at Mr. C., I watched Oscar for any signs of attack. When he gave none, I began copying the notes for both of our benefits later. I didn't want Oscar to fail a class, especially this one. He was too smart.

The minutes ticked by in a forever slow pace, and I only looked up again when I had the entire assignment transcribed. The bell rang loud enough to rattle many of us in our chairs. As I walked outside, I noticed Oscar was close behind. If he didn't want to break the ice first, I was willing to step up and ask him how he really was.

CHAPTER 29

We spoke in fragments across the day, passing notes and sticking them into the slits in one another's lockers. The first one from him simply read 'My house after school.' The one I wrote was a little longer, and I tried apologizing erratically and realized it probably sounded like a desperate zombie babbling incoherently. I think I even signed it 'Your friend, Star.' I scolded myself for sinking to such crazy lengths. It was only one bad ending that time at break. *Surely he'd forgive me of that, wouldn't he?*

I sat beside him at lunch, and he ate slowly, munching on some green beans from who knows how many years ago. As I watched him, Angie took a seat across from us and began to open her milk carton. She remained silent and eyed both of us in turns. I imagined that it would have to be me who broke the ice, but Oscar said, "We need to wait until we're at my place. I got a bad feeling about all of this. I'm not feeling too well."

His face did look pale, and I could see bags under his eyes. He stabbed at the few remaining beans, and they fell apart at his quick jabs, turning to a sickening mush. Oscar picked up a stale piece of cornbread and took a reluctant bite. He swished it around with a gulp of milk and tried to not cough. I always found humor in how close to choking the lunch room always made us. My smile fell short because he quickly stood and dumped his tray without a word. We ate mostly in silence, and I realized the sliced ham with supposed brown sugar was not going to cure me of my hunger. I dumped my tray as well and Angie followed, asking over my shoulder, "Is he okay?"

I shrugged, trying to think of what I should say. He was my friend, and I honestly didn't know. Angie said, "You going over there after school? I think maybe it should be just you two," smacking her tray against the trash can, watching a few beans cling to the plastic for dear life.

I surveyed her and shook my head, "He wanted *both* of us to be there. You *and* me."

She nodded in assent and left her tray on a stack gathering there at the metal receptacle where a lunch lady scrubbed and sprayed with an industrial hose, knocking food remnants all over the cleaning platform. We walked back and saw Oscar gathering his backpack; he reminded me of a hiker readying himself for a long journey across the Appalachian Trail. I gathered my stuff and followed him out the door.

"When you get over there, I'll let you in. Make sure no one follows you, okay?" he said, sounding bewildered and unlike his usual self.

"Followed?" Angie said first, her voice sounding shrill in my ears. "Who would—"

"I'll tell you at the house," he added, his voice more a whisper. "Not here," he added, looking down the hallway behind us for something.

I turned to follow his gaze and saw only the usual high school crowds leaving the cafeteria and making their ways to lockers and third blocks. It was completely ordinary except it wasn't now. *Who would follow us beyond our imposter teacher?* My mind fell on Randall Tolley of all people, and I felt as sick as Oscar looked. *Something was up. Or, maybe he was just overreacting?* But Oscar climbed mountains and was way bolder than anyone I knew. He didn't spook easily, and I felt his hand grip my shoulder before separating for class. He spun me slightly, and leaned in to say, "Apology accepted, Star. See you in a bit."

As he walked the opposite way, I took a sliver of paper from my notebook and wrote in my most convincing voice 'See you at the Lake. Tell Melanie to bring the flash drive. We'll throw it into the lake and pretend it never happened. XOXO Corine.' Then, I marched to Mr. C.'s classroom, checked to make sure no one was waiting in the room yet, and placed the note underneath Corine's chair, trying to make it look like it had fallen innocently to the floor. As I turned to leave, I noticed a gear bag like a backpacker would use to go on a long hike resting against the inside of Mr. C.'s desk, where the chair went. It was hidden from anyone's view, except for someone sitting down at the teacher's chair.

A large part of me wanted to rummage inside the pack, but the smart, keen part of my brain said *Get out you dummy* and so I did. I left and made my way to third block. When I sat down at my desk, I took a sheet of paper out of my notebook, ripping it in my haste. I began to pencil what I had seen but thought better of it. It was better to leave zero of a paper trail.

So, I wrote "O, it means so so much that you said what you did. I never wanted to put this on you or make you feel like it was in some way your fault. You are my best (crossed out) only real friend. I mean, Angie is a friend now too, but I only trust you. And I do. With every bit of my life. You helped me climb a freaking mountain, I mean. You could've left me out there for dead. Hah. And what happened to Andrea is . . . is the crummiest thing a person could ever have happen. And you still believe in God somehow. Amazing! I wish I could be more like that. I question EVERYTHING. And I don't have faith in almost anything except what I see, and I see you. And you're a good person. For something to bother you this badly, it has to be BIG. If you feel like we need to talk about it before the end of the day, meet me at the lockers. I can skip fourth. You know I'm good at that, at least. But if I don't see you then, I will see you at the house. Star."

I folded the paper up three times and made sure it was all but tucked fully inside the locker slit. Only a small fragment stuck out, just enough to be visible to someone looking for it. I didn't want some knucklehead to spot it and read what I'd written. I'd never hear the end of it from snoops like Corine or someone she ran with. Pleased with myself, and my 'tenacity' for thinking things out, I walked back to third and knocked on the door. My teacher gave me a stern warning and an unexcused tardy was entered beside my name on attendance. *The tally keeps growing,* I thought.

The only noises I heard were bits and pieces about political systems and government. I imagined a country that kept tighter surveillance on its citizens. Cameras around every corner. Someone like Edmund Munson wouldn't have such an easy time doing whatever he did under the ever-watchful eyes of Big Brother. I'd heard Dad talking about how many cameras existed in present-day England and could hear his voice booming, amazed, "Over twenty million CCTV cameras in the UK alone! Can you imagine, Star? Cameras on every street in London watching you pick your nose. What's the world coming to? Soon you won't be able to look at your own boogers." Then, I remember disgustingly tuning Dad out and checking Mom's reaction. She had been cleaning plates off the breakfast table that morning and shaking her head. Her exact reply escaped me, but I knew she was as displeased with government patrolling as Dad. "Where was the freedom?" she might've asked.

A funny thought popped in my head, and I saw a scene playing out where Jennifer Lawrence of *Hunger Games* fame was stepping out of a Hollywood limousine and cameras were flashing everywhere. The paparazzi were bustling to get a glimpse of the red carpet darling, and she was shielding her eyes. Instead of wearing a gala gown or something sleek, she was suddenly aflame and her dress was the one from the *Hunger Games* all aglow and she was trying to get past the bustle into whatever building stars went into for the Grammy awards. Her escort was none other than the actor who played Peeta from the novels, Josh Hutcherson. He tried to help her inside, but she tripped on a bump in the carpet and her high heel caught in a way sending her to the ground. As she fell, I saw Woody Harrelson lunging to try and catch her from making impact with the surface in slow motion. The bulbs of the cameras flashed in succession, and Peeta's face went into an 'O' shape. There was a collective groan when she met the Earth, scuffing her elbows. The tabloids, I imagined, would read 'Rug Burn for Katniss' or something the next day. But, as I thought of this, I saw smiles across the crowd and Woody was helping her to her feet. The crowd clapped in unison, and Ms. Lawrence shook the mishap away, straightened her flaming dress.

Suddenly, my body lurched from Hollywood and flew magically to somewhere dark, grey, and overcast. I was dodging a double-decker bus and lunging for the sidewalk. Cars honked their collective horns, and I threw up my hands in anger. My eyes scanned the street, and I saw people walking with heads down and hands firmly lodged in their pockets. Even though rain began to fall, no one reached for an umbrella or seemed to have one on them. I blocked the rain with my t-shirt, pulling it up above my head, my stomach exposed to the cold, whipping wind. With everyone's eyes cast down, I followed a few gentlemen making their way into a pub. None seemed to be in a hurry, and the rain fell faster and people kept their usual pace. The clothes of those passing by were all of the same muted, monochromatic style. No one wore bright colors or floral designs on the street, and I looked down at my faded Nirvana tee, my holey jeans. I laughed at the circumstances and every head snapped in my direction.

Even with the hard, freezing rain falling, no one else seemed to notice the absurdity of how everyone was dressed for funerals except me. I laughed at myself and my rock-n-roll style, and I tried to point at my shirt and help them understand. Then, I pointed to the gentleman closest to me who had paused before entering the pub. He looked at me like I had zero brain cells, and I pointed at his clothes and then mine again. When I opened my mouth, he held his finger up to his lips and pointed to the pub's edge. Affixed to the wall about two stories high was a camera pointed directly where we stood. Others on the streets paused and looked at the corner as well and pointed in unison. *What is going on?* I frantically began to think, my smile dropping to a frown.

The fingers continued to point to the building's edge, the camera affixed to the grey bricks, pointing downward at us, rain falling in rivulets off the mounted display. I scanned the gathering crowd; no one was moving or looking down now. All eyes were fixated on the camera at this pub, and I looked from their blank expressions to the surveillance and back again. As my humor disappeared, I saw that they now were the ones smiling and laughing. But they were laughing at me, and I dropped my shirt down from my head and watched them laugh and giggle with mirth.

My gut reaction was to flee, and I turned and pushed past several who blocked my path away from the pub, its camera and watchful eye. As I did so, I saw the camera swivel on its mount and begin to follow my chaotic pace down the sidewalk. When I felt safely outside of its reach, I looked up at the next street corner and saw a camera turning atop a stoplight to monitor me now that the last had lost visual of me. I ran on and on, and when I saw an opening, I turned across a street without looking and heard a car horn before I saw the headlights and felt the impact. The vehicle met my body with a sickening crack, and I felt myself flying through the air in deafening silence. The images of the Hollywood scene and Katniss falling felt similar to my midair theatrics, and I felt imaginary flash bulbs searing into my pupils. Then, I saw Woody picking her up, and the crowd applauding, and I felt the heat of her dress and the peacock feathers or whatever they were. In my impact with Earth, I was flung forcefully to the asphalt and then ricocheted off a car screeching to a halt from the opposite direction. Rather than taking note of who was gathered around me, I saw the cameras above their heads, and I thought how odd that they still watched and monitored even this on a rainy street. My body felt no pain, but I knew every bone was now in pieces. The rain hit my face and pelted my forehead, and I felt like an alien to it all. Then, I heard an odd, disconnected voice say, "Star! Star! Move," and an elbow was pushing me hard.

The bell rang, and I saw the teacher writing a note and tearing it off, handing it to me. It was a detention note, and I saw it was dated for today. *Not in a million years,* I thought defiantly. I was needed elsewhere, and I would face the consequences with Mom and Dad later. Wiping drool from my cheek, I stood and gathered my backpack. The class was empty save for me and the teacher. I gave her a dazed look and tried to clear my head of the dream. It felt like I was still laying in a street somewhere in London, and my stomach growled at me for not eating lunch.

Chapter 30

Angie met me at the doorstep, and Oscar let us in. His face remained a pasty white, and I saw that he looked both left and right down the street as we entered his home. The street remained vacant, and no cars passed in either direction. We took off our shoes, because Oscar had his off and the floor looked newly cleaned. He pointed at the fridge and offered a drink. I was thirsty, and I wanted to do anything to help him feel more at ease.

"Juice?" I asked.

"Help yourself," he said, over his shoulder, already getting his dad's laptop from the living room.

"Angie?" I said, adding as I stuck my head inside the fridge, "Orange or cranberry?"

"Orange, please," she said politely.

"Where are the cups, Oscar?" I asked, through the wall separating kitchen from living room.

"Top shelf beside the fridge," he hollered.

I took out both jugs of juice and poured Angie's and then poured one for myself. Once the drinks were in hand, we sat at the kitchen island and waited for Oscar to rejoin us. Angie eyed me skeptically above the rim of her glass; she sipped hesitantly and gave me her, 'What's going to happen now?' look. I frowned as I didn't know.

Oscar brought in the computer and opened it on the countertop. He held out his hand for the flash drive, and I fumbled in my jeans for it. Somehow I had forgotten it was there. It had been in there for so long, I was beginning to feel like it was a part of the fabric. When Oscar took it from me, he plugged it into the laptop without ceremony. It was odd how comfortable we'd become in using something that wasn't even ours. Oscar typed in his dad's password 1,2,3,4 and clicked open the familiar file. I laughed at the irony of an engineer using the most common password in the world. Oscar swiveled his head to me, and a slow grin spread across his face, because he was thinking the same thing as me. It felt like a Christmas present just seeing him do that, be himself again for a second. Then, just as quickly the smile fell away, and he was all business again. He opened all of the two columns onto the computer's desktop and left them there for easy toggling. His callused fingers scanned the files twice to ensure they were all still there, and I didn't take issue with this. It was the first time he'd seen them since before break. Then, he paused on the extraneous bottom file for longer. He ran through the profile of his father, Edmund's SSN, and the Cayman account. As he did this, I felt a surge of adrenaline rush through me and a simultaneous shiver cross my neck. *What was he looking for?* When he got to the bottom of the PDF, he went back to page one and lingered on his dad's face. Slowly, he scrolled through the details connected to Mr. V.'s work, his company, his profile, and love for history and how he spent his free time exploring. *How much did Oscar know about Idaho?* I wanted to ask. *Why was Oscar suddenly wanting to do this when he'd said he was out at Christmas? Didn't want any part of it.*

Oscar left the screen centered upon Mr. V.'s profile paragraph, and then he turned to both of us. He clasped his hands together and closed his eyes. Oscar sat like that for a moment, and I thought he was having a meltdown or something. Then, he opened his eyes and looked somewhat relieved, less pale.

"What?" he asked, looking from me to Angie slowly. "Haven't you all ever prayed before big decisions?" he asked incredulously.

Angie looked at me dumbly, and I shrugged my shoulders.

"I know I left *this*, and you guys in a bad place last time," Oscar exhaled, speaking to us, then pointing to the screen. "It was wrong of me to just throw up my hands and walk away. I almost did," he admitted, his cheek contorting to a cute dimple on one side. "But that wasn't fair to you all. And besides, this wouldn't just go away, would it?"

Neither of us spoke in the affirmative, but I knew he was right.

"I asked Dad one night about it. If he had any enemies, you know?"

"You asked him about the file?!" I half-shouted in disbelief.

"No, I'm not stupid," he replied, not getting angry, putting a hand on my forearm, soothing me. "We don't keep secrets in my family, and it was eating me up that Dad was in some sort of trouble. So, I asked him if anyone ever got mad about the projects he worked on," Oscar said, taking his hand away from me, the warmth still there.

"Dad said no. His work wasn't like that. It was all 'take a project, see it through' and customers were happy or his company made it right. And, I asked him about other things like his philanthropy and how he gave back to the community. He said he always tried to make it better, not worse. So, no, there hadn't been any enemies that he could 'see.' And he had asked me why I was asking these sorts of questions, and I thought he knew something was up," Oscar said, pausing to look at the screen again.

"If he doesn't have any enemies then why—" I began, but he held up his hand to cut me off.

I wanted to tell him about the story I'd found online, but I didn't want him to think I was a snoop or push him away again. So, I stopped.

"He told me that 'sometimes' people got angry with his work in preservation," Oscar said, waiting for us to acknowledge the development. When he saw our looks of disbelief, he said, "He sometimes tries to make sure history is protected, you know?"

Angie shook her head 'no,' and I played dumb.

"Dad likes to explore and sometimes he looks into how cultural artifacts and stuff are preserved. One time, he said he got into a scuffle with a community over how Native American artifacts were being trampled over out West. He said he had to go to court with a group to make sure everything was given back to the reservation. It didn't go easy, and the judge eventually had to *make* them give everything back to its rightful owners. It didn't make the community too happy," he said, tapping his fingers against the marble countertop.

When Angie sipped from her glass, I did likewise and waited for whatever else he'd learned. It was hard, because I wanted to tell him about the article so badly, but a bigger part of me wanted him to say it.

"The Native American group deserved that," Angie said, between sips of her juice. "That was a good thing, Oscar," she soothed. "People get away with too much," she added, putting her cup down on the counter.

"I was proud of him for standing up for what's right," he agreed. "He said it wasn't the only time, and I asked him about others. He talked about land rights and stuff mostly, but he mentioned one in Idaho that got out of hand and never felt quite right," Oscar admitted.

"Idaho?" I pried, feeling he was on the cusp of telling me just what was on the tip of my tongue.

"Yeah, it was before we moved here. He was working out of Boise, and he always tried to keep himself busy with work, but we'd gone camping around the state. He took Mom, Andrea, and me to various cities, and we explored together," he said, his voice falling away.

I reached for his hand, and he let me take it. Angie saw this and smiled for a second, then looked away.

"On one trip, we were visiting Massacre Rocks State Park near Pocatello, and Dad saw a newspaper mentioning something about a local man finding a rare Chinese vase. He read up about it and saw that the town wasn't too far. Being a lover of history, he asked if we could detour to Pocatello so he could ask the reporter about it. So we did," he said, looking at both of us to see if we were lost.

Angie bit her nails, unsure if she wanted to hear the rest, but I nodded and urged him to go on. It felt weird knowing this already, but I wanted him to say it aloud.

"We drove to Pocatello, and Dad asked this guy with a funny name, Herbert something or other, about the story. He said it was true. A dude found a super rare, expensive vase in his backyard and didn't want to give it to a museum. He wanted to sell it to the highest bidder and claimed it was his right. He would do whatever he wanted to with it," Oscar admitted.

"And what happened?" Angie asked. I looked at her and thought the same thing. *This was the edge of my understanding as well.*

"Dad said he couldn't let it go. He needed to get Herbert in touch with the Idaho Preservation Society or he would. If it needed to be returned to China, Dad was ready to make that happen as well. The guy called Dad at work and told him to leave it alone. It wasn't none of his business. Dad said the guy called three or four times, and the last had been the worst, because he said he would make sure Dad's life would be 'difficult' if he saw this through. Never being one to back down from a threat, Dad kept at it and had the vase rejoined to a group in China. And to keep the Pocatello guy quiet, Dad opted to not let this story make any other news. It was his belief that insult to injury would only make it worse. Then, he drove us back to Boise, and I think that was the last he heard about it," Oscar said, looking at the screen again.

"So your dad ticked him off by sending it back to its rightful place?" I asked. "How much was it worth?" I added, looking from Oscar to Angie. "It had to be a lot of money!"

Angie agreed and said something about rare pieces in Asia being worth a fortune.

Oscar said, “Who knows, but it’s over there now, and get this, there’s an article about it online,” he rejoined, clicking on a search browser and bringing up the same article I had found during break, the picture of the blonde mustache staring back at us. “It’s him!” Oscar said emphatically. “It’s Mr. C. He’s Edmund Munson!”

We all looked at one another, and I kept my face in what I imagined was a surprised state of shock. Angie’s face flushed, and she had a thin line of perspiration above her lip.

“So, what do we do now?” I asked, forcing out the question I’d held for what felt like weeks.

Oscar gritted his pearly white teeth and tilted his head back. Angie took another sip of her orange juice and wiped it and the sweat from her lip. I conjured up images of us taking the only course of action that made sense, and before I could speak, Oscar answered with, “We go to Wolf Island and find whatever he’s after before he does and take it.”

I smiled and clapped my hands together, and Oscar stared at me. I downed my juice in a single gulp and set the cup down on the marble too loudly.

“He’s messing with my family, and I want to be the one to tell him he’s all out of luck,” Oscar said defiantly.

As I admired his sudden commitment, I thought of the backpack and my heart immediately dropped several feet. Mr. C. was already planning to go out there. *Maybe he already went?* I steadied myself by holding onto the countertop and said, “Guys, I think he has plans to get out there ASAP. I saw his gear beside his desk today.”

The two looked at me, and I told them about my quick deception and letter from earlier. Oscar congratulated me on ‘good thinking,’ and Angie agreed. Even if Mr. C. took the bait and went to Chartreuse Lake to try and thwart Corine, it wouldn’t be long before he was on his way to Wolf Island, and we needed to get there before he did.

Chapter 31

Oscar rummaged in a thousand closets and went down to the basement. He returned with a heap of old flashlights, a tent, and a flare gun, spreading them across the kitchen island. He opened the drawers beside where I sat and flung things around in the drawers and found a few batteries that worked. We had enough for two of the flashlights, and I unscrewed the ends and added the batteries. When they were reattached, I clicked one and Oscar the other and both lights came to life. As soon as I clicked mine off, I heard Angie ask, "We're going now? It'll be dark anytime now."

We looked outside and the January light was already almost below the tree line. The lake provided a little more time, but we needed to move swiftly. Oscar packed up some snacks in his biking pack and bottles of water. He took the flash drive out of the laptop and stuck it in his back pocket. I wanted to ask 'What for?' but thought better of it. Oscar seemed to know something I did not.

Leaning over the counter to Angie, I said, "He already had the bag. He's going out there tonight, and we can't let him find whatever he's after."

Angie pressed back a little from me and took her glass to the sink. Not sure why, other than having something to do, she took mine and did the same.

"Should we tell anyone where we're going?" she asked, adding, "You know. In case . . . "

Neither Oscar nor I finished the sentence. He gathered the two flashlights and pushed them down into the other gear. The tent took up more space than anything, and he had to press down on it to make room for the flashlights. Then, he opened another drawer and held a pack of waterproof matchsticks to the light. Pleased with this, he laughed a quiet laugh and stuck them into the front pocket of the pack. As soon as the bag was cinched together and buckled into place, he hoisted it behind his back, and I realized it all but matched the one Mr. C. had behind his desk.

"We're going to come back," he reassured Angie, finally looking her fully in the face. "Star, hit the lights. Angie, would you lock the door on our way out? I'll grab something out of the garage and be right there."

Angie followed me as I clicked the light switch, and I heard the door shut behind her. On the steps, it felt suddenly real. She timidly hunched her shoulders and shivered in her puffy jacket. I kicked myself for not bringing more than the jean jacket. It was already falling below freezing, and I knew Oscar had something else in his mind. He was prepared, or at least he seemed so. As I clenched my teeth to keep them from chattering, I heard the garage door spring to life and slowly rise. We walked around the corner to peer inside at whatever he was doing. No sooner had we turned at the edge of the house, we could see the light on in the illuminated garage and an old Jeep roared to life, headlights glaring at us. Angie stepped back and was almost completely behind me. I stood my ground, because I didn't know what else to do.

Oscar's head popped out from the driver's side and he said, "Hope Dad doesn't kill me. It's his old toy," he added.

I could see something jutting out the back hatch, the door raised, and I saw what looked like life jackets jammed in the front seat.

"Get in," Oscar called over the noise of the old engine. "We gotta get out there."

He pointed to the backseat, and Angie and I filed in beside the biker pack. Angie inadvertently put her hand on mine, and I didn't move it away. The closeness felt good, and I was comfortable that Oscar was driving. He knew where the island was, but he plugged the address into his GPS anyways. We sped out of the garage, and he hit the door closer button. I looked back to see the garage slowly closing and saw that the kayak was wedged next to Angie. She had next to zero space on her side.

"Your boat, too?" I asked, half-shouting above the engine's groan as Oscar navigated a hill and then went around a roundabout intersection.

"We don't use it much," he admitted, shouting back to us. "We did out West, but here Dad's only been out a time or two. I was at your house both times," he added. "He thinks he's lost me to you or something," he laughed.

"Don't blame me. You were the one who said 'yes' each time I asked you to stop by," I said, smiling as the warm heater's air hit my face. *It felt amazing compared to how cold the Jeep's window felt against my hand.*

"He's gone out around Wolf a time or two, he told me," Oscar admitted. "But I think he just played around and fished some. He didn't say anything about exploring on the island," he said to himself more than us, his voice falling to a whisper.

"What's the plan when we get out there?" I asked. "The kayak is a two-seater," I pointed out, proud of my observation in semi-darkness. "She going to swim?" I joked, pointing to Angie.

Angie's mouth froze in horror at the suggestion, and I told her I was kidding.

"There's a paddleboard underneath it. I'm going to use that, and you two are going to steer the kayak. It should work, but if one of us falls in, it's hypothermia. So don't fall in," he said, voice serious and detached. "I'll take point, and you two can row behind me. It's not far from the bridge, and we can get there in a matter of minutes."

I looked from the kayak beside Angie to my denim jacket and tried to shake away chilling thoughts of the water. *If it was barely above freezing now, what was the water like?* As if reading my mind, Oscar shot back to us, "I put some blankets in the garage in the bottom of the kayak."

"You think of everything," Angie's voice uttered, shocked at how quickly all of this was happening.

"Won't matter if you fall in," he repeated. "So, don't."

"Yes, Dad," I attempted to joke, but it fell flat, as I imagined Oscar didn't want to think about the six hundred commandments he was breaking right now.

The Jeep roared and strained around the curves and dips leading to the water's edge. The bridge creaked and groaned from the weight of cars going across it. My mind thought back to bridge signs and suddenly realized what 'Bridge freezes before road surface' meant. The exposed air beneath it felt frigid, and the wind whipped across my cheeks in cold blasts. I longed for the comfort of my room and warm blankets. Oscar tugged the kayak out onto the rocky ground making a clanking sound on the frozen ground. The oars jostled in their wedged spaces inside the kayak. He unclipped two life jackets from the kayak's hull and handed them to each of us. Like children, he took time to make sure each clasp was secured on us and then asked me to help him lift it and place it in the water. It felt 'cumbersome,' and I walked awkwardly to the water's edge. Then, he helped Angie step into the first seat, steadied it, and assisted me into the backseat. Once we were sitting awkwardly in it, he waited for us to test our balance and handed us the oars.

"If you row in unison, it'll be easier. Star, the back is where steering happens. You can keep the boat pointed toward Wolf, and Angie will control the pace. I'll be in front of you, guiding us across," he said, his voice almost parental. "Please, don't tip over," he said a third time. "If it happens, we'll only have so much time to get back to shore."

Again, I imagined hypothermia and scenes from that Titanic movie when Leonardo DiCaprio freezes to death. But what made me most nervous was watching Oscar lift the standup paddleboard and carry it to the water beside us. He took his oar and readied himself for something I hadn't considered before. He would be trusting his skill in not falling off the narrow board the entire trip across the channel. *What if he fell?* I thought in a panic. There was no way Angie or me could get to him in time, let alone drag him to shore. Time seemed to freeze like the air I exhaled from my lungs. I watched as visible smoke came out of my lips, and I stifled a cough. The air seemed entirely capable of freezing my lungs mid-breath.

Oscar bowed his head and closed his eyes for a second, and I knew he was praying this time for real. Rather than ridicule him, I realized it wasn't such a bad idea, and Angie leaned back and squeezed my hand. Before I knew what was happening, she said, "God, help us make it across and back in one piece. Amen."

"Amen," I said, my breath coming out in an icy single burst.

Oscar pushed himself away from the safe shoreline with his oar and stood to full height. Thankfully, the surface of Chartreuse was like mirrored glass, and nothing stirred on its grey, forlorn surface. Gone were the fishing herons, and it felt like snow could fall at any second. Instinctively, I put my oar across my lap and shimmied my bottom forward. The boat moved a little at this moment, and Angie did likewise. Then, I put my left oar paddle into the water and heaved against the deep color. Angie did the same, and as she came down with her right paddle to scoop the water backwards, I matched her stroke. The boat propelled forward, and I realized that steering largely was done from the back. I took this responsibility Oscar gave me seriously, and I began to tell Angie 'left' and then 'right' and we rowed this way in tandem. The going was much easier for us than Oscar, and I saw him wobble on his board a time or two. When it happened, I held my breath and prayed he wouldn't topple into the abyss. Each time he wavered, he quickly found his footing and recovered in the middle of the board. He kept his feet shoulder width apart and looked as balanced as a pro. Oscar didn't look left or right but only focused on what was directly in front of us—Wolf Island. Not wanting to overtake him or disrupt his balance, I told Angie to rest between each succession of rows, and she assented willingly. Her chest heaved in front of me, and I knew this wasn't a strength of hers, and I couldn't blame her. I had never trained for kayak conditioning either. It was foreign to both of us.

As we rested, Oscar paddled downward on his left side and right with supreme intention. If he pushed too hard, it showed in his balance, and he was quick to check his center ground each time. I could only imagine how hard this would be on a summer day when everyone flocked to Chattanooga with boats. The wake alone would be enough to send a seasoned pro into the choppy waters. I gave 'thanks' to a higher power for letting today be tranquil. Absolutely freezing but calm. My teeth chattered in my mouth, and I bit down on my bottom lip to still them. I could feel the top lip cracking, and the pain felt terrible against the wind.

"Okay," I heard my voice telling Angie in a small voice. "Let's take a few more strokes."

She assented, and we paddled this way for the next long interval. We paused, Oscar gained in the lead, and then we paddled some more. The boat felt surprisingly stable, and I was proud that it was a wider kayak. Some I had seen were shallow, and the kayakers looked to be riding level with the water. In this one, we were half-encased inside the boat, and the protection felt equally good. I kept my eyes focused on the oars as much as I could. A great part of me didn't desire to check our progress with the approaching bank of Wolf. But Oscar needed us to be watchful. *He needed me to keep watch,* I thought. Angie was tasked with pacing, and I was responsible for steering, but I wanted to make darn sure that we didn't ram into him either. The yards ticked by, and I discovered we were only a few more pushes to the island's shore.

"When I get up here, I'm going to skid onto the bank and land far enough to drag it out, and then I'll pull you guys to shore," Oscar said, almost losing his balance as he semi-turned in his planted stance.

"Just get there," I called. "We can manage," I added, trying to sound confident.

Oscar nodded his head and delivered on his promise. He stroked downward two more good times using his left and right sides, and his paddleboard skidded onto the embankment almost three-quarters length. When he was clear of the water, he jumped off and dropped the oar a few feet away. He turned and checked our progress, and we were almost parallel to his board. I heaved a last paddle stroke on both sides, matching Angie, and we crunched onto the shore beside Oscar. He stooped and picked the front end up, dragging us farther into dry terrain. When he gave the 'all clear,' we handed him the oars and dismounted one at a time. Angie wiped her hands on her pants and zipped her puffy jacket all the way up to her neck. I put my hands in my denim jacket and tried to warm them. They felt frozen stiff, and when the pockets didn't help, I took them out and cupped them, blowing into them every bit of hot air I could muster.

Oscar dragged the kayak the rest of the way out of the water and placed the oars down inside our seat spaces. Before he stood up, he took the tightly folded blankets and draped them across our shoulders in a way they wouldn't drag against the ground. It felt settling to have him press the fabric against my semi-frozen jacket, and I clung to the edges of the blanket like it was a shawl. He turned and exhaled loudly. Then, he scanned the shoreline and said, "I don't see any movement on this side. Let's get into some of the tree cover and figure out where we're going. I'll try to get a fire started later."

We stamped our feet to get some blood flowing, and Angie and I followed after him into the coverage of Wolf Island.

Chapter 32

The dense overgrowth made our way through the forest of trees all but impassable. Coupled with this, the freezing temperatures made the trees resistant and prickly like the plastic Christmas tree put up in my home each year. The evergreens were the worst, and I felt the snags against my blanket repeatedly. Oscar received the bulk of it, pushing and smacking branches with his forearm and trying to not let them fly back into Angie's or my face. It was slow going, and I wondered if we were making progress at all. In here, the sky grew darker than dark, and it looked like it was midnight rather than sunset. The cold January night enveloped us fully, and I knew it was going to be the longest night of our lives.

Angie's teeth clattered in front of me, and I watched where she walked. Oscar unfastened his pack and clicked on one flashlight and then the other, handing it to me. "I should've done this at the start," he admitted sheepishly, voice croaking at his rookie mistake.

As he led on, his light cast a beam out in front of us, and mine cleared the space between him and me. Angie walked in a glow, and I mimicked her movements, swaying left and ducking right behind her puffy purple coat. She walked like someone completely unfamiliar with trails, and I caught her a time or two when her foot caught an exposed root. The tangle and her near falls caused my mind to lurch to the nightmare I had about Oscar, and I tried to shake death and drownings away from my mind. I couldn't help but see Andrea going under the water again and again, and the frozen surface we'd just traversed brought the circumstances too close for comfort.

Oscar high-stepped over the roots and tried to warn Angie about any others ahead. He gave as much warning as possible in the collapsing darkness and pointed with his flashlight to anything that barred our way. Even though the air was icy, the enveloping pines and growth helped make us feel hugged on all sides. It played a trick on my mind, and I was okay with that as I felt slightly warmer with the coverage and protected with the two of them in front of me. My flashlight flickered a time or two, and I smacked it against my leg to make it hold steady, praying it was only a battery connection thing. The light did hold, but I felt the stinging sensation of where I'd smacked my leg, and the warmth traveled up my leg trying to make its way back to my heart.

"We're getting there," Oscar said over his shoulder, attempting some form of confidence as his voice rattled against the tree limbs. "I think I see where the trees open up ahead," he shouted, his voice echoing throughout the creepy foliage.

The trees looked like arms and hands trying to stop our progress, and I kept my limbs as close to my body as possible. When one swooped in from Angie's release of a branch, I shielded myself and fought against any skeleton trying to cling to me. The prickliness went through the blanket and jacket and stuck against my skin. I fought against it and freed myself from an evergreen branch. The slight cut hardly registered, and Angie said, "Sorry, Star. I didn't mean to hit you with that."

I said don't worry about it. This was uncertain terrain for all of us, and I knew only Oscar felt confident that we would get to wherever this blocked path was leading. He stepped and paused as we navigated the dense copse, and he held the final limb for Angie to pass through and then me. We stood to full height, and Oscar said, "Good," like he was proud that we were still with him.

I rubbed my hands and cupped them again, blew into them with what little air still resided in my lungs. Angie walked into the clearing and spun in a slow circle. Oscar said, "This is where the pictures were taken."

Looking around at the trees and the open ground, I scanned my flashlight for anything familiar. "Did we pass the wooden sign?" I asked, feeling uncertain about the entire trip. "I didn't see it."

Oscar turned the flashlight onto me and then held it below his face, pointing upward at his chin like he was about to tell some twisted ghost story. I remembered Dad doing this to me when we camped out in the backyard one night. I could hear his spooky voice ringing with, 'Star, Star, there was once a very old lady who lived alone in a cottage in the forest . . .' and I shook the memory from my head. Oscar's chin and cheekbones cast eerie shadows within the light, and his spectacled eyes were reflecting the light in an odd way, making me think of terrible things. But his voice brought me back with, "Guys, it was at the first signs of the overgrown trail. Didn't you see it? I should have pointed it out. The tangled shrubs had almost overtaken the side of the tree where it was."

Angie looked at me and shook her head; she hadn't seen it. I did the same, and Oscar said, "Well, it was there. You have to trust me."

It felt like this entire evening was one of trust with Oscar. He knew how to get us over here, and he had the gear, and he stole his dad's Jeep. It was all we could do now, trust him. And normally I would've argued the whole way with anyone else, but Oscar had a way of getting me to do just about anything. I clung to the blanket's fabric and breathed in the smoky, woodfire smell it still held from some campsite in his past. I wondered if this very blanket had been with his dad, his family, at Massacre Rocks. It felt cozy, and my eyes watered from the chill air. I tried to blink the water away for fear of my eyeballs freezing shut.

"Now what?" Angie asked, arms raised in a stance of forfeit. "We're here, and I'm about to freeze to death."

I wanted to whine with her, but the silence and surroundings willed me to stay calm. Oscar sat his flashlight on a low, naked tree limb that might have been a maple or oak. If I had a leaf, I could tell you in a heartbeat. But, he wedged the light and stepped back to analyze the terrain. His gloved hand went to his chin, and he held it there for a moment, looking like Rodin's sculpture. I wanted to laugh, but it didn't feel right. He was looking for something we couldn't see. Then, looking down at his glove, he saw my hands wedged firmly into my pockets, and he took the gloves off. He had been the only one smart enough to carry gloves, and he said, "We can take turns," handing the gloves to me, and I gave them to Angie. She looked like she was about to topple over from the chill.

She hesitantly put the gloves on and pulled them all the way flush with her fingertips, then shivered and said, "Star, you can have them in exactly fifteen minutes. I just need to get feeling back."

Proud of his discovery, Oscar put his hands in his pockets and walked the circumference of the opening. He looked into the darkness surrounding our circle for something, and we waited in silence. The silence was a good omen, I imagined because he said, "Nothing looks disturbed . . . yet. He's not been here today."

The realization that he studied our space for Mr. C.'s whereabouts unnerved what little resolve I had. We were locked in a race with our crazy English teacher, and the discovery made my knees shake. Angie twisted her torso right and left and froze when she made eye contact with me. It had dawned on her that we were genuinely doing this, and her face fell into an expressionless gaze. I avoided eye contact as best I could and went to Oscar's backpack resting beside the bare tree.

"I'm hungry," I said, opening the clasps and uncinching the drawstring.

"How can you think of eating at a time like this?" Angie asked, her voice rising into a panic.

"I never ate in the cafeteria," I admitted, and I hadn't. My stomach gurgled now that I was so close to the snacks. I opened the pack and fumbled for whatever had settled to the bottom. My fingers went across Oscar's other belongings and found two granola bars. "Want one?" I asked, offering them.

Angie turned her back to me, and Oscar appeared to be too lost in thought, and I pocketed one and opened the other, taking a big bite. It had chocolate chips, and my mouth watered as the sugar and oats hit my taste buds. I choked them down without any water, and my mouth felt suddenly dry, but my stomach was pleased. I ate the entire bar in four bites and scrunched the wrapper up, tucking it into my pocket.

"Water's in the canteen," Oscar said, turning back to where I crouched beside the pack. "We can get a fire going. It doesn't look like Mr. C. has made any efforts to get out here, but that doesn't mean he won't be coming later. If we hear or see anything," he said, scanning the perimeter as if his words might conjure a ghoul or our intruder, "then, we will dash it out as fast as possible."

I opened the canteen and took a too big swallow, water streaming down my frozen face. Instinctively, I wiped the water away, and my cheeks felt numb. After recapping the lid, I sat the bottle on the ground beside the pack and asked Angie if she was thirsty. She kept her back to me, but I knew her mind was suddenly on the same thing as ours. *Fire.* Oscar mentioning it had invaded warm thoughts and comfort into my brain, and I could feel the heat against my limbs already.

"Can I help?" I offered more out of selfishness than genuine goodness of my heart.

Oscar assented, and we gathered as many dry sticks and small limbs as possible. He took the waterproof match box from his coat and began to strike the first one when the makeshift fire pit was protected from the wind. The opening where we stood, being protected from higher gusts of winter air, helped considerably. He got a flame going on the first attempt, and it puttered out as it hit the first good-sized stick. On the second match, the fire took, and I frantically searched for bigger, fatter limbs I could pull over and break into sizable pieces. The dead branches worked best, and Oscar said scraps of river birch worked amazingly to start a fire almost anywhere. I committed this bit of knowledge to my delirious brain. Angie only turned and reluctantly walked over to us, when the fire was casting a nice warm glow onto our legs. I could feel my pant legs beginning to thaw, and I was suddenly okay with a first-degree burn. *I could hold my legs here all night,* I thought. Angie must've thought something similarly, because she inched closer and closer to the flames, and might've gone all the way into it, had Oscar not held out his hand to her knee and said, "Too close. You won't feel the burn until all of this is over. It's working, but you have to remember that it'll burn you."

Angie stopped and backed a couple of inches away again. I matched her distance and held my swollen knuckles out to the fire. The heat felt as if it could cure cancer, and I wanted to let it warm me all night.

Oscar brought over more firewood, but his focus was constantly over the woods beyond us. He went deeper and deeper into the tangles beyond our clearing and came back with less and less wood. His focus was on what lay ahead of where we'd stopped in our navigation, and I tried to imagine what was north of our improvised campsite. My mind latched onto monsters and dragons guarding stockpiles of gold coins. As I felt enlivened by the heat, I decided to sit on the leaf-strewn ground and felt the chill beneath my bottom. Angie sat beside me reluctantly at first, and then as the minutes ticked by, I felt the weight of her head against my shoulder. Her sweet-smelling perfume nestled against my body, and I thought of cinnamon and vanilla. It was a welcomed bit of nostalgia and something I imagined her parents buying for her at the mall. The Hamilton Place Mall felt a million miles away from this spot, and I knew it must've felt even farther for her, out here on Wolf Island. She took the gloves off slowly, and said, "Sorry, it's been way longer than fifteen minutes," extending them to me.

I took the gloves and put them on my hands, and I suddenly felt as warm as I had in a hot tub I once sank into on vacation. The artificial scents of Angie's perfume coupled with the warmth sent my eyes slowly downward, and I tried to steel myself against sleep. She began to breathe heavily against me, and I felt the slow rise and fall of her lungs. It felt safer in this space, and I imagined Oscar would return from the surrounding woods with another armful of logs at any minute. With this blurry vision, I let my eyes close fully with the heat of the inviting fire against my slowly thawing face.

CHAPTER 33

I dreamed of a hot tub big enough to fit Angie, Oscar, myself, and everyone else in our English class. For some reason, I sat opposite Oscar and was immediately beside Corine and Melanie. It felt close and yet disorienting to be all in the hot tub together. My mind tried to place where in the world a hot tub would be large enough to seat all of us, but I knew it was a dream. The hot tub was a figment of my imagination, and I was still asleep beside the fire.

As soon as I realized this, I felt additional heat, and the pool of water where we all sat began to be exceptionally hot. *Too hot,* I thought. My skin felt like it was boiling, and I didn't want to become a cooked chicken. I fought against Corine and Melanie's shoulders, but we were wedged like sardines in the tub. As I fought for purchase against the side of the pool, Melanie's hand came up and seized my wrist. 'We're not done yet,' she insisted. Shaking her away, I felt Corine's legs entangle mine, and she said, 'Yeah, things are just getting warm,' snaking around me so that I couldn't move. I looked from one to the other and pleaded with Oscar across the pool. He equally was ensnared by someone else from class, and he struggled to free himself from the tentacle-like grips of others. I didn't see Angie, and I wondered if she was the one thing missing from this puzzle. But as I looked past Corine, I saw Angie's pitiful gaze pinned against the left side of the pool. She bit her lip and had hands pushing her under the surface slowly. 'No,' she cried out, but the hands kept pushing her down and down, until she relented and went under. I felt Corine's hand and then Melanie's, and they pushed me under as well, the warm water meeting my hair and causing it to float.

I held my breath for as long as it would last, and when I could bear no more, I took a big inhale of water and was met with zero resistance. My lungs, rather than filling with hot, bubbly water, were instantly clear.

My eyes opened and didn't burn from chlorinated chemicals. It was a suspended state, and the air and some kind of room were completely blank. *Was this heaven?* I thought, still knowing I was safely beside a fire built by Oscar. So, I let the dream continue. No one else was in the blank space, and I shouted and heard echoes in all directions. My shrill voice rang out again, and it continued for way longer than a normal echo would. It kept bouncing from wall to wall, and I knew something sinister was about to happen. Instead of someone appearing from the ether, I heard only my cries of 'Hello, anybody there?' distorting from a high pitch to lower and still lower to almost a hideous growl. It sounded animal, and I thought of a big cat in a remote forest stalking its prey, cries like a baby and remembering someone once telling me that rabbits sounded that way when they were about to die. *The deception of the natural world,* I reasoned. I moved my shoulder blade minutely and felt what I knew was the weight of Angie still resting on me.

The echoes rang so low it sounded like a bass drum, and I imagined Oscar and me trying to recreate it at his house. When the sounds emitted in the blank space almost shook me, vibrated my feet from the ground up, it all went deathly silent. My ears felt plugged with the world's best noise cancelling ear plugs, and my head felt congested. As I was about to shout out again, the room spun around, sending me in cartwheels, end over end like a box carried by a strong wind. Then, I was flung away from the sterility of the white space into literal space.

Great, I thought. *Now, I'm beyond all hope of humanity.* I laughed at my imagination as I slept soundly beside the fire still. It was my grounding with reality, and I ensured this with the weight of Angie's head against me. The weightlessness of zero gravity for some reason caused me to doggie paddle against the darkness. I felt lightheaded and realized I was holding my breath. *You can't breathe in space, dummy. You'll die,* I heard my brain say. The seconds ticked by, and I felt my lungs filling up with carbon dioxide. I was about to burst because I couldn't hold it in any longer. I gasped a long exhale and dreaded what would happen on my equally frantic inhale, but as I took in air, I realized nothing was killing me. Space was cooperating, and I laughed. I reached up to my face and discovered a helmet covering it, my hands in a spacesuit. *Ha! At least my dreams didn't screw me over here,* I reasoned. I breathed a few more deep times, and I took delight in not meeting a quick demise. Then, once I was recovered, I doggie paddled some more toward literally nothing. Like the room before, there was nothing in this space except me and my panic.

I tried to calm my heart as I'd done my lungs when discovering the space suit. The oxygen levels on a profile screen in my helmet registered as ninety-eight percent. My pulse showed 170 bpm, and I watched it decline to 150 and eventually settle below 100. I was pleased with this as I swam slowly and pointlessly in the direction I was headed. The lack of stars, and planets, baffled me. *Was this even the Milky Way I was in?* I thought. Maybe I had invented some other place. If so, I didn't like it and scolded myself for putting my dreams in such terrible places. Space was cold, and it felt completely alien to the fire where we slept. *Why was I thinking of it? Was it even worth asking at this point?* The darkness was everywhere, and I was in it, and my white suit with an American flag stood out as loudly as anything I'd ever seen. If there was a villain out here, I didn't want to imagine it seizing hold of me. I could go nowhere and see next to nothing. *Where was the sun? Our sun or any sun?* My mind thought of Dad playing Pink Floyd's "Dark Side of the Moon." The sounds of that album radiated across my brain, and I was suddenly at peace with my surroundings. The guitar riffs and drums took hold of my head, and I smiled inside my space helmet. There was always music, and I was thankful for it. *Why couldn't I dream of Saturn or Jupiter? Something to look at?* I thought, paddling toward nothingness.

Then, I felt the grip of some unseen vine thrashing at my leg, and I felt my knee twist in an unnatural way and a pop like a champagne bottle being opened by Mom at her New Year's party with Dad. I squirmed and cried out in pain, knowing I had to get away from this hidden monster. I couldn't look down that well in my suit, and I didn't want to. I knew the knee was torn, and there was nothing I could do about it now. The vine-like grip released and went away. I doggie-paddled as fast as I could in a comical swim through space. My breathing became a pant, and my blood pressure spiked on the helmet gauge. I knew it was only a matter of seconds before the vine thing snapped onto my body again. I heaved and squirmed, but the leg kicks were all but impossible with one leg. My injured knee throbbed with each lunge in the darkness. I swiveled onto my back and began to do some odd form of backstroke in space. I stared at the clear helmet display, my only source of illumination out here. The oxygen levels were diminishing quickly falling to fifty-four percent. *How?* Then, I heard the faint hiss and an alert that my suit had a leak, a tear somewhere. *Probably the knee,* I thought.

I waited for the inevitable vine to return and puncture my suit somewhere else, and I found myself longing for it to attach itself to me and get it over quickly. I realized I would rather have a quick snap of my neck than have to float like this watching the numbers plummet in my oxygen, slowly suffocating to death. *Please don't toy with me,* I pleaded to the void. *Come back and finish what you started, Leviathan!* I screamed in my head. But the vine hid itself under his Hades cloak. The silence deafened me, and I realized screaming in space was true like scientists said. No one could hear it and no one was in communication with me. Even though I was warmed, almost burnt by the fire and knew Angie must be too, I felt cold and alone. My body was turning blue, my lips like a fish on land searching for its home state. Homeostasis.

The percentage of O_2 drained to single digits, and I wished for a small kind mercy from the monster. *Please come back,* I pleaded. *Just finish what you started.* And just like that, I felt a whip ensnaring me across the throat, a precision hit beneath the bulky helmet. There was almost zero space between my helmet and sternum. The vine tentacles enveloped my thin, birdlike neck muscles and twisted tight enough to leave little breathing room. Then, in one quick flick of its snaking grasp, it snapped my neck, and all I felt was a burn much like the fire before us.

Chapter 34

Angie shook my numb shoulder and said, "Get up!" Her face was noticeably pale even in the glow of the fire. "Oscar never came back!"

Her words rang hollow as I tried to clear my head, "What do you mean? He's just getting more firewood," I muttered, wiping drool from my lips, thoughts of space still lingering in my mind.

"No," she said, pleading with me this time, gripping my shoulder blade and jostling me where I sat. "Look," she pointed, and the fire was about to die out. The flames were now just embers dwindling out of air.

I rubbed my neck still thinking of the vine from space, the other ominous dreams I had. The fire was the concern, because Oscar wouldn't let it go out unless he meant to extinguish it, and he would've done that in a hurry. *Something was definitely wrong,* I knew. I stood on numb legs, and my butt was numb, slightly damp from the ground. I dusted off my pants and turned to scan the tree line. The flashlight, the one he'd balanced in the tree, was missing. He had taken that with him the last time he went out for wood. So that made sense. The darkness was less thick, and I knew we were somewhere approaching dawn. The canopy surrounding us made it difficult to determine exactly how close to daylight we were. I noticed Angie was panicking as she walked to different sides of the opening and stared blankly through the tree coverage. I walked over to her and peeled the gloves off, extending them to her.

She took them slowly and put them on. They were extremely warm now, and I knew that might help her focus more on what was happening. As she patted them together, her palms made a light clapping sound, and I smiled at her, my attempt at a smile at least.

"I'm sure there's a reason he's still out there," I soothed, my voice feeling false as the words came out. *Oscar wouldn't leave us unless it was serious.*

She unzipped and zipped her coat in a nervous manner, and I tried to listen for anything out of the ordinary. The trees surrounding us on the island felt as calm and surreal as they had the night before. Not a bird sang a single note, and the trees creaked and swayed in the chilling air above our coverage. I looked up and noticed our smoke traveled past the tree canopy and was visible for anyone within a short distance of us. It would tip off anyone looking that we were nestled in these woods.

Staring at the way I'd seen Oscar go the last time, into the dense trees ahead of where we'd paused to rest, I knew it was where we needed to go next. I took a painfully deep breath and cleared my throat. I was hoarse from the night air and the woodsmoke, and my lungs caught inside my chest. "We have to go that way," I pointed, feeling the circulation in my fingers already slowing since giving the gloves to Angie. "It's where Oscar went before I fell asleep," I said.

Angie gulped and put her chin down into her purple coat shyly. I didn't offer the other option, going back the way we'd come, getting in the kayak and trying to see if Oscar's paddle board was still there. *It didn't happen like that,* I thought.

I took my flashlight from beside where I'd slept and clicked it on. I was thankful it came to life, and that I hadn't left it on while I slept. Angie stayed close behind me, so close it removed fear that I would accidentally smack her with branches. We moved in greater silence than we had with Oscar, and I felt responsible for whatever happened to him. It was a wild thought, but my dream felt oddly tangible now that he was missing. From the drowning hot tub to the blank room to the vine in space, I felt attacked on all sides, and this island was slowly driving me mad. *Where are you?* I screamed at myself, not sure if I meant Oscar or something nefarious.

The branches yielded no more reply than the creaking sounds they made at the tops of their highest reaches, scratching against one another in the wind. I surveyed the treetops for any birds or squirrels and nothing stirred. Angie's teeth chattered again, and I felt my chapped lips with my empty hand. The way ahead was completely barred, but I pushed through one obstacle at a time, and my stomach churned again. Rather than stop to take the other granola bar from my pocket, I bit my lip, feeling blood from one of the chapped sections split open. An iron, metallic taste flowed into my gums and onto my tongue. I swirled it back and forth and spit it onto the ground, and Angie stepped over it.

"You okay?" I heard her ask behind me.

"No, but we have to keep going," I uttered, scanning the flashlight around the limited field of vision.

We trudged through the next acre, or what I imagined was an acre, and the evergreens thinned out and most of the growth was sparse, naked deciduous trees. It gave us a lot of extra breathing room, and Angie began to walk alongside me hesitantly. I welcomed her presence beside me, and it added to what little confidence I felt remained. She took her cell phone from her pocket and said, "Zero bars."

"Do you think that girl really disappeared or something worse happened?" Angie added, pushing her phone back into its place.

"Let's not scare ourselves," I replied.

"No seriously," she said, continuing, "no one just completely disappears anymore. There's usually some reason they go missing. It's usually someone nearby, and they almost always know them," she added, trying to get a reaction from me.

"Disappeared or kidnapped, what's it matter now?" I answered, wanting her to drop it. The woods were exposing us in a way I didn't like. Angie was talking too loud.

"I'm just saying no one can disappear with all the maps and searches now. Not really," she admitted, pointing to her phone, her pocket. "*Nothing* gets lost."

She had a point, and it wasn't one I could argue. Human trafficking was a big problem along I-75 from Atlanta, and Chattanooga was a stopping point along the way. I had heard Mom and Dad talking about it in whispers inside their bedroom before. People went missing because other creeps took them. It was kidnapping of the worst kind, and many of the children or teens were never heard from again. I shook away images of what supposedly happened to them, how they fared. My lips felt broken and my mouth tasted rusty. I spit again but this time sending it toward the bare tree trunks.

Angie paused like she needed a rest, and I turned the flashlight off. The light surrounding us was now bright enough to orient us to the paths ahead. It was barren, but I imagined some footprints would become visible now. So, I turned my head to the ground and tried to think of what Oscar might say to look for. Angie reached inside the backpack I was carrying, and she took the canteen. After taking a long pull, she offered it to me, and I did likewise. The water burned my lips, but I welcomed the hydration.

"Where to now?" Angie pointed ahead. "Did Oscar leave us?" she asked, but her voice sounded flat, and I knew she couldn't be serious. Oscar wouldn't do that.

I pointed to the ground, and to my delight, the day was dawning enough to reveal dirt and leaves in plainer sight. I clicked the flashlight on and realized it wasn't helping that much, and so I clicked it off again. Once my eyes readjusted, I stared at the dirt path in front of us and recognized a boot tread, then a second pair of larger sneakers. *Oscar's,* I thought.

My heart sank, and I put my finger to my lips, instinctively crouching and pulling Angie off-balance beside me. I hunkered over the tracks and pointed at one and then the other. *Edmund Munson had him,* I knew. *Who else would even be out here?* A large part of me wanted to blame myself for falling asleep, not offering to get the firewood myself. But I knew the sentiment was silly. Oscar knew more about the woods than either of us combined, times one thousand. If anybody could elude Munson in our party, it would be him.

Now, we were on our own, and Munson had him out here somewhere. I kept crouched, and Angie didn't protest as I scanned the trees. Gone was the protection of the dense foliage from yesterday. I waited and watched the sunlight slowly fill up the spaces between sections of the forest. The footprints pointed us onward, and I slowly rose and stared ahead to note the gait of the prints. Both were firmly planted, boots and sneakers, and it told me that they were walking rather than Oscar being dragged. My heart swelled with some hope at discovering this.

"You watch straight ahead, and I'll keep an eye on the footprints," I told Angie, not caring that my voice came out more like a soft bark. She nodded slowly.

We walked on in this manner for a time, and I was as stunned as she was when we abruptly saw the footprints end at the shabby remains of a cabin, smoke pumping up from its decrepit chimney. Both Oscar's sneakers and the dirt caked boots were resting outside the cabin's front door.

"What's a cabin doing out here?" Angie said.

I shushed her and half-pulled her behind a river birch not nearly wide enough to conceal us. She stared at me quizzically, and I said through gritted teeth, "He has Oscar in there. Right now."

Angie said, "But I thought—" her voice was much too loud.

I cupped my hand over her lips to stifle her, and she became mute.

"Shh, he's there. Trust me. See the shoes?" I said, pointing to the porch.

Angie nodded slowly.

"Edmund has him, and we gotta get him back," I said, with no clue as to how to do it.

Angie saw my face and must've realized the same thing, because she crouched lower to the ground and put her gloved hands over her eyes.

"Hey, hey. We need to get a plan together. Do you see any trees big enough to hide behind? All the way, I mean."

Angie uncovered her eyes slowly and scanned the tree line. I needed her to cooperate, or she was a liability out here. When I scanned the opposite direction of her, I saw nothing close to proper coverage. But I felt a slap on my arm and felt her grabbing my elbow. She pointed to a giant oak not too far from where we stood in that direction. Without waiting, we sprinted toward the tree and ducked behind it, out of sight of the cabin. Once settled, we turned and began to survey everything we could around the tattered cabin. I tried to think of what our next move might be, but I was drawing a giant blank. Angie's breathing remained heavy, and I prayed she wouldn't hyperventilate. Oscar was so close to us now, but it felt like a million light years from here to the safety of home.

Chapter 35

The cabin's front door hung by a thread, and I could see a dim light escaping the front holes. Sounds of footfalls and a creaking of old wood made itself known in the stillness of the morning. I saw the smoke dissipate from the worn brickwork of a dilapidated chimney. *Edmund must have put the fire out,* I thought. As I formulated how Oscar must look inside the cabin, possibly tied with ropes or chained to a wall, I was surprised to see the cabin door open and both Oscar and his captor step outside. To my bewilderment, Mr. V. was with them, and his expression was bitter, his shoulders rigid. Edmund did not hold a weapon, and he was tossing the remains of a cup of coffee over the railing of the cabin. When he sat the mug down on the rickety wooden railing with a *clank*, he stretched and popped his back. The carefree attitude of Edmund unnerved me further, but I noticed that Oscar was looking back in the direction we'd camped. His eyes roved the woods and gave off a pleading look like he hoped we were long gone. Then, it hit me, *He was trying to keep Edmund away from us!* He had spotted Edmund during the long night and tried to make peace with him, distracting him from our presence.

"You can let my boy go," I heard Mr. V. spit, eyes focused on Edmund's sly, beady countenance.

Edmund straightened to his full height and slung his hiking bag, the one I'd spotted in the classroom over his shoulder, "Now where would the fun be in that?" he asked. "Three pairs of eyes are better than two," he admitted, gesturing for Mr. V. to walk in front.

"He's just a kid, Munson. Whatever beef you have with me is something we can settle and be done with," he offered, turning to look at the false teacher.

"This isn't just about the vase," Edmund chuckled. "No, you can be my eyes for this treasure. The both of you. And this time, I don't think you'll be so quick to call some society to take it away," he beamed, surveying the woods.

Instinctively, I ducked down and kept Angie's purple jacket, her head, as close to the ground as I could get us. *Were we fully hidden beneath the leaves? I prayed so.*

The crunching of boots broke the icy silence as the trio before us made their way back in the direction of our makeshift campsite in the clearing. I waited for what felt like an eternity until the clodding, clumping sounds fell away. Every fiber of me knew that Edmund would recognize the scene for what it was—more than Oscar being there. My mind tried to consider multiple scenarios that involved me overtaking Edmund while the rest got away. I didn't want anyone to get hurt out here except our phony teacher. He was who I tried to will into submission, but the results were empty. The boot sounds dwindled to nothing, and I felt the silence of the forest overtake my hearing. A shrill pecking rattled me where I sat, and I looked up with Angie to see a woodpecker smacking the tree above us for food or a better roosting spot. I removed some of the leaves from around us and told Angie to sit up. She breathed heavily as her purple coat became exposed to the sunlight once again. I dusted her off and told her we needed to move outward from the path and close back into it from what I imagined was above the clearing, closer to the shore we'd first banked on. She started to resist, but I told her it was the only way.

The traipsing was much slower due to the resistance from limbs and brush, but we made steady progress. I scolded myself for letting Oscar get as far away as he had, but I knew this was our only course of action. Trying to surprise them directly from the trail might make Edmund do something really sudden and put Mr. V. and Oscar in danger. *Why didn't he have a weapon?* I wondered. *Maybe it was stored away in his pack, only to come out if absolutely necessary?*

As we navigated the thick brambles and thorns resting in their own forms of hibernation, I felt resistance as sharp edges still stuck to my pant legs and tore at the already holey fabric. At certain branches, I held them as long as I could before Angie made her steps forward but some still lodged in her puffy coat and tore at the down fill, exposing goose feathers. When I turned to survey her progress, the loose white feathers looked silly escaping from her sleeves and shoulder. I tried to wipe these away, but she said, "Just leave it."

I wedged us forward and around the trail as best as I could, and we made slow progress to what I thought was enough ahead of the clearing. When my dry mouth longed for a sip of water, I paused to rest and put the canteen to my mouth. Then, I stretched back to Angie, and she took a long pull and capped the lid closed. I fitted it back into the pack, and we began our slow creep toward what I prayed was our abandoned campsite.

The tight branches and thicker foliage suggested we were approaching the right spot. I stopped to listen for voices, but nothing was discernible save for a thudding sound and what sounded like the scraping of something against the ground. Then, I heard a loud exhale, and my heart dropped into the soles of my Converse sneakers.

Angie paused behind me, and I turned to see her lips quiver. A large part of me wanted to tell her to stay put, and I would come back for her. But an even greater part wanted to keep her in sight. *If we became separated, would that be helping her at all?* I shook the image of her frantically running, cutting herself on thorns and thistles away. But I found myself pointing to her puffy coat, saying, "Take the coat off."

She shook her head, but I continued to ask for it, my hand extended. Slowly, she unzipped the warm covering and handed it to me. My idea was simple, and I scolded myself for not thinking of it sooner. Angie folded her arms against her exposed midsection, and I wrapped the coat in a bundle and told her to sit still. My effort to walk around to what I thought was directly in line with our first path from the lake was painstakingly slow. When I found our semi-broken path, I displayed the unzipped coat on a low-hanging branch and stepped back to see how visible it was. If Edmund came this way, it would be spotted quickly. I retraced my steps in a semi-arch back to where Angie waited impatiently.

"Now what?" she said, her lips shaking from the cold.

"Diversion," I uttered, looking down to see cuts and new blood on my pant legs.

"Think it'll matter?" she asked, her voice in a pout now.

"It's four against one, if I can scare him enough," I admitted, sounding less confident by the second.

"What if he has a gun on him?" she asked, pointing in the direction of the clearing.

"This is where Oscar would say to pray," I muttered.

No sooner do I admit this, she closed her eyes and looks to be doing just that. I wait for her to open her eyes, and I make a point to not scold or ridicule her. I wish I could be as faithful as that. A large part of me wants to look up and admit I am doing something I have no control over, but I think of Mr. V.'s face from earlier, Oscar's tired eyes, and I know I have to stay with this and see it through.

"So, how're you going to get Mr. C., I mean, Edmund, to take the bait?" Angie asked, pointing toward where I'd just gone to hang the coat.

"It's not much," I offer, picking up a hefty rock, one I can palm and somewhat toss. "I'm going to chuck this toward where your coat is on display, and then, we are going to sprint toward the clearing that way once Edmund goes to check it out," I point, imagining a bee line straight into the open space.

"What if he doesn't check it out?" she countered, hands now hanging down at her sides, teeth chattering from the cold or fear or both.

"What else can we do?" I admitted, scolding myself for being so honest, putting everything out there for her to see.

She stared at me, and I felt the heft of the rock making my arms suddenly very tired. When she broke eye contact, I shifted the rock from my weak hand to my dominant, and I listened for anything discernible in the clearing. When my eardrums felt strained and I thought I might be making sounds out of nothing, I heard a stick break and then the scraping of metal against the frozen ground. *They were digging,* I realized. I didn't know if it was Oscar, Mr. V., or Edmund, and prayed Edmund was keeping watch. I tossed the stone up in the air and felt its heft when it fell back into my palm, bringing me down somewhat with it. *Here goes nothing,* I thought. I reared back as far as I could and heaved the rock toward where Angie's puffy coat hung from the trail path. The ensuing *thump thump* was loud enough to get the clanking sound against ground to pause, and the rock broke a few branches as well.

"What was that?" I heard Edmund ask his two inmates.

Mr. V. exhaled loudly, and Oscar said, "Go check it out."

"Don't be getting any dumb ideas," Edmund spat into the silent January air.

"Where would we go?" Oscar asked, loud enough to be heard through the branches.

There was a painful silence, and then I heard the sweetest reply imaginable to my ears, "I'm taking the pack with me. I'll be right back. Keep digging," Edmund grunted. "If you so much as move away from this spot, you know I only need one of you to finish the job."

Then, the hard steps of Edmund's boots fell to loud crunches in the direction of my rock's path. I didn't wait, as I sprinted toward the opening and felt branches thwack and cling to my denim jacket. I fell into the clearing with limbs still wrapped around my forearms and torso. When I crashed to the hard ground, I felt Oscar's hands on me, and I felt him pulling me to my feet. It was only after I was inspected and dusted off by him, I heard Mr. V.'s voice ask, "Star, are you by yourself?"

I spun on my tired feet and noticed Angie was not beside me or anywhere within sight. She had frozen in the moment, I realized, and my stomach lurched a sick realization. Just as quickly, I realized Edmund would realize the coat was just a ploy and would come straight back to this spot. It was all for nothing, and I was now as much in the way as anyone. Mr. V. put his finger to his lips, and Oscar tried to force me back into the branches.

"There's still time," he said, his tired eyes scanning me for something I couldn't see. He pushed his long hair back from his glasses, and he held my face in his strong hands. Then, before I could protest, he thrust a shovel into my hands and said, "He has to sleep sometime. Go!"

My lip quivered at the fierce tone, tears forming at the edges of my eyes. I gripped the shovel and stood frozen to the ground. I noticed Mr. V. still held the shovel he used on the excavation and this extra shovel was my only weapon against a madman. I panicked and started to say something else, but I heard a loud laugh erupt from where Angie's coat hung, and Oscar pushed me with his full strength. I stumbled and stood upright. Before I could protest, I bit my lip and fled back in the direction where Angie last stood.

CHAPTER 36

She stood motionless where I'd left her, and my first inclination was to berate her to kingdom come, but her face was locked in fear, and I heard a loud cackle in the trees behind me. Edmund was now no doubt back where Oscar and his dad had struck at the frozen ground.

"I see your ladies have come to try and save you," Edmund hollered through the trees. "That was real smart in you trying to keep them away from this," he roared, laughing again. "Real quick. Mr. Villanueve, you've raised a son that's almost as sharp as you," Edmund spat. "What you forget is that I've got a little extra reassurance in my bag," he added, my thoughts leaping to the supposed gun in his bag.

Angie mouthed an 'I'm sorry,' and I ignored her frozen shock, pulling her deeper into the trees and away from this menace. Before we'd gone fifty yards, I heard, "And you gave away a shovel?" Then, I heard Edmund's booming voice laugh a sinister sound and add, "A shovel isn't much match for this," and I pictured him brandishing a firearm and pointing it at either, or both, of the men before him. "Let them try to shovel their way through me. Maybe I can trap them into helping you dig?" he boomed through the eerie January silence.

I pulled Angie deeper into the growth, and my mind raced from where we stood to retracing us back to the lake. *Should we get on the kayak and risk going back to the mainland? Getting Chattanooga Police to take this maniac down?* I thought of the frigid lake, and my mind flashed through scenes of us toppling over into the water and drowning or succumbing to hypothermia. Most of my working mind knew we could do it successfully, but the larger part of my animal instinct didn't want to leave Oscar in a lurch. *How did Edmund get Mr. V. out here? Had he tracked the northern parts of the island with Edmund, been a prisoner before this?*

There were so many questions whirling around inside my addled brain. I felt sick and bile rose into my throat.

Angie put her hands up and said, "I'm so so sorry, Star. I—"

"Forget it. You froze up. It could happen to anyone," I heard myself say, scanning the tree line for our best path back to the lake.

"When you took off, I saw my life flash before my eyes," she admitted, her face dropping into her gloved hands. I was thankful she still had the gloves.

"We lost your coat, but we have this now," I said, sounding cheerier than I felt, as I displayed the shovel for her to see.

"We need to go home," she said, her eyes red and tears staining her cheeks. She wiped at the water with her gloves and then smeared it onto her pants. "We are just causing more harm to them," she added, gesturing toward the clearing. "Mr. C., I mean, Edmund, is going to do something bad, and we can't help either of them."

I shifted the shovel from one hand to the other and looked in the direction of the lake. Hearing her say this same sentiment aloud caused me to think about possible outcomes. If we left, we would all but seal Oscar's, and his dad's fate, if Edmund got whatever treasure he was after. For all I knew, there was no prize, and they were simply digging their own shallow graves on Wolf Island. I tried to shake this morbid image from my brain. I thought of Edmund palming Angie's purple coat in his hand and walking back to our makeshift campsite. *He felt he had us completely,* I imagined. One of us was without a coat now, and all he was missing was an extra shovel. It was still largely his plan, and he was in control. *Let him think that,* I reasoned. On one side, we were all 'missing,' and the longer we were gone, the more it would become noticed. If Edmund requested leave, it would mean a substitute teacher at Idyll. With Angie, Oscar, and me missing, it would show up in three separate homes and be 'unexcused absences.' And the best news in my mind was Oscar's home, because Mrs. V. would be sure to go to the authorities with both her husband and son missing. It felt like the best thought I'd had in a while, and I relished in the image of Oscar's mom picking up a phone and calling CPD. Our faces would be on the news in no time. I took a big, icy breath into my lungs and held it there until it became uncomfortable before releasing it.

The sun began its afternoon descent as best I could tell beneath the tree line, and I longed for a drone I'd seen a boy using at Idyll High one day. The ability to hover above the clearing and check Edmund's whereabouts teased me. I stuck my hands into my denim pockets and tried to get circulation going in my hands again. If only we'd not separated from Oscar that night, we might've still been able to get out of here together. The notion was silly, and I scolded myself for thinking it. Edmund was already at the cabin by the time we were settling in for the night. He probably intercepted Oscar, and Oscar's only thought had been to go willingly into the enemy's lair and make peace. *Especially if Edmund already had Mr. V. there with him,* I realized. *There was nothing you could do,* I thought. *We're lucky he didn't come in the way we did to the clearing.*

As the daylight diminished through the forest, I looked up and watched the sky shift from visible to grey and saw thin wisps of clouds move determinedly through the air. Angie held out the gloves, and I didn't refuse, slipping them onto my cold digits and clasping the Velcro in place. As I waited for circulation to return, I realized returning to the kayak and paddleboard were efforts at retreat, and I didn't want to leave them here. With no fire to warm us, Angie sat down with her back against mine, and we surveyed the growing darkness around us. I took off my denim jacket and handed it to her. She refused at first, but her will diminished and she took the thin layer of protection. I studied the space between where we sat and the clearing somewhere a few hundred yards away. It felt dangerous to remain so close, but I knew Edmund misjudged us, and his focus was on the ground where Mr. V. worked.

The *clank, clank, shovel, toss* sounds were all that remained as dusk settled into pitch black. At times, I thought I could see the flashlight flicker and rejoin the ground. The *clank, clank, shovel,* and *toss* noises continued, and I heard Mr. V. grunt and imagined black, frozen dirt being tossed back from the hole. When he paused, I heard what I thought was, "You take over," and I imagined Oscar getting into the narrow pit and prayed it wasn't his own grave they were digging.

The noises began again, and it went on this way, and I felt my eyes growing heavy. I took the gloves off and handed them back to Angie. She offered my coat reluctantly, and I took it for a short interval, telling her we should switch out every fifteen minutes again. In this way, it gave us something to do, and it helped stave off hypothermia. She agreed, and we began this new shift. I pinched myself when my eyes drooped again sometime later, and I winced at the pain, realizing it should hurt worse than it did. *What if Edmund realizes nothing is there and decides to turn the gun on them?* I worried. I prayed that a gunshot wouldn't be the sound heard next in the quiet hours of night.

Clank, clank, thump, I heard through the woodland, and shook my tired brain awake. The *thump* sound was heard again, and I heard a shovel rattling to the ground.

"Get out of the way," I heard Edmund's tired voice scold. "Give me that."

Instinctively, I leveraged my frozen legs into a crouch and left Angie resting where she was. Her voice groaned, "Star, what're you—"

"Shh," I said, behind me. "Stay put. Be right back."

I skulked blindly through the growth to where the clearing was, and I came to the edge as I heard, "It's just under this, if the map is true. I've searched every other piece of this dang island," Edmund spat. "Don't try anything funny, or I'll use this," he said, patting his pocket.

I kept low to the roots and watched Edmund scoop remaining clods of dirt from the object giving resistance in the ground. Mr. V. sat on his edge of the dirt mound and eyed his assailant skeptically. Oscar sat opposite with his back to me, his face hidden.

Edmund tore at the ground with exposed fingers, and he removed chunks of earth like a man possessed by something unholy, a demonic force willing him onward to whatever he believed his rightful possession was. He scooped and pried at the January soil, and when his fingers bled, he picked up the shovel and hoisted against a rectangular object until it cleared its space in the ground. Edmund picked it up like a precious baby, and he sat it on the ground beside Oscar and wiped away the grime. He trained the flashlight on it, and he said, "Here, hold this," to Mr. V.

I ducked down for fear the light might hit me, and I waited for Edmund to turn his back to me and rifle in his pack for a crowbar. When it was visible in the light, I inched a few feet away from the forest edge and waited, holding my breath. He grunted and heaved at the corners of the box, not trusting his captive audience with the discovery. I looked at the pack and wondered if Oscar was bold enough to consider taking the bag and sprinting away. Then, I saw Mr. V. and knew Oscar wouldn't chance leaving his dad behind with this lunatic.

I knew this would be the most distracted Edmund would be out here. The box was his sole focus, and he inched away from the two in his detention to the far side of the clearing, the flashlight wedged between his teeth. I crept closer to the opening and knew I only had seconds. With the shovel gripped in my hands, I tiptoed into the clearing and kneed Oscar in the back. He started to fight me, but I pushed the shovel into his hands in the darkness and said, "Use this." Then, I stumbled over the open pit and fell awkwardly into Mr. V.'s hands. He steadied me, and it felt like time stopped. *Edmund's back was still to us but for how long? Where's the pack?* I wondered, fumbling in the dark.

Mr. V. pivoted out of the hole and came up with the pack and began digging into its bottom portions, throwing gear out of the way. When he met a strong metallic handle, he brought it up and held it outward from his body. Edmund pried the box loose on the ground and went, "Aha!" As he made this exclamation, he took out what looked to be a small posterboard with tissue paper surrounding it. His eyes swung from the art piece to me standing beside the empty backpack, Oscar beside me with a shovel, and Mr. V. holding a handgun trained on Edmund's gaze.

At first Edmund looked confused, and then his face went from alarmed to unconcerned. He waved a dismissive hand toward me. Then, his gaze went back to the tissue paper covered posterboard. He slowly took the paper away to reveal a lopsided sketch of some sort. "Star, I'm glad you're here. This is what all the fuss is about. I was just telling your friend that I'd let them go once I got what I came for," he said, trying to sound genuine. His fingers held the sketch up to the flashlight so that he might analyze it better. Pleased with the results, he turned again and said, "Gentlemen, thank you for joining me on this hunt. It has been a worthwhile endeavor. And, Mr. Villanueve, I believe you can see that this time I was able to get what I came for," Edmund said, pointing to the sketch.

"What is that?" I heard my voice ask, before adding, "And why did you have to kidnap Mr. V. and Oscar for such a dumb child's art piece?"

Before I realized what I'd done, I noticed the veins rising on Edmund's temples. He took the sketch and held it up to the light again for further inspection. Mr. V. held the gun unsteadily in his outstretched hand. Oscar gripped the shovel beside me, mouthed, "Star, please don't say anything."

"Dumb art?" Edmund asked exasperated. "Child's piece?" he added, walking toward me with no thought of the gun or anyone else in the circle. "Miss Crowley," he spat, disdain in his voice, "I wouldn't expect you to have a clue what real genius it took to make this," he scolded, holding the sketch up to the light. "This is a *genuine* Warhol sketch done when he was just nine years old. See the signature down here?" he answered with venom. "It's worth more than your soul," he said, only halting when Mr. V. clicked the hammer back on the pistol.

"Edmund, let's stop right there," Oscar said, finding his voice and answering for his dad. "This is all over. You are going to turn yourself in, and I am going to make sure you stay there for a long time," he said, sounding sure of himself. He looked to Mr. V., but he was silent, even while holding the gun. His face was pale, as if he were seeing a ghost he hadn't seen since Pocatello.

"I'll do nothing of the sort," Edmund laughed, clutching the sketch close to his chest now. "I didn't come all the way out here for you all to gloat about how brave you are. I intend to leave with this fortune, and I'll do it with or without you all still drawing breath," he laughed. As he said this, he reached for his pants pocket and unbuttoned a side pocket and drew a second pistol, this one a revolver, and took aim at Mr. V.

Stupefied, we all stood there and gazed at someone truly unhinged. *Edmund was willing to die for this simple sketch done by a child!* I shook my head and looked from Oscar to his dad. I wondered if Angie was still sitting in the forest, clutching her frozen legs with her arms. The darkness took over, and I watched as Edmund's flashlight flicked from each of us and back to the box where he gently placed, according to him, the priceless piece of art.

Chapter 37

We could just turn and make for the shoreline, our boats. I didn't see a single bit of resistance now. Edmund was focused on the wooden box more than anything else. Mr. V. kept the gun trained on him, but there was no need for bloodshed. It was a classic stalemate between us, and neither party wanted to turn this into more. At least, that's what I hoped. Oscar scanned the tree line in the direction of our boats, and I glanced in that direction with him.

"Where's Angie?" he asked, from the corner of his mouth, his breath in icy fragments. "Is she okay?"

I nodded, then realizing the light might not be strong enough, said, "She's fine. I left her just back there," I pointed in the direction of my last theatrics.

I wanted to search for her puffy jacket, but realized it wasn't of vital importance right now. Edmund gazed downward at the box as he placed it on the ground. His flashlight clicked off, and I heard a click as I realized he'd secured the worn wooden box clasp. Edmund tucked the box under his arm and readjusted the revolver in his right hand. He pointed it more assuredly in our direction and said, "Let's try to be civil, Villanueve. You know how this is going to go, don't you?"

Suddenly, I wanted to take the gun from Mr. V.'s grip and point it at Edmund myself. The pride I felt in such confidence fell flat as I saw the pistol begin to shake in Mr. V.'s hand again. What was going on? Was it something I missed?

"Let Oscar and his friends go," Mr. V. groaned through clenched teeth. "This isn't about them anymore. Just us," he pleaded. Gone was the familiar, confident tone I'd heard him speak with at dinner that night at Oscar's house over intoxicating smells of chili mac and cheese.

"It's as much to do with them, my pupils," he sneered, "as anybody. I have you to thank for that," he said, waving his treasured box outward to us. "Where's your third?" he asked me.

I bit my lip and realized I would never tell him. To my chagrin, I didn't get that pleasure, because I heard a sniffling sound and realized Angie was now beside Oscar at the edge of the pit. "I'm so sorry," she apologized to no one and all of us at once.

"Now it's a party," Edmund said, clapping the top of the box, the gun making a clanking sound as it made contact. "I was just telling everyone how glad I was that everyone was here to witness my achievement," the false teacher beamed. "I found it, Angie dear!"

Angie looked bewildered from Edmund to the group, and she kept her gloved hands wedged against her ribcage. Her teeth chattered, and she actually said, "Good. Can we go home now?"

Edmund, caught off guard by her question, looked around at all of us and decided to place his box on the ground for safekeeping. Thinking of something else, he waved Angie toward the shallow grave and said, "Lie down in that and see how much deeper I need to make it, darling."

Angie looked bug-eyed at Edmund and he said, "Go on. Be a good girl."

She began to sniffle again, and she wiped snot from her nose. I prayed she would play along, because I didn't want to test the limits of this maniac's patience. "Just do it, Ang. We're right here," I said, through clenched teeth.

Angie hesitantly walked over the mound and stepped into the hardened earth where Oscar and Mr. V. had dug it up. Once her feet were both inside it, she knelt down and laid supine in the gap. Her entire body was hidden from view, but it was nowhere near six feet deep. *Maybe two or three feet max,* I thought. She kept still and tried to make herself as small as possible.

"That won't do, will it?" Edmund laughed, shoveling some dirt over her for sport. "The buzzards, when they return, won't have to work at all will they?"

"You've made your point, Munson," Mr. V. scolded, raising his pistol to eye level at Edmund. "Let these kids go, and we can sort out whatever you want afterwards."

Edmund's teeth flashed white, and Oscar clicked on the other flashlight and tossed it at Edmund's head. The madman ducked the object, and it flew just above his head landing in the branches. Immediately, I heard Mr. V. roar, "Run, kids!" and I heard a gunshot ring out across the dark circle, the sound splitting the night air and leaving me half deaf. I grabbed Angie's arm and pushed us in the direction of where we first made landfall. Oscar was close behind swinging his shovel in a wild fashion and making contact with what I prayed with Edmund's thick profile. There was a lot of confusion, and I felt my breath choke itself midway into my lungs.

"Get Angie to the boats!" Oscar screamed in my dulled eardrum. "I'll be right behind you!"

I wanted to protest, but there was a second report and this time it came from farther away—Mr. V.'s gun. I heard a piercing yell, and I knew someone was hit.

Rather than heed Oscar's advice, I turned to see a shadow lying in the clearing with a box clutched tightly to its breast. Mr. V. was kicking the figure, and Oscar was prying the box out from Edmund's grip.

"Take this with you, O, and get the girls to safety," Mr. V. said, his voice odd, sounding miles away. "Do it for Andrea," I heard Mr. V. half-shout into the darkness. "Now, go!"

Oscar turned and pushed me farther along the path. I did the same to Angie in front of me, and we jostled one another for what felt like an eternity. When I tried to pause and get my breathing settled, Oscar stuck the dirty, wooden box harshly into my chest, and I realized the wind was completely gone from me. When I started to hyperventilate, he put his hand on my shoulder and guided me along. He pointed in the direction he thought we should go, and Angie kept going and I did likewise for what felt an eternity. I heard groans and clenched mutterings, and I realized Oscar was talking to himself. When I calmed my nerves to a deafening roar, I realized he was saying, "For Andrea, for Andrea, for Andrea," over and over again.

As we fell into the vast opening at the lake's edge, Oscar pushed our kayak into submersible depth and twisted it around in one swift motion. He took the oars out and handed them to us one at a time. Then, he backed the boat upward onto the shore and Angie got into the first seat instinctively. I did likewise with the backseat and neither of us clicked the lifejackets onto our bodies. We kept them buried in the bottom of our seats and waited for Oscar to slide out onto the water with his stand-up paddleboard. Before he did, he leaned over to me and handed off the wooden box again. "Keep this close," he mouthed in my ear. Then, he deftly took to his board and began pushing himself away from Wolf Island.

No one spoke as we traversed the placid waters on our return across Chartreuse toward Chattanooga's mainland. A primal part of my body watched the back of Oscar's head to see if he would chance turning around, if it was my dad I would've, but he kept his eyes focused on the water ahead. Since there was zero wake on the water's surface, he laser-focused on our landing spot and paddled with an Olympian's focus. Angie set a steady pace and none of us talked for fear of breaking some spell that seemed to exist on the lake. I collected my breath and took swoops into the water with my left and then right-side oars. The water parted and collapsed repeatedly, and I wondered what happened in the chaos behind us. *Was Edmund alive? Was Mr. V.? What would we find when any of us went back?* I wished I was standing behind Oscar on the board so that I could lean in and tell him I was praying, too. He looked stoic and immovable on the board, and he heaved determinedly into the water until we rejoined the familiar shoreline. Without saying a word, Oscar collected our gear and flung it into the backside of the Jeep hatch. Then, he cranked the engine to life, and we fled the scene not toward Oscar's house but the Chattanooga Police Department.

Chapter 38

The police station appeared devoid of life, and I checked the old Jeep for some clock to indicate what hour it was. Angie pulled her cell from her pocket and said, "One thirty." Her phone chirped to life with whatever cell coverage suddenly sprang to life and a gazillion messages clicked onto her screen. I watched as she fumbled to scroll through them in the backseat. One she hovered over was from her mom or dad, and it was all caps reading, "WHAT IS GOING ON? ARE YOU OKAY?!!!"

She frantically typed a reply and hit send. An instant response came back, and she replied to that one as well. She said my parents were worried too, and I told her to tell them I was alive. I didn't like the idea that Mom and Dad came home to a bleak house, no visible sign that I was okay.

Angie typed and typed and clicked send multiple times. I looked up to the front seat and noticed Oscar wasn't moving much. He looked to be locked deep in thought, and I was afraid to jar him from his reverie. Before I could lean forward and say anything, he instinctively took the key from the ignition and shut the driver's side door. Not looking backward, he began climbing the steps two at a time. I got out and followed him quicker than I thought my legs could go. Angie was left in the comfort of the backseat, and she didn't get out of the vehicle so fast. When she lingered at the Jeep's door and finally shut it, I went into the police station without her. *She could catch up,* I thought. I needed to help Oscar get this story delivered to the authorities and fast. With the time ticking by, I knew he must be thinking only about his dad still out there with a psychopath on Wolf Island.

As we signed in at the front, Oscar tried to get someone's attention, but no one was moving from their desks, there were only two officers on site, offering to take his statement. I leaned over the counter and half-shouted, "Excuse me! Listen up. We have a situation here."

"Miss, I'll ask you to step back or I'll have to get physical," a gruff voice said at the desk farthest from the glass window.

"Are you listening? We have a serious threat we need to report!" I said, gazing through the partition to a sleep deprived officer and his co-worker, rubbing her eyes. The Styrofoam coffee cups were situated beside each worker, and I saw a smear of lipstick on the female officer's cup. I tried to angle the conversation toward her, hoping the female urgency would strike a chord. "Officer, ma'am?" I asked, trying to get her to look up from her screen. "It's urgent! Please?"

The lady officer slowly stopped typing some note, and she pulled herself away from a phone that began to ring. As she made sleepy eye contact, I said, "My friend, his dad, he's in trouble . . . "

"Domestic disturbance?" she asked.

"No," I replied.

"Car trouble?" she droned, running through a familiar repertoire.

"No, listen—"

"Friends partying too—" she started, but I cut her off.

"My friend here," I said, pointing, "his dad is in serious trouble. There's a guy with a gun and there's been shots fired out on Wolf Island!" I exhaled all in a rush. "Get some people out there now!"

She looked from me to Oscar and then her dazed co-worker. "Gunfire? Somebody shot?" she said, seeing me nod frantically, my mouth completely dry now.

"And how do you know this?" she said, looking us over with new focus.

"Because, we . . . we were out there," I admitted, seeing no sense in lying to police.

She looked us over again, and said, "So much for a slow night, Henry," she said over her shoulder. Then, begrudgingly said into her radio, "10-32 reported Wolf Island. Be advised. Witnesses present. Use extreme caution. Two possible suspects, 10-20 Wolf Island," she added, clicking the receiver off and turning to us again.

"Now, I need all of the details. Was it just the two of you to make it off?" she asked, looking from Oscar to me and taking a sip of her stale coffee, grimacing at the taste.

I looked at Oscar and he said, "There was one other person. She's out at the Jeep," he pointed back out the main entrance.

"Well, bring her in. We'll need to go over all the specifics that way we can rule you three out of suspicion," she grinned, taking some delight at being able to turn the tables on us, salvaging some form of her early morning hours.

Angie walked into the police station and gawked at the memorials on the walls like it was her first trip into any such building in her life. I imagined it was. My long, familiar trips to detention and administration offices had thawed my nerves a lot compared to hers. Plus, I was dead tired from spending the better part of two days on Wolf Island. Angie let me lead her to a small desk where the officer, her name tag read Spivey, wrote in quick fragments anything (and everything) that we mentioned about our trek out to Wolf. She tried to turn the legal pad away from me, but I caught phrases like 'scared sick' and 'children hiding from parents' until she all but told me to stay on that side of the desk and pointed at a chair beside Angie and Oscar.

"Aren't you going to put us in different cells and make sure our stories line up?" I heard myself ask. "Can I have a cup of coffee?" I asked the one named Henry. He looked daggers at me and hoisted himself from his chair to venture wherever the ancient coffee pot was located.

"We don't need different rooms unless . . . you aren't being truthful?" she said, voice going up two octaves. "You're not lying are you?"

I shook my head no, said, "That's preposterous. We're just wanting you to get it down and get out there," I said, pointing beyond the memorial wall to the lake. "Oscar's dad is in real trouble."

She soothed us and gave Angie an unasked-for Little Debbie snack cake. Oscar licked his lips but refused to give in to food when his dad was still outside and in harm's way. Henry limped back into the room, and I had misjudged him. It wasn't just a sedentary existence that gave him his laid-back physique, but he had a real prosthetic leg. Without thinking, I blurted, "How'd you get that?"

Angie elbowed me between bites of her first cake, and I said, "Ouch. Just making conversation."

He sat the steaming cup of coffee down on my side of the desk, and Officer Spivey paused in her writing.

"Thanks. Sorry," I apologized. "Please continue."

Henry ambled back to his desk behind the glass partition with the front room, and I realized Officer Spivey was still eyeing me.

"What?"

"Nothing," she said, putting her pen back to the pad and writing something about me that I couldn't see.

Two could play that game, I discovered. I leaned across to her side of the table and said, with hideous breath I imagined, "Don't you want to know what all the fighting was about?"

By the way Officer Spivey inhaled, I knew I had her. It was the tidbit I was holding closest to my sleeve in case she didn't want to take us seriously. When she looked up, I knew I had her by the cast of her eyes, glossy and somewhat looking past me and not directly at me. I folded my arms across my denim and waited.

"You better not be withholding evidence," she stammered, gripping the pen tightly. "Because that could be the difference between whether this Mr. Villanueve lives or—"

I cut her off with a wave of my hand, not wanting Oscar to hear any 'conjecture' from this woman's lips.

"Share what you've been sitting on," Officer Spivey spat.

"The criminal behind all of this," I said, gesturing to Oscar, Angie, and myself, adding, "went out there with a treasure map . . . and he found what he was after. We just happened to put up a fight against him."

"But didn't start this fight?" Officer Spivey asked, looking down the bridge of her aquiline nose at me, my friends.

"We're wasting time," Oscar finally spoke, standing to his full height. "My dad is out there, could be dying," he said, lip quivering as he uttered the last part. He looked through the blinds of the window to the abandoned, dark streets we'd just fled.

"We've got officer en route, Mr. Villanueve," she said. "They—"

"My father might not last that long," he admitted, putting his head against the cinderblock wall.

"Have faith," Officer Spivey said, and her words jarred Oscar back to the present. Someone he didn't know was telling him what he might tell me or Angie. He stepped back from the window and sat down at his chair again.

"What else can you tell me about this map, what the criminal found, why you all were there?" she said, eyeing me, avoiding contact with Angie. She looked like eating her snack cakes was all she could manage.

"He was pretending to be our teacher," I began, gesturing to all three of us. "Only it was all a big lie."

"Teacher where?" she interrupted.

"Idyll High," I replied.

"Grade level?"

"Ninth."

"How do you know he was pretending to be a teacher?" she asked, looking only at me this time.

"We, er, I mean, I found his identification, and it didn't match the name he was using at the school," I said, suddenly proud of myself and for not getting Oscar or Angie into more trouble.

"How did you find his identification?" Officer Spivey asked.

I let the question hang, because this was the one that was going to drive all of this into uncharted territory. As if it wasn't enough for our trio to sleuth against someone really trying to hurt us, one of our parents, I was now about to fess up to stealing a flash drive from a teacher and looking into their background. *This was where it could all go belly up,* I knew. I asked Officer Spivey if she'd ever read *Alice in Wonderland* before. She nodded in the affirmative that she must've in grade school or something. The one with all the twisty turns and mad hatters and caterpillars smoking hookahs. I told her that was the one. She said she felt like she was traveling down a rabbit trail right now, and I laughed with her. Then, I admitted that I had snuck into this man's classroom, picked his desk drawer lock at lunch, and rummaged to find a flash drive. Afterwards, I went home and (acting alone) looked up files he had on the drive and differentiated that he planned to 'acquire' something out at Wolf Island.

She asked, "How much did Angie and Oscar know about any of this?"

I said, "Only the bare minimum. I didn't want to implicate them in any of my wrongdoings."

She laughed, and I told her about my internet search into anyone I could find named Edmund Clarence Munson and what I found about a man in Idaho. Officer Spivey, to her disdain I imagined, leaned forward and almost toppled my cup of coffee. When she found her posture again, she began writing down bits and pieces of what I told her on the yellow legal pad. Suddenly, I had her focus off of us and more directly situated where it should've been this entire time—on the criminal.

When I paused to see if she was still processing this, she wrung her wrist and chuckled to herself.

"What?" I asked, flustered that she was still laughing at a time like this.

"You're different, Ms. Crowley. You know that?"

"It's Star," I corrected. "Only people who don't know me call me that."

She went to write again and circled the word 'Star' more than once on the legal pad. I smiled at that gesture. *Maybe she was warming to us?* I thought. *One could hope.*

"So, Idaho to here, because of some grudge? That seems a bit far-sighted for a criminal, don't you think? Why not keep doing mischief out West, if he got away with it?" she asked, genuinely thinking of it, because her eyebrows stayed furrowed, her teeth biting down on the ink pen.

"You're missing the point," I said, tapping the legal pad, encouraging her to write this down, too. "He was duped by Mr. Villanueve, and the Ming Dynasty vase wasn't something he got to hold onto or sell for big bucks. It all went overseas to its rightful family of owners. So, Edmund Clarence Munson got zilch, and he never let the grudge go. So, he tracked Oscar's dad, his family, and when they moved out here, after they lost . . . " I trailed away, not sure how to mention Andrea to this recent connection.

Oscar looked outside again, and I knew he was giving me permission to finish my dissertation with this woman no matter how much the account hurt him. I tried to tread lightly and only said, "Oscar's sister to an accident. They moved here to start over, but Munson wouldn't leave it alone. He had to retaliate in the only way he knew how. He stalked them across country, and when he learned of a potential treasure tied to Wolf, he had to drop hints to Mr. Villanueve and get even by luring him out to this forsaken place and making him look like an idiot. At least, that's what he thought was happening," I said, stifling a laugh that quickly turned to shock when I saw the horror on Oscar's face.

He stood and quickly exited the area, walking to a bathroom and entering without a word to Henry.

Angie crumbled her snack cake wrapper and stuck it in a trash bin beside her chair, wiping crumbs from her face, pushing a stray strand of hair from her eyebrows.

Officer Spivey kept her gaze focused on me and finally replied, "That's a lot to take in, Star. You know I would throw someone half this stark-raving mad into a cell without batting an eye, but you don't come across as mad. You are something else," she said, tapping her pen against her forehead. "You think differently, and I wonder if you have a career in law enforcement in your future," she added, chuckling to herself.

"Detective more likely," I said, not wanting to offend her, but I was always partial to detectives and protocols they followed, how their brains operated around crime scenes.

Officer Spivey held up her hands, said, "Whatever you want, girl."

"But it's definitely a financial heist, too," I said. "Edmund is willing to kill for it. That sketch by Warhole or whoever," I said. "He wanted to embarrass Oscar's dad, but now that the treasure is real, I imagine he won't part with that box for anything . . . even death," I admitted, feeling a chill like I'd felt on Wolf the night before as I said it to the room.

"Warhol," Officer Spivey corrected.

"Yeah, that's what I meant," I said, adding, "some sketch he did when he was just a kid or something. His name was signed on it, Edmund said, if you can believe him."

"I don't know what to believe at this point," Officer Spivey said, looking at Angie. "Want another Little Debbie?"

Angie shook her head no, but I could tell she meant yes. It had been a while since our last real meal if you didn't count the granola bars.

"But I will say, you all have made our night a whole lot more interesting, haven't they Henry?" she called to the front office space.

Oscar came through and retook his seat opposite the police officer. Before Officer Spivey could say anything else, he said with cold calculation, "I'm glad our lives have entertained you two in the Chattanooga Police Department. If you don't give us an update on this case," he said, pointing to her legal pad, "in the next ten minutes, I am going to commandeer one of those squad cars myself and drive it to the lake. Am I making myself clear?"

Baffled by his tone and his change in demeanor, Officer Spivey checked her holster for her gun and was relieved to find it was still there. In the same instant, Henry limped down the hallway to check if everything was all right. Spivey waved him away, and she leaned in and said in the politest way the force had trained her to, "If he's half as strong as you, he'll be fine."

Oscar breathed a deep trembling breath and leaned back in the uncomfortable metal chair to gaze at the ceiling. I looked upward with him and wondered how many criminals had contemplated their lives from this very spot. Then, I felt Angie beside me, and she leaned over to Officer Spivey and asked, "Could we have more of those snack cakes?"

The police officer left us alone, and it was the first time we'd shared a moment without fearing for our lives in what felt like ages. Angie put her head on my shoulder, and I reached down for Oscar's hand. He tried to brush me away the first time, but I persisted, and he eventually gave up and let me envelope his large calloused hands in my own as we waited on Officer Spivey to return.

Chapter 39

The police station played a mournful rendition of some old hymn at the memorial plaque when someone first entered the building. I didn't notice it when we first came in, and since no one entered the room, the room remained silent. Only when Henry limp-walked to the front of the room for something to do did bagpipes begin playing at the wall to signify honor to some fallen heroes on the plaque. It sounded like something I remember hearing in church once, but I couldn't recall the song. My eyes grew heavy, and I found myself resting my cheek against the uncomfortable chair turned backwards to me for support.

"Amazing Grace," Angie said to no one in particular. "My grandma always sang that song when I visited her house." Her voice felt forever away, and it gave insight into something akin to remorse that we might not ever see our homes again. At least, not in the same ways. I wanted my parents here, and I looked outside for anything on the street to indicate they were alive. As if reading my thoughts, Henry turned from his assessment of the fallen and said, "Your folks called," looking at me, then Angie and Oscar for a second. "I told them we could let you go once we know more about what's happening . . . " he fell away.

Officer Spivey sat another cup of nasty coffee before me, and I shook my head. "It'll keep you awake," she soothed. "And Henry's right. We'll let you go as soon as we know something," she added, lips trying to smile a thin, birdlike look.

The bagpipes started again, and I realized Henry was shuffling in place. Officer Spivey cleared her throat, indicating that Henry should step away, move back to his desk. *Please,* I thought. *I don't want to think about death right now.*

He read the room and limped away from the picture, casting three friends in uniform all with arms around each other's shoulders. "They were the best," he muttered below his breath, his path past us creating a stir of frigid air.

I shivered and realized the recirculated air was making me sick. I fought down bile rising in my throat, before I could stop it, I dry-heaved and ran to the trash can in the corner.

Oscar was up on his feet, holding my hair back from my face and soothing me with, "Hold fast, Star. We'll know something soon."

I wanted desperately to believe him, but my mind flashed to Wolf Island and it sent shock through my body. *Why Oscar's dad and not someone else's? Why couldn't it be Randall Tolley or someone, anyone else?* But I knew it was selfish, and I felt instantly worse for trying to throw someone else into this mess.

Angie's chest rose and fell, and I knew she was asleep and propped against three chairs placed together, her body turned toward the backing. I watched her for a second and still heard the bagpipes in my head. Rather than focus on what I couldn't control, I focused on my surroundings and listened to my heart hammering against my ribs. Slowly, I felt the thumping subside, and I walked with Oscar back to the chairs.

"We can't do anything now, but pray," he offered, sitting me on three chairs he pulled together, mimicking Angie's spot.

"You can pray," I said, sounding sterner than I felt. "What good is it going to do?" Instantly, I wanted to grab Oscar's hand again, but he had already turned from me and bent his head downward.

"That's not a bad idea," Officer Spivey agreed, and she sipped from her cup and let the room fall silent.

I turned toward the chairs and tucked my legs toward my chest and decidedly closed my eyes. The room fell to a hush apart from an occasional click from the police radio. I felt the chilly air, and my mind rushed back across the lake. I shivered where I rested, and I thought of the purple puffy coat hanging from the branches of our last silly ruse.

My legs pumped the air and found little purchase on the mucky terrain, and I was running toward something or away from them. My heart leapt in my chest cavity, and the air felt frozen in my nostrils. I wiped away sweat from my forehead, and it burned in the icy winter air. I was on Wolf Island but somewhere else, too. The land looked flatter than I remembered it earlier, and instead of trees smacking my legs and arms, the ground tried to suck me under. The mud gripped at my ankles and squelched with each effort I gave of trying to free my Converse sneakers.

I heard a high-pitched whistle, and it signified that someone was calling others toward my position.

Like a great hunt scene I'd once seen on someone's wall, a painting with horses and riders, I heard the tramping of hooves, a thunderous roar and it all came toward my spot. I heaved one foot upward from the mire and felt my shoe come off. With only a sock, I placed my foot on the ground and tried to not sink deeper. As I struggled to free my other foot, the remaining shoe came off, and I looked at it buried in the sludge. Now shoeless, I looked around me and saw bogs as far as my eyes could see. The place was a wasteland, and I couldn't imagine horses making much better progress than myself. The whistle rang out again, but closer this time.

I felt helpless and alone and realized all I had on were my usual things—rock tee and wasted jeans. I felt my pockets and realized all I had there was a single whistle. I took it out and blew on it, not sure of why I did such a thing. I was leading them right to me. I blew out three more quick bursts and crawled to the nearest bog. Sinking into my elbows, I barely kept my chin above water. The horses thudded closer and closer. I heard a rider yell out something indiscernible, and the hooves fell in thunderous waves one after the other. Then, the sounds hit my eardrum like cannons, and I knew they were close. *About to put me out of my misery,* I realized.

I drew a deep breath and went under the water and sank as far down as the pool permitted. I buried my hands in the muck and dug enough to feel the bog bottom snag my arms with squishy satisfaction. The ground thundered and came to an eerie halt, and I thought I heard a rider dismount from the herd's front, the leader. The footfalls came to within an inch of my bog, and the rider's eyes reflected a golden hue. He stared down at my bog and stood motionless. I closed my eyes and willed my body to become one with the terrain. The chilly water tickled my nose, and I fought back anything that might cause a bubble to rise to the surface. *He has to see me,* I realized, fearful of ever opening my eyes again. Then, I realized I knew no one else out here, and I wouldn't have a clue where to start if I let this party leave. I was about to open my eyes, lunge to the surface and take a life-altering gasp, when I remembered the whistle, the hunt. A bigger part of me still didn't want to die. I fought the urge to yield, and I waited past what I thought my lungs could take. When I started to go numb, my lungs burning for a taste of air, I slowly let my scrunched eyelids go lax, and I peered through the murky waters to see the leader's body turn toward where his mount was. He stuck a foot in his steed's stirrup and remounted. Then, without warning, he offered a shrill whistle and rode onward in the direction of nothing but desolation. I waited for what I prayed was the last rider to thunder past, and I freed myself from weeds and ooze and thrust to the surface for the sweetest-tasting air.

As I cleared my eyes of silt and slime, I wiped my hands on my drenched pants and stumbled for purchase on the edge of the bog. The riders kept going with no signs of turning or slowing down. The thunder shook the foundations of the earth, and I rubbed my pruny fingertips together. This desolation expanded in every direction, and I looked up at the sky and thought, *Why would you create such a place?* Not getting an answer, I continued to stare at the heavens and noticed not a bird was in flight. *What now?* I wondered. As if in reply, the faint sounds of an awkward instrument blurted to break the silence, and I knew it wasn't from a rider. The sharp whistle was as different to this sound as anything on earth. The blurting sound clanged again, and I knew it was building to join other awkward notes, and I heard the funny sound of a song taking shape.

I slowly opened my eyes and realized the bagpipes were trying to play "Amazing Grace" on the wall again. Standing in front of the plaque, I saw a small, stoop-shouldered woman discussing something with Officer Spivey, and I realized Oscar was rising to join them. Before my head could fully clear, I realized Mrs. Villanueve was the one asking the questions, and Oscar all but fell into her chest for a tender, sad embrace.

Chapter 40

Mrs. Villanueve asked Spivey what was taking so long. She wanted to know how many officers were on scene and whether her husband was safe. Officer Spivey held up her hands and tried to deflect with what she knew, which was little beyond what was shared at the start of this saga. Mrs. Villanueve raised her voice for the first time I'd heard, and she flung her hands around the air. She grew into hysterics, and Oscar hugged her again, trying to soothe her. I watched as she fell into Oscar's arms and sobbed that more must be done. She said between breaths that her husband was the best, no one of better substance. I agreed with her, wiping sleep from my eyes.

Snowflakes began to fall outside the station, and Henry swayed back and forth almost mimicking their movement in the air. Even though the heater kicked on again and pushed stale air around the room, I shivered at the sight of snow beginning to stick to the Chattanooga street. I stood and walked over to where Oscar hugged his mom. She saw me and gave me a big squeeze, and I pointed to Angie still asleep on the chair cushions.

"You all are so brave," she consoled, her voice too tight for comfort. "When I saw the Jeep missing, and no one at home, I . . . " her voice fell away.

The bagpipes tried to kick to life again, and I steered us away from the plaque. Officer Spivey seemed pleased because she walked beside us to the chairs I'd just awakened from. We all sat down, and Officer Spivey asked Mrs. Villanueve if she wanted coffee. Mrs. V. shook her head, and I was grateful she would dodge the black sludge. The taste still lingered in my mouth.

Oscar stood again and joined Henry at the window. The two stood in fixed gazes looking outward at the scene beyond. The snow stuck to the streetlight and the sidewalk, and I wondered how much was expected to fall. The temperature was perfect for a nice blanket. Instead of feeling protected inside, I suddenly imagined Mr. V. alone in the woods of Wolf Island trying to hang on for help to arrive. I knew Oscar must feel similarly, because he stomped his foot and said, "What's taking so long?" his foot shaking the old tile flooring.

Henry gave a noncommittal reply about these things taking time, keeping his gaze fixed on the falling flakes. Oscar pushed his hands deeply into his pockets and fumbled with his dad's Jeep keychain. I realized he was so much like his dad in this moment, his stance, his glasses, and keen awareness to do the right thing. I wanted to hug him, but I knew he needed a moment to himself. If it had been any other night, under any other circumstance, I would write him a note and tell him everything was going to be fine. *But was it?* I wondered. The snow accumulated on the street and began to wipe the lane markings away. It would be dangerous for a city with few snowplows soon. I prayed for the officers searching the woods, and I wanted to know Edmund was no longer a threat. As I sat at my chair, I gripped Mrs. V.'s hand and waited for something good to happen on this torturous night. She returned my squeeze and closed her eyes and sat in silence.

As Angie turned in her fitful sleep, the police radio went off, and I saw Officer Spivey reach for her walkie. There was a disconnected voice rattling out from the radio, and I missed what it said at first. Officer Spivey took the walkie to her lips and said, "Go again."

"10-13," the voice replied. "Suspect in custody. 10-32 apprehended. 10-33 at ER. Be advised," and squawked to silence again.

Officer Spivey said, "10-4. Station okay," and she clicked the walkie back onto her belt. She turned to us, and Oscar's face glared at her for answers. I stood and joined him, watching her for any hints.

"There's no need to panic, but we need to go over your stories one more time. The suspect is detained now and will be brought here shortly," she said, her voice measured and solid.

"No," Oscar argued, pointing to her walkie. "If Dad's at the ER, we are going there now!" he shouted, pointing to the door. "I heard that about the ER," he repeated. His stance was firm, and I knew there was no budging him on the subject. Officer Spivey must've noticed this too, because she put the yellow legal pad down on the desk and stood to her full, squat height.

"That's not protocol," she said, sitting her lipstick-stained Styrofoam cup on the desk beside the pad.

"I don't care about your protocol!" Oscar spat.

"Don't get like that," Spivey interrupted, turning to look for Henry's assistance.

Henry turned from the window and reacted like a weather forecaster might, saying, "It'll be dangerous to go anywhere."

Officer Spivey bit her tongue and swore to herself, cursing her co-worker. The room fell silent, and even Angie leaned forward and looked at us for some recap. Not getting it, she stood and straightened her chairs.

"Let's go, now," Oscar said, panic rising in his voice, tears forming in his eyes.

Mrs. Villanueve rose and grabbed his hand. I walked behind them, and Angie hurried to join us at the entrance of the station.

"You'll just end up stuck or worse," Henry said, pointing toward the fresh snowfall outside.

"I'm not getting a tow truck called after you all," Spivey said, through clenched teeth. She grabbed her keys from a key holder behind the main desk and searched for one in particular. Satisfied that the key was attached, she pocketed the keys and walked to the entrance begrudgingly.

If Edmund was en route to this police station, a large part of me wanted to be here when he arrived, see him marched in handcuffs into the cell, hear the lock clanging shut behind him. But there was something in Oscar's face that won out. His dad was in the ER, and I tried to think of Mr. V. just getting stitched up from minor injuries. *But the ER wasn't reserved for simple fixes, was it?* I thought. It was serious, and I followed Officer Spivey, and our crew, single file outside the glass doors. As Angie brought up the rear, the bagpipes began to chime once more, and I noticed Henry standing before the plaque once more.

He held a hand up, and he signaled to Spivey that he would be fine in her brief absence. She took the keys from her pocket and unlocked a solitary squad car beside the building. Oscar filed into the passenger seat without waiting for permission. I opened the backdoor and Mrs. V. scooted all the way over to the far side, then Angie. Once I seated myself beside them, I felt the chill of the frozen leather against an exposed part of my jeans. I shook with cold as much as the fear of what lay ahead of us. Officer Spivey brought the car to life with a turn of the ignition, and the heater blasted us with still-frigid air.

Oscar scolded the police officer to *go, go, go*, but Spivey told him to take a deep breath. She said this was largely out of our hands, and I imagined her telling countless victims a similar story. Then, she pushed a lever turning the main overhead lights on, flipped a switch to create a loud siren wail, and exited the parking lot with as much speed as possible, without causing a wreck.

CHAPTER 41

The squad car shrieked to a stop at the ER entrance and Oscar hopped out of the car first. I banged on the door and realized getting out of the back of a police car needed assistance. I kept tapping the glass, but Oscar was already halfway to the ER doors. Officer Spivey put the car in park and got out to open our doors. Mrs. Villanueve caught up to Oscar, and they went to the front desk for help. Angie and I hung back, and I felt her hand squeeze mine, and heard her voice say, "Let's give them a minute."

I looked at the clock and tried to register the time with where we were, what day of the week it was. The time on the island felt like it'd taken years of life away from us. Angie hugged my arm, and we lingered in the lobby for a bit. Every time the front doors slid open on their automatic sensor, arctic blasts churned across the open ER room, completely vacant save for us. In jogged an ambulance team with a gurney with someone on it. I avoided eye contact with the team, but Angie pointed to the bed and said, "Look. Car wreck, I bet," she breathed, too close to my ear.

I felt myself tug away from her arm, and I walked to the main desk to ask where our party went. Putting my arms up on the counter, I rested my head on my arms and waited for the receptionist to get off a phone call. When I heard the click of the receiver, I looked up and said, "Mr. Villanueve, please. What room is it?"

"Family member?"

"Of course," I lied, not feeling nearly enough energy to discuss my relation to anyone involved in this mess.

"Please fill out a check-in form and return it to me," the lady said, pointing to a stack of forms in a holding tray. "Do you have your ID on you?" she asked, looking from me to Angie, now standing behind me.

"It's urgent," I said, pushing tangled hair back from my face.

"We've not slept in a while," Angie adds, trying to smile.

"We still need to get you checked in," the receptionist replies.

"Listen, we need to see our—Mr. Villanueve—and we aren't filling out any forms," I said, finding my voice, hitting the counter with the bottom of my fist. The canister holding a stack of pens bounced as I did it, and the receptionist swung her head back.

"You can point us in the direction, or we can find it on our own," I said, glaring at her for some defense against our plan.

She hesitantly took the ink pen receptacle off the counter like an opponent would move a weapon away, and she pointed toward the elevators. She said, "Take it to the third, turn left, follow it to Room 403. If he's out of surgery, he'll be in there."

We were already past the desk, and I punched the 'up' button more than once with my outstretched finger. Angie turned and mouthed, 'Sorry,' to the lady doing her job.

When the elevator dinged and the door swung open, I hung a left and walked to the designated room. Angie hustled to keep up with me doing a slight lope, and I paused at Room 403 and peered inside. No one was there, and I considered lingering in the hallway. The other elevator pinged, and the door opened. Two nurses came out and one pushed a wheelchair with an elderly lady in it. Rather than risk more confrontation with the ER staff, I pushed the door open, and we went into the immaculately clean room and sat down in two vacant chairs.

Angie kept her eyes fixed on the empty hospital bed, the gadgets illuminated on the digital display. I watched the door for any signs of movement and took a deep breath. *Now what? Do we sit here and wait for whatever news comes our way?* I thought. Not knowing proper ER etiquette, I sat with my hands clasped in front of me and tried to steady my thoughts.

Oscar and his mom were somewhere in the ER with Mr. V. If he was still being operated on, they were probably right there. My mind flashed to images of Edmund Munson walking up the steps of the station we'd just left manacled and bound for a cell. I tried to envision how Wolf Island looked now that all of us had cleared out. *Were cops still canvasing the place looking for clues? Had Edmund given any confession or was he claiming to be innocent?* I laughed at the notion and stared at the blank wall in front of us. Angie fumbled for a TV remote and clicked the power button. I was about to scold her for wanting to watch TV at a time like this, but I stopped when the news station van popped on the screen and a headline appeared with 'Suspect apprehended on Wolf Island, one person injured.' My mouth froze in a shocked O-shape, and Angie elbowed me. I elbowed her back, and she turned the volume up.

The newswoman said that details were incoming, and the story was still developing but what they knew so far was that a person was responsible for severely injuring at least one person during a gunfight on Wolf Island. The snow fell harder behind the woman, and the camera blurred with the gusts of wind and flakes obscuring the lens. The reporter tossed her hair from her face and tried to reposition herself in front of the camera. She said the suspect was in custody with Chattanooga Police, and the area on Wolf Island was being swept for clues as to why this skirmish happened. No mention was made of us or the treasure that Edmund Munson was after. The station went back to its main crew, and the story continued to spin inside my head. *The treasure was not mentioned,* I thought. Then, I remembered that I left the box. *It was still in the bottom of the kayak!* I knew this 'evidence' would be brought up later, when police questioned us fully, and I felt somewhat guilty for not having the box on me.

Angie turned the volume down, and she looked at me expectantly. I knew I should offer some hope for her, but I didn't have any words to give. She said, "I'm hungry," and sat the remote down on the hospital bed. Instinctively, I picked it up and put it on the doctor's table. The bed was for Mr. V., and I was certain he would be joining us soon. I prayed he would. That would mean that Oscar would be there, too. I tried to will it to happen, but the doors remained closed. Angie bit her lip and asked, "Do you think they have something to eat? My stomach is in knots."

I wanted to scold her for thinking of food, but my stomach felt terrible as well. *Maybe if she found something, she could bring it back?* I thought. I waved her toward the door, and she said, "I'll go look for a snack station or something."

When she was gone, I went to the sink and turned it on, sticking my head under. I tried to pull my hair back but some of it still fell into the water. I gulped several times at the lukewarm water, and I tried to push images of the whole ordeal away. Please come back, I pleaded with the water falling in a stream straight from faucet to drain. When my thirst was sated, I turned the knob off and wiped at my hair with a paper towel from the automatic dispenser. The clock read 4:30 AM, and I knew the sun would rise in a few hours, even with the snow blotting it out. I longed for the comfort of my room, my parents asking me to breakfast. *Where were they?* I wondered. I picked up the room's phone and listened for a dial tone. Even though it was early, I knew neither Mom or Dad was asleep. I tried the home phone and Dad picked up on the first ring, his voice frantic, "Sweet pea?!"

"Dad, I'm at the ER," I said, fighting back tears.

"Are you—"

"I'm fine," I cried, not stifling it at all. "It's Oscar's dad," I said, staring at the hospital bed.

"We're on our way," he exhaled.

"Is she okay?" I heard Mom ask.

"Fine," Dad replied, voice distorted. "Stay put," he added.

I promised and told them what room I was in. He hung up, and I felt better and worse all at once. The silence of the room deafened me, and I hummed the bagpipes from the police station. Realizing what I was doing, I laughed at myself. The tears fell onto my torn jeans, and I wiped at my face with my dirty palms. When Angie came back, I pointed to the phone and said, "Call your parents. The phone works," realizing I sounded like a moron. Angie picked it up and did the same. We, at least, now had the peace and comfort of knowing our loved ones knew where we were, what had happened. When Angie sat down beside me, she offered a bear claw in a napkin and a juice box. I laughed at her resourcefulness and took them both greedily. As we ate in silence, I felt the sugar coursing through my body, and I wanted to walk in the snow just to feel human again. Before I could let such a bizarre thought take complete hold, the door shook, and I heard a hand twisting the knob, trying to hold it open for a party of hospital staff.

The person in front, dressed fully in scrubs, held the door as another wheeled a bandaged man into the room. The two stopped beside the bed and helped lift Mr. V. into the hospital bed. Oscar and his mom joined the throng of people, and Angie and I stood to give them ample space. The male nurse who entered first began talking fast and saying that everything was here, all they had to do was push a button on the bed and someone would be here in a second. The female nurse took her face covering from her mouth and smiled at all of us. She beamed at how well the surgery went, the entire bullet came out in one piece, just missing an artery. She said, "I'm going to check on another room, and I'll be right back." She smiled and turned to put Mr. V.'s chart on the holder affixed to the room.

Mr. V. leaned back to rest his head on the pillow, and Mrs. V. smiled at all of us, leaning in to whisper, "He's heavily medicated," and laughed a mirthful, buoyant laugh.

The room came to life, and Oscar gave me a gigantic hug. I held him and felt the weight of his muscular body against mine. It was the first hopeful moment in what felt like days, and I let him stand close like that for a while. Angie cleared her throat and said, "We're glad you're back."

Oscar gave Angie a hug as well, and we stared at Mr. V. resting peacefully on the bed. The male nurse checked the vital signs on the display and hooked a few remaining loose tubes away from Mr. V.'s bed. I felt joy in knowing everyone was alive, and we were no longer stuck waiting for something bad to happen.

CHAPTER 42

The attending doctor stopped by to check Mr. V.'s wounds. He had lost a substantial amount of blood and had lots of pints of O negative now added to his body, Oscar said. We watched and Oscar prayed with his mom for what felt like hours. The nurses asked if he needed anything, but Mrs. V. filled the gaps with requests for more water, a thinner pillow. He liked a skinny pillow to where his head almost touched the bed. Officer Spivey stuck close by in the hallway and watched the happenings through the glass divide. She did a fantastic job, because I knew it was procedure to stay with the people connected to a crime, even if they weren't suspects. *I guess she hasn't ruled anything out yet,* I thought. I held Oscar's hand so tightly I left nail marks in his palm, but he didn't wince. He kept his eyes glued to Mr. V. when he wasn't praying.

Angie scooted her chair to the far corner and observed the happenings in the room. I knew she wanted to be useful, but our words were insufficient here, and I felt equally helpless. *Is this how doctors feel all the time after a surgery?* I wondered. The male nurse leaned in and checked a plastic tube beside Mr. V. leading to a receptacle beside his bed.

"Catheter," Oscar whispered. "After surgery they have to make sure he's regaining some use of his organs."

I squeezed Oscar's hand and gave him my best side hug. He held me, and I could see Spivey staring through the glass at us. She gave me a head nod, beckoning me outside in a minute. I acknowledged her and broke from Oscar to wipe tears from his face. Then, I tried to straighten my super grimy tee and opened the door to the hospital hallway.

"All good?" she asked, scanning the hallway for some would-be perpetrator I couldn't see.

My face must've looked like the confused dog gaze I felt, because she answered her own question by toying with her gun holster. I noticed she had gray hair at her roots, and the black hair dye sprouted beyond the one-inch source. Her crow's feet at the corners of her eyes more pronounced now that we were under the scrutiny of ER fluorescents. My head turned to survey the room I'd just left, and I knew it felt infinitely more breathable here in the hallway. I took in a gigantic breath of air and released it in a rush.

"There're snacks around here somewhere," I offered the police woman. "Angie found them earlier."

Officer Spivey shook her head, "Listen, Star, I spoke with Henry a second ago," she said, pointing to her walkie. "He said Munson is now locked up at the station."

"Good," I mustered, thinking of my last image of him holding a gun, standing off with Mr. V.

"We've got him. You can relax, if what you've told me is the truth," she said, her voice falling an octave, her eyes squinching even more to reveal just slits.

I put my palm against the eggshell white wall and noticed a large print of an Audubon bird, framed on the wall beside us. It was a Californian vulture, and I laughed at the choice for an ER hallway. People were supposed to recover in here, not think of death, I laughed to myself. Spivey's gaze held me in place, and I noticed she wanted more. *But what?* I racked my brain for what all we'd told her at the station, and I knew she still didn't think the full story was out.

"I'm telling you the truth," I pleaded, tearing my eyes from the vulture to face the officer. "Why do you have to sound like that?"

"Like what?"

"Like you still don't believe us," I said, hands stretched out to her in supplication. "After all you've seen and heard since we met you."

"It's a lot," she admitted, scratching the chapped lips and thinking of more. "You three come into the station, half crazy, and telling us about a revenge plot against Oscar's dad."

"You see him, don't you?" my voice rising into hysterics, pointing to the hospital bed inside Room 403.

"That I see," she said, shifting from one police issued boot to putting her full weight on the other. "But, I've been around long enough to know there's always more. You said something about a treasure on Wolf . . . " she trailed off.

"Warhol sketch," I said, feeling less confident than I had all throughout the ordeal. "I think that was his name anyways. Not sure who Warhol is or was," I added, looking her fully in the face. "Was he some big shot artist? Munson seemed to think he had a fortune," I said, laughing at one sketch causing so much trouble. "It better be worth a gold mine, because Oscar's dad isn't something I'll let you make into a joke," I stammered, fighting back more venom in my throat, trying to calm my voice.

Officer Spivey took what I said and chewed on it for a second. She pointed at the framed print and acknowledged my thoughts with, "Odd choice for a hospital, huh?"

I laughed to split the tension between us. When I didn't offer more, she reached out and touched my hand. My instinct was to pull away, but I let her hold my clammy hand for another second.

"I ask all this not to grill you on things I think you're lying about," she soothed. "I've just been around long enough to know that usually the full story doesn't come out until everything settles a bit. You have time now to think about things you might've inadvertently left out. You said that Munson followed your friend's dad East from Idaho. They had a falling out over something like this once before. Mr. Villanueve duped him out of a lot of money? That's reason for retaliation, isn't it?" she tried to coax.

I held her gaze and watched the wrinkles at the edges of her tired eyes crease and relax.

"But if Munson did all of this to get back at Mr. Villanueve, why was he willing to kill over a sketch worth a supposed fortune? I'm not an art collector myself, and so I don't know a bunch about Warhol either. Why bring his target to the island or kill him or do any of this to end up where he is?" she asked.

My sleep-deprived brain tried to see the whole episode from her view, and I tried hard to shake the fogginess away. I shivered thinking of Wolf Island, the chill we met in crossing the lake. My arms still felt like they rowed in tandem with Angie in the kayak. I grounded myself by freeing my hand from Spivey and pointing to her walkie. She looked down to see what I pointed at.

"My walkie?" she asked.

"When you heard from Henry, you knew his side of it. I get that. And it must have sounded the same when we rushed into the police station. We told you all of it from our side, but I promise you that it's the truth. And we tried to not leave anything out. Oscar's dad did tick off Munson and made him return something, a vase, he found in Idaho. It made Munson so mad, he traveled all the way to Chattanooga to get even.

It sounds stupid, but he even impersonated someone else, going by Mr. Chethers, to get close to Oscar, at our school. He was a maniac and went from Jekyll to Hyde on a daily basis," I spat, thinking of the classroom. "He made our lives hell at Idyll," I admitted. "And I did break into his desk drawer to find these things out. If I hadn't, he might've done even worse . . . " I trailed off, hearing the gunshot in my head again.

"So, I have you to thank for spying on the teacher?" she asked, voice confident, not accusatory.

"I was the only one to break in and steal the flash drive," I said, not mentioning Angie's and Oscar's lookout roles.

"And it did give you a lot of material to work with," Spivey admitted. "If I didn't have to play twenty questions, I would say that you have a promising career indeed," she smiled. "It was really brave, and some would say stupid, to go out there where you knew he could be," she said in what I imagined was her attempt at a motherly tone.

The elevator dinged, and I saw Mom and Dad as soon as they exited and turned toward us. Before waiting for Spivey to say more, I sprinted toward my parents and fell into their outstretched arms. Dad said, "Sweet Pea! You're alive," as only he could, and it felt funny and warm unlike anything I'd ever heard in my life. Mom kissed my forehead a million times, and I lost count at which one mauled me worse. I let them hold me, and I put my full weight against their arms. My body felt ancient, and I knew they hadn't slept from the bags under their eyes. Looking at them both fully, I cried when I saw Mom's tears, and she wiped at my grimy eyelashes, sweat encrusted on my eyelids.

"Oh honey," she said, taking in my clothes, my scrapes, and bruises. "Why didn't you call?"

I fumbled for some answer, but I knew they would never believe all the antics from Idyll to this moment. Instead, I shook my head and laughed that we were all together in this ER hallway. Dad tossed my mangled hair into a greater frizz, if that was possible, and he said, "Pea, it might be time we get you a cell phone."

We laughed, and I checked behind me to see Spivey still leaning against the wall, pretending to survey the vulture print.

"Are you in trouble?" Mom asked, the color in her checks falling to a sickly pale white.

"Not really," I said, holding out my arm to Spivey for some explanation.

The officer strolled over and shook hands with Mom, then Dad in her best professional manner. She introduced herself and gave a condensed version of the events, leaving out large chunks about what happened on Wolf and anything to do with Munson, I noticed. Of course, police procedure to treat everything as factual and grounded in what was available. Then, she took Dad and Mom away from me and asked if they had any need for coffee or a snack like their placement was still at the police station rather than the ER.

When Mom and Dad cleared far enough away, never breaking sight with me completely, I looked in the hospital room to see Mr. V. stirring, reaching for his water cup. Angie stood beside him and was surprisingly tipping the cup straw toward his lips. Oscar laughed as some of the water spilled on Mr. V.'s face. Angie put her hands to her face in embarrassment, and Mr. V. encouraged her that she was doing fine as a nurse.

I laughed and knew he would recover, even though he was far from well at this hour. A nurse brushed past me and entered Mr. V.'s room. It was the female nurse from earlier, and she carried a food tray with small snacks situated on it. My stomach lurched, and I wanted another bear claw or something substantial. As the door opened, the beeps on the monitors beside Mr. V.'s bed chirped and flashed. He held his hand out for the tray, but Oscar intercepted the nurse and took it from her. I watched the scene unfold and was about to reenter the room when I felt a firm hand on my elbow. Instead of Dad gripping it or Mom wanting to look at me again, I saw Spivey at my side again, and her gaze looked one hundred percent through me. I pulled back because her face sent daggers into me.

In a determined pause, she held me and finally said, leaning into my ear, "Munson's agreed to give a full confession . . . but he wants to talk with you first."

I stepped back, pulled at her grip, but she held tight. *No way! I didn't want to ever see that creep again.*

"It's not protocol, but he means to tell us exactly what happened. I spoke with Henry, and he says we should do it. I don't like it, but I know that Munson must be an odd bird," she said, lips curled inward, biting them with her teeth. "Your call, Star."

"His side," I said, my voice feeling light years from the ER hallway. "You're willing to listen to his side now?" I asked incredulously.

Spivey said, "Listen. I don't take sides," digging into my elbow deeper now. "Ask anyone. But, if he's willing to tell all, I think you should do it."

I pulled away and considered her request. *This could end everything,* I thought. *Or, it could be another trick of his.* Suddenly, I knew what I had to do. I shook her vise-like grip from my elbow and followed her to the elevator. Oscar and Angie would protest, and I knew this was a rare moment. My parents hugged me again as I walked past what must have been the snack room, and I gave a less than confident thumbs-up. The elevator dinged, and Officer Spivey followed me into the lift to return us to the Chattanooga Police Department.

Chapter 43

When we arrived, snow hit my face as Officer Spivey held the front door to the station. I entered and Henry handed me another stale cup of coffee. Before I could protest, I realized I was suddenly their best hope at making this case go away fast, maybe even avoid unnecessary phone calls from news reporters and fielding agents from beyond the Hamilton County jurisdiction. Normally, I would pride myself on being able to help, rattle off knowledge I held about the case. But the sleep deprivation sent me in an angry direction. I thought of Munson robbing Mr. V. of his dignity and hurting him. I could still hear the gunfire ringing out in my head. I wanted to see this guy squirm. *What could he do to me now, anyway?* I reasoned. I marched past Henry's arm pointing down the narrow corridor to the cells at the end. We went through a set of double doors, and I waited for Henry to procure a key and open the solid metal door. Before walking in, I steeled myself for whatever monster would bare its teeth at us.

Officer Spivey leaned in, said, "Let me set the tone," and she sat her yellow notepad down on the polished aluminum table, bolted to the ground.

Munson leaned forward and tugged at his handcuffs lightly as if to stretch his arms. He straightened himself to an erect posture and eyed me with the same green orbs from English class. He said, "All right. This is nice."

Officer Spivey sat down across from him, and I did likewise, reluctantly. I balled my fists as tight as I could make them and felt the fingernails draw blood. Spivey said, "Mr. Munson, you've been read your Miranda rights, haven't you?"

Munson gave a jerk of his head in the affirmative, but his eyes remained locked on me, my fists on the table.

"You have the right to an attorney. Do you waive that and wish to speak to us of your own accord now?" Spivey asked, tapping her ink pen on the paper.

"It's funny how things can get out of hand, ain't it?" he laughed and tapped his leg against the floor. "I mean, it all looks so bad, but it's really explainable when you think about it. I am just a guy trying to get what is rightfully his," he sneered, bad breath forced across the small space between us. "And it is mine," he admitted, pointing an accusatory finger at me.

Unable to hold it in any longer, I stood from my chair and took in the pathetic man before me. I was emboldened by the chains, and I said, "You tried to kill him. And for what? Some stupid grudge? Look at you now. You'll be rotting in here, and it won't matter how much you almost had a treasure. You failed, and we get to go home," I said, crossing my arms to leer at him.

Munson began to laugh at something unsaid, and I felt my palms stinging. I looked down and saw droplets of blood where I'd torn the skin with my fingernails. I wiped the blood on my tee and folded my arms again tighter against my chest.

"You brought us here, Mr. Munson," Officer Spivey suggested, encouraging me to take a seat. "Why don't you go ahead and say your piece. You said you'd confess, and we might as well get on with it. Tell me what happened in your plan, and I can maybe help you out," Spivey added.

"Help him out?" I countered, refusing the offered chair. "He's the cause of all of this!" I roared, considering what might happen if I flung the chair at him. I wanted to see him squirm.

Officer Spivey held up her hands and then took me by the shoulders and guided me to the chair. I reluctantly sat, and I clenched my teeth not wanting to hear anything else from this liar's mouth.

"You found something valuable, and you wanted to protect it. Is that right?" she offered to the man in handcuffs. "Tell me why it was so important to you."

"I found a treasure in my backyard," he said matter-of-factly. "Did she tell you that?" Munson asked, looking from me to the officer. "It was worth a fortune. And that punk's dad took it away. I never took to thieves," he spat. "And I could've been set for life on that one find," he added, licking his lips and staring at the wall behind my head. His face went from friendly to a scowl, and I saw the change I'd seen in the classroom so many times.

I leaned back so that he couldn't lunge for me. He bared his yellowish-tinted teeth and cleared his throat. There were snowflakes sticking to the sliver of a window in the top, right-hand corner of the cell. I remembered the cold Jeep ride to the station and shivered in my seat.

"But no. Her boyfriend's dad had to open his big trap and tattle on me. Whatever happened to 'finder's keepers?'" he air-quoted to me and Spivey. "I was entitled to sell it or do whatever I wanted. It's a free country, and it was in my backyard. So, why couldn't he just leave it alone?" he growled, his voice an angry cry. He slammed his fists down onto the aluminum table and jarred both of us. "Now, I'll just have to find another way," he added, scanning the room for some additional map he could tack to a wall and begin his search anew.

"So, you what? Drove thousands of miles, pretended to be a teacher, found a new search, and wanted to murder your enemy once and for all?" Officer Spivey asked, wanting to put a neat bow on the whole ordeal, I imagined.

"No, I didn't plan to kill him," Munson groaned. "He was collateral damage. His stinking kid couldn't keep his nose clear of it, and they got in the way. His dad came looking for them, and I was suddenly in a place I couldn't help but defend," he confessed. "I had to make sure they didn't get my reward this time," he added, grinning to the officer. "See, I was set up. They did this to me," he beamed, pleased with some turn of events in his mind I couldn't see.

"Liar!" I roared. "We weren't out to get you. You tried to put all of us in the ground. You would've shot all of us and left us for dead if we hadn't escaped!" I screamed at him.

Officer Spivey held her hands up and tried to restore some order to the mayhem. She told Munson to leave me alone, and she scolded me for losing my cool. I felt it was understandable given what he was accusing us of. When silence fell over the room, I walked to the back of the cell and rested my back against the wall—eyes fixed solely on Munson.

"I only shot the one person," Munson admitted, flashing a grin to me. "And he didn't die," the man proudly broadcast. "So, it's not a big deal. I don't see why it's even worth all the hysterics."

"It's worth all this," Officer Spivey said, gesturing to the prison walls, the cell, "because you did shoot a man. Plain and simple. So, Star's right about that part," she admitted, smiling and turning her to me.

"I'll be fine," Munson mumbled. "It wasn't anything more than friendly fire, a warning shot," he claimed.

"You impersonated someone and stalked a man!" I yelled at him, my voice cracking, and my throat suddenly sore.

"You broke into my personal belongings. Inadmissible evidence in any court," he laughed, cackling like a hyena. "And you're lucky I don't have you expelled," he boomed, pounding the desk again. "You aren't exactly squeaky clean."

I pushed off from the wall and began to trudge to where he was chained, but Spivey halted my progress with a forearm blocking my path. "He already confessed to pulling the trigger," she soothed. "Whether he changes his tune later or not is irrelevant. Just step outside with me," she said, pointing beyond the cell door.

Munson spit at me, and I felt actual saliva hit my tee shirt and arm as I walked toward the cell door. He roared and shook his chains and yelled, "Just wait until I see you again Freida Crowley!"

Hearing him use my actual name unnerved me more than anything else. I wanted to go back to the Jeep and burn the Warhol sketch just out of spite, even if it was worth a ton of cash. He didn't deserve the satisfaction of even thinking it was somewhere safe. I pictured the childish sketch engulfed in flames, bending inward and turning a charred black. *You lose, jerk!* I thought with as much hatred as my small frame could create.

"You're lucky he didn't die," I said through the cell door. "Otherwise, you'd be in here for life."

Munson sat with his face straight ahead, and I waited for some other retort but none came. Officer Spivey clicked the lock into place, and I felt my emotions fighting to take over. She spun me away from the cell and guided me along the corridor back to the station's entrance. When we sat at her desk, she said, "He said enough, and you heard it. I know Henry will back everything I write up in the report. Plus, he processed him earlier. So, it's a good place for now," she said, reaching out to squeeze my shoulder.

I shook her away and looked outside. The snow accumulated to an inch or two on the street, and I was suddenly aware of what Randall Tolley told me about the treasure, the missing girl. I wanted to ask if the other girl was ever found. *Was it something that could be pinned on Munson?* But I couldn't open my mouth to talk. The timelines were off, and I knew it was no good. Munson, like Mr. V., hadn't moved West yet. The girl was another missing case likely to never be solved, and my heart sank. *How many go missing like that? Like we could've if no one had been there to interrupt Munson?* I bit my lip and felt my chapped lips cracking under the pressure. The iron tasted familiar, and Spivey handed me a napkin to wipe away the blood.

"You need to go home and get freshened up. Since your folks know I'm with you, and everyone else is still at ER, I can have Henry take you home or—"

"No," I said too quickly. Then, looking at this oddest of new connections said, "I'd rather you took me back."

She eyed me skeptically and said, "We're not going back to ER, Star."

I shook my head, "No, not there. I would rather you took me home. It's nothing against Henry, but I would rather you took me back," I said, thinking of the cold leather upholstery, the squad car noises and my empty house.

She relented and entered her notes into the system as quickly as she could. My stomach gurgled, and I knew I wouldn't touch the food at home until Mom and Dad got there. A silly part of my brain thought of Dad's credit card lying on the counter and how many times I'd taken instant food for granted. My pulse quickened at the images of Oscar eating takeout with me, and I relished in the hope of more memories like that. But these thoughts were just as swiftly swept away, because I knew nothing would ever be the same once his dad got released from ER. *Would we even be the same people again?* I prayed that we would, but the snow's attempts to purge the night seemed ineffective, and I felt anything but pure.

Officer Spivey glanced up once her notes were saved on the computer, and she told Henry of our final rendezvous. She took her coat from the rack and said in her matter-of-fact tone, "You need a winter jacket, you know that?"

Instantly, I thought of Angie's somewhere in the woods on Wolf collecting snow. I fake-smiled and said it would be top priority when I went back to Hamilton Place mall. She collected her keys and made sure the walkie was attached to her hip. Thinking better of taking her lipstick-stained cup with us, she left it on the desk. Wrapping a wool scarf around her neck, she looked older than when we'd first met, her salt and pepper hair more pronounced in the early daylight. Her hazel eyes scanned me for something else, then she said, "You could use a whole makeover actually," fixating on my holey jeans and then my unkempt hair. She laughed a genuine laugh, and I felt my anger from earlier subsiding a little.

"Anyways," I interrupted her muse, thinking this must be her attempt at a parenting voice. "Let's just get away from here," I added, pointing indirectly toward the corridor we'd just left. Knowing Munson was locked away just a couple hundred yards past us, I felt relief and still no small amount of revulsion.

"He's not going anywhere," she soothed. "One less person to mess with us."

I did a rare thing and buttoned my metal buttons on my denim jacket. I usually kept it wide open so people could see my bands proudly displayed on my chest. Plunging my sore palms into my pockets, I turned and let her lead us out of the station. Only when the car had heated and put into gear, did I fully release my fists again and allow myself to relax in the squad car as it rocketed toward home.

CHAPTER 44

A few months later . . .

The sunshine fell heavy on my shoulders as I stepped outside Idyll High and waited for Oscar and Angie. When they joined me, we walked in step down to Chartreuse Lake, and I kicked rocks on the path leading to the water's edge. Angie hugged a binder to her chest, and I felt like we were light years away from what'd happened that winter. Our substitute for Mr. C.'s class, I refused to now call him by his real name, the remainder of the year was a mousy woman named Ms. Young. Her height (and everything about her) was so opposite to our last teacher that it was easier to deny it'd ever happened. We made sure that administration checked her name, and that she was Ms. Henrietta Young. She actually taught English at a school in Nashville before moving to us, and her credentials were impeccable according to administration.

Still uncomfortable being in the American Literature classroom, Oscar made a point in removing the creepy map from the wall himself, and Angie helped tear down the posters of great American novels. Oscar scolded her and told her to be careful with *The Old Man and the Sea*, and we both laughed at him for this—his love of literature still intact, despite all of this madness. When the trappings of Mr. C. were removed, the classroom suddenly felt more breathable and static. Ms. Young brought with her a love of literature, and she was the one thing we all wanted more than anything in 9th grade—stability. She spoke in a calm, tranquil-like voice, and she never rose above a whisper. If we wanted to speak, we raised our hand, and she only had to point to the board or look at us for us to know what was next. She was consistently herself, and her brown wavy hair fell to her shoulders like ocean waves meeting the shore. Corine told us that she must use an entire bottle of mousse to have that look, and Angie waved her away. Corine was still, very much, herself.

Now with bare walls, Ms. Young encouraged us to plaster the classroom space with posters of our takes on the books we read. Students drew flaming images of Guy Montag from *Fahrenheit 451* and white whales battling Ahab from *Moby Dick*. We didn't even complain when she challenged us to read big classics like *War and Peace*. Oscar took it as a personal challenge to read all 1,296 pages of Tolstoy's masterpiece before summer break. If anyone could do it, Oscar could. We spoke up in class with reports and analytical assessments and were genuinely thrilled to have a class no longer reminiscent of a prison.

Melanie stood and delivered a great argumentative speech about racism in *To Kill a Mockingbird* and Atticus' attitudes as a parent to Scout and Jem. We clapped at her enthusiasm, and she beamed no longer looking solely to Corine for approval. When our grades came out, the entire class was averaging ninety in the gradebook. Our fear of finals diminished, and we focused on where Ms. Young would take the next year's class, or, if Mrs. Bottleheim would ever return. Suddenly, I found myself not wanting to leave the safe place and move into a new 10th grade ELA teacher's room. The blank wall behind Ms. Young was confirmation that good things happened in the year.

Oscar's dad healed completely and was released in the aftermath of Wolf Island. His parents invited all three of us over for chili mac and Mrs. V. did every bit of the cooking, as Mr. V. instructed her about what to add and said, "Taste test it," repeatedly. We laughed as Mr. V. hobbled around the kitchen, and my parents even joined us for dessert.

"We heard how much Star loves French toast," Mr. V. grinned across the table, removing a lid from a dish still steaming as it left the oven. The smell blew through the kitchen and hit my nostrils full force. It was cinnamon goodness, and I could see a terrific glaze on a type of bread. "This is a recipe I wanted to try out, and I know my wife made it even better than I could've," Mr. V. beamed, watching his wife put a massive metal spoon into the dish and placing generous portions on each person's plate.

"Sweet pea, what do you say?" Dad asked, like I was still a toddler.

"I can't wait," I said.

The room collectively laughed at this for some reason.

"She means, 'Thank you, Villanueves,'" Dad answered, not hiding his smile at all.

"It's a casserole version of French toast with cream cheese thrown in," Mr. V. replied.

"And if it's not any good, you can blame the cook," Mrs. V. chimed in.

"Never," Mr. V. soothed, stroking the back of her hair.

We took our plates ladled with this delicious offering and sat down to a wonderful last course. Mr. V. winced a little as he sat down, but other than that, his accident was completely invisible. I took a bite and wished everything tasted this good. It was cinnamon-y with sugar, and the cream cheese made it smooth and slightly salty. My mouth was full, and I wiped my lips with a napkin on the table. As we ate in silence, I thought of how warm this room was, and it felt like an alternate universe to the chill in January. Pollen fell and clung to the vehicles as they baked in the Chattanooga sun, and I was thankful to leave my denim jacket behind, much like I had any thoughts of Wolf Island.

Mr. C., no longer Edmund Clarence Munson in my mind, went from the initial cell I saw him chained in, to a quick court proceeding. The Chattanooga judge found him guilty of everything except for the one thing I really wanted him to be held accountable for—lying to us. It felt silly, but that was really what stung me more than anything. Sure, the 'trying to kill Oscar's dad' made me feel hatred, and his verbal abuse and Jekyll and Hyde mood swings was equally awful, but the dishonesty hit hardest. There was something in my mind that I just wanted closure with, and I felt his admitting that he lied to everyone, including himself was the greatest injustice. *Just tell us the truth!* I wanted to shout during the case. But he held firm, resolute, and he still laughed when accused of all his misdeeds. The sentencing caused him to shut his trap, but he went right back to saying, "I'll get mine," as he was led from the courtroom. *Maybe the hush following his exit from the courtroom was the best part?* I reasoned. At least, he won't be able to do this with anyone else.

What he didn't get was the Warhol sketch. Much like the Ming dynasty vase, it went to a fitting museum that specialized in displaying Warhol's work in Pittsburgh. I laughed when the judge made mention of this, and I knew Mr. C. fumed at his 'second loss' to Mr. V. But Mr. V. claims this one was all us.

As we stopped at the edge of Chartreuse, I felt the tiny plastic device inside my pocket. Angie offered to do the honors, and I felt reluctant to let it go. *Would we all still be friends after this?* It felt silly to think, but I was nervous about all the lonely years at Cascade Middle, even before that, being friendless as a kid, returning. Oscar stood and faced the choppy water stoically. His hands were on his hips, and he looked like a salty fish captain, his own Ahab of sorts. The wind whipped his long hair up, and it stood at an odd angle like a rooster tail. I reached with my free hand and pushed it down.

"Get it over with," Angie said, more as an exhale than anything.

I stood on tiptoes and planted a childish kiss on Oscar's smooth face. He kept his eyes cemented on the water, the bend leading to the Walnut Street pedestrian bridge and Coolidge Park. I traced the contours, and dimples, on his face with my eyes. He bashfully agreed with Angie, looking from her to me. It was time to let go. For all of us to move on. But I didn't want to move on too far. The summer months would test us simply by distance. Oscar had a job lined up with a fishing charter, and Angie planned to babysit and housesit for people in Red Bank. I was the only one without a job, and I didn't have a cell phone. But we made a pact to keep close and meet up for pizza once a week—a necessity. *At least until we were back together as 10th graders,* I thought.

The water sloshed at our feet, and I took the flash drive from my pocket inspecting it for some defect, some sign of all we'd been through. It still looked like the same black plastic piece that had opened our eyes to so much. The images of Mr. V. in business attire, the ground at Wolf, and coordinates all came flooding back into my mind. I thought of the nine digits that represented the maniac responsible for all of this. It was traumatizing to think that a social could be blotted out with a flick of the wrist. At least when stored on a flash drive. But I smiled as I considered the Cayman account sitting empty, and I knew it was important to celebrate the small wins. Turning the slim gadget over in my hand, I felt for a groove and flicked the metal aluminum USB piece outward. The hardware was outdated just like its previous owner. Instead of rearing back and launching it into the lake, I dropped it in the rocky soil and stepped aside, beckoning Oscar to take the first stomp. He grinned a sheepish grin and arced his foot up high in the air. With the full force of his leg, he slammed his sneaker down on the device and watched it break into several fragments. Angie stepped up and did the same. Then, once my two friends had taken ample turns and tired themselves, I stepped onto the obliterated drive and brought down all my hurt onto it as well. The crunch gave my heart a satisfying jolt, and I stood with my foot covering it, aware that I'd killed a sizable insect much larger than myself.

www.ingramcontent.com/pod-product-compliance
Lightning Source LLC
LaVergne TN
LVHW050629100826
845148LV00011B/1794

* 9 7 9 8 3 8 5 2 7 6 5 5 4 *